A WORLD BETWEEN US

A WORLD BETWEEN US

LYDIA SYSON

HOT
KEY
BOOKS

First published in Great Britain in 2012 by Hot Key Books
Northburgh House, 10 Northburgh Street, London EC1V 0AT

The poem on pvii, 'To Margot Heinemann', by John Cornford,
is reproduced by kind permission of Jonathan Cape
(*John Cornford: A Memoir*, ed. Pat Sloan, 1938)

A CIP catalogue record for this book is available from the British Library.

ISBN: 978-1-4714-0009-4

1

Typeset by Palimpsest Book Production Limited, Falkirk, Stirlingshire
This book is set in 10pt Berling LT Std

Printed and bound by Clays Ltd, St Ives Plc

FSC

Hot Key Books supports the Forest Stewardship Council (FSC),
the leading international forest certification organisation, and is committed
to printing only on Greenpeace-approved FSC-certified paper.

www.hotkeybooks.com

For Antonia

Heart of the heartless world,
Dear heart, the thought of you
Is the pain at my side,
The shadow that chills my view.

The wind rises in the evening,
Reminds that autumn is near.
I am afraid to lose you,
I am afraid of my fear.

On the last mile to Huesca,
The last fence for our pride,
Think so kindly, dear, that I
Sense you at my side.

And if bad luck should lay my strength
Into the shallow grave,
Remember all the good you can;
Don't forget my love.

'To Margot Heinemann'
John Cornford 1915–1936

Her fever lifts and Felix finds herself in an open truck. A swaying muddle of people; no one she knows. There are soldiers with trench beards and filthy bandages, and civilians too. She is crammed between an old woman with emaciated fingers which feel like ice against her arm, and a mother with a baby who cries and cries.

She hasn't felt so alone since she came to Spain. From where she sits, knees to her chin, hard metal bars at her back, she can't see the driver, but she knows it can't be George. If only. What wouldn't she give to surrender herself to him now.

Over the church bells' urgent ringing comes the roar of engines up above. Nuestras? Are they ours?

Felix squints into the sun, and the light knifes her eyes. The planes are diving towards them, then levelling out, and there's no sign of Republican red on their wingtips. These are German fighters. You can almost see the airmen's faces – goggles over guns. The truck brakes, screeching, and the people pour out. Felix reaches a ditch by instinct, rolls up like a foetus, bracing herself. The planes swoop back over and over and don't stop firing. A few feet away someone has lost control of their bowels. The smell is slightly sweet and acrid and familiar.

The silence after the planes have gone is worse than the noise. Felix thinks again of the silence in the snow. It only took one shot. And then there was nothing Nat could say or do to make things better. But how could she have left without meeting his eyes? Why had she denied herself a last look at his face?

Felix watches the others – the old woman, and the mother with *the child in her shawl – as they move back towards the truck. The baby is quiet now, because he is dead. Felix watches and can't speak. Her mouth is dry. She is burning up.*

OCTOBER 1936

LONDON

1

Crowds had never bothered Felix before, so she was surprised to find herself shaking. She really shouldn't have come this way, not when the Fascists were marching. She realised that now. Stuck in the thick of the protest, she wasn't even sure why she'd persisted. Curiosity, perhaps, or something about the singing. Or just her stubborn streak. Anyway, it was far too late to turn back. She'd never get through all these people.

The closer she came to the police line, the louder the chanting grew.

'One . . . two . . . three, four, five. We want Mosley, dead or alive!'

A new cry went up, less familiar.

'No pasarán! No pasarán! No pasarán!'

'Excuse me. Excuse me.' Nobody could hear her through this racket. All she could smell was overcoats and sweat. Unease turned to fear, and she began to struggle for air. A battered homburg and then a bald head shifted, giving Felix another breathless glimpse of the row of helmets ahead. Not far now. Such a relief. She could explain to the police. *I'm not meant to be here. My tram, you see . . . I was just trying. The station . . .* They'd let her through, wouldn't they? She didn't exactly look like a demonstrator, not in her uniform. Everyone loves a nurse.

She stuck out her elbows and pushed. A few steps further

1

and she saw the policemen's faces. Set and grim, they might have been rounding up wild animals, not protecting people. Behind the line, a mounted policeman made a show of holding his nose, acting out his disgust at the stink of the East End. No point in trying to catch *his* eye.

And then the wall of police officers parted, and Felix knew she'd made a terrible mistake. The horses were coming straight at them. They weren't going to stop. The police hadn't come to defend the crowds from the Fascists. They were clearing a path so the Blackshirts could march.

Felix tried to turn and run, but lost her footing at once. Hurtling into a stranger, she was rammed against three more. Everyone was falling over each other in their efforts to get away, but there was nowhere to go. Hooves thundered on cobbles. Batons slashed through the air. Her head filled with screaming, and the icy smash of plate-glass windows shattering, and loud Yiddish curses, and the high-pitched keening of a weeping woman.

Felix glanced back to see a huge brown horse skittering towards her, skidding and sliding on marbles thrown in its path. Foam from its muzzle hit her face, and then she felt a shove in her back, pushing her away from the animal's iron shoes and rolling white eye.

The truncheon came down like a sledgehammer. The horse ploughed on and Felix saw a dark-haired young man stumble back, dazed. He clutched his head and blood flowered from beneath his hands.

'Nurse! Nurse! Help him. Quick.'

People started pushing her towards him. *They think I'm a first aid post*. She wiped her cheek with the back of her hand. He saw Felix's uniform, looked her straight in the eye and grinned.

2

'Hello, nurse. Will I live?' he yelled. Then his knees gave way, and he collapsed against her, and she staggered, held up only by the crowds behind.

'You're all right, love, I'll give you a hand.' An Irishman, built like a bull, stuck his head under the boy's shoulder. 'Get him out the way before they charge again.'

She gulped back a sour taste, and nodded, and they pushed back through the crowd together. Missiles kept flying overhead – saucepans, bottles, rotten vegetables, God knows what. It was like a tide on the turn, with banners and placards dipping and rearing. There were all sorts here, not just East Enders. Even the side streets were packed with protestors. Most gave way to her uniform though. By the time they found an empty doorway, the young man was walking without support, though Felix couldn't quite stop trembling. With a clenched fist salute, the Irishman left.

They were on their own. After a fashion. Something inside her hammered so hard that Felix thought it must show. She swallowed, and got her brisk voice working.

'Let's get you sitting down.'

He was very pale now, grey and obedient. He looked up at her, eyes expectant, trusting. She wondered if she could get him inside somehow, somewhere clean and safe, but this shop front was boarded up like all the others. You could just make out some old graffiti: *Kill the Jews*. It was covered over now with another whitewashed slogan. *No Pasarán! They shall not pass!*

Felix sat on the doorstep next to him.

'Put your head between your knees. That's right.' Now she could get a better look at the wound. She began to clean it up with her hanky. 'It's not too bad. Is it throbbing?'

'Bit.' She dipped down to catch his reply and their hair touched.

3

'You have to be careful with head injuries,' she said. *Keep calm. Do what you'd normally do. This is what you're good at.* 'They make a lot of fuss. Lots of blood. But it's what you can't see that's the problem. You may be concussed. What's your name?'

He rolled his eyes vacantly, then smiled at her frown. 'I get it. Don't worry. I'm all here. Nat Kaplan's my name. Mr Stanley Baldwin is our Prime Minister, God help us, and it's October 4th 1936.'

The loudspeakers of a slowly moving van began to blare out a message.

'What are they saying?' Nat screwed up his eyes as if it would help him hear, while he peered through the forest of moving legs. 'Not sure. Hang on. Wait. Cable Street! Mosley's going to Cable Street.'

There was a surge towards the docks, and the singing started up again.

Arise, ye starvelings from your slumbers . . .

It is just like a hymn, thought Felix.

All at once Nat pulled her to her feet, and began to bellow out the words. His singing voice was very deep. He stood so close she could feel it vibrating through her.

And the last fight let us face.

The Internationale unites the human race.

There was something about the tune, and the words, and the way everyone sang them together: Felix felt herself brimming over and light-headed. It was like nothing she'd ever known before.

'Let's see if we can make it to Cable Street. They might need help there,' said Nat, and before she could answer he had stepped out of the doorway. She followed without thinking and they were both swept right back into the current of people.

4

'Hold on to me,' he shouted, sticking out his elbow for her, as if it were the most natural thing in the world. 'You'll be all right.'

This time she was. It was the same crowd, but it felt completely different now. Felix didn't mind the jostling any more, or the press of bodies against hers. The force was just as determined, but no longer threatening. She was breathless again, but not afraid. They weren't really getting anywhere though. She couldn't see how they could hope to get across Whitechapel Road.

'Best stick where we are, eh?' Nat grinned at her. And then he said it again, closer to her ear, so she could hear properly this time.

'Don't think we've got a choice.' Felix smiled back, absorbing the warmth of his breath and worrying about his wound. At least the bleeding had definitely stopped. This wasn't very responsible nursing, but she didn't have much of a choice about that either. Singing and chanting, the two of them held their position with the others. Until the news finally erupted, shouted from voice to voice.

'He's called them off! The Blackshirts have given up! We've won!'

Felix looked at Nat, and saw the excitement in his eyes. He picked her up without a thought and whirled her round, while her cape flew out like a matador's, flashing its red lining. Suddenly there was space. They could all breathe again. Fists punched the air, and hats went flying. In the explosion of back-slapping, she was enveloped by stranger after stranger, passed from embrace to embrace. Felix finally careened away from the immense bosom of an old lady whose black shawl reeked of pickled herring, and turned to laugh with Nat.

He's gone, she realised instantly, her laughter freezing. In all this giddy rapture, he had vanished. With mounting panic, Felix ducked under the joined hands of a line of young men. They were all singing loudly, and made a move to encircle her, but she darted away in time. Weaving in and out of the crowd, looking out for Nat's face, she kept imagining the relief of finding him. She had to find him. Surely she would see him, any moment now, and he would smile at her again.

But it was hopeless. There were so many people still milling around, and it was getting so late. Oh, what was she thinking? She knew she'd pushed her luck already, and she had quite a walk ahead of her still. Well, that was that then. She had to be sensible about it. Just one of those things. Heading for the station, Felix braced herself for her monthly visit home. Disappointment settled in her stomach.

The sun was beginning to go, but there was a lingering street party feel in the air. Happy groups kept stumbling by, half-drunk with the wonder of it all. Snatches of song and coal smoke and the noise of traffic starting up again. Felix saw a father walking with his arm round his son's shoulders and imagined him telling the boy how they had just saved the East End from the Fascists.

The crowds were thinning when she felt Nat's hand on her arm again.

'Don't go yet. We never said goodbye,' he said. 'I thought I'd lost you.'

Felix tried to keep her smile under control, and felt dizzy with the effort. It wasn't a problem she was used to.

'I thought . . .' she began to say, not knowing how to finish. 'I'm glad you found me.'

'Me too. I might not get a chance to see you again.'

'Look . . . there's a café I know, just by the station,' Felix said quickly. She didn't have a chance to wonder what he had meant. She just knew she couldn't let him go again, not right away. She couldn't quite believe her own daring. 'Do you have time for a coffee or something?'

Nat smiled again, and took her arm to cross the road.

'I reckon I've got time.'

2

While he held the café door open for her, she ducked under his arm, and his elbow knocked her starched cap askew again. He looked down at her. Felix was already looking up at him, and noticing more and more. A jacket that was old but well-cut. Blood on his collar. The length of his eyelashes. Their gazes were afraid to hold each other for long.

There was an empty booth near the counter, so they squeezed along the benches opposite each other, knees briefly touching under the white marble table. The windows were clouded with steam from the huge urn.

'Thought I was about to be arrested back there. Just before I got clobbered. That would have scuppered everything. A mate from the YCL's in prison right now. Wormwood Scrubs. Four months. He was heckling at a Fascist meeting in Victoria Park. The police carted him off to the station and planted a brick in his pocket. That I didn't need.'

Criminal elements. Felix heard her brother's voice in her head.

'The YCL?' She knew she ought to know.

'Young Communist League. Stepney branch.' As if it was obvious.

'Oh.'

'Don't look like that. It's not what you think. You should

8

come to our meetings. They're dead lively, very mixed, you know. And plenty of girls come.'

As Nat talked, a dart of jealousy surprised Felix and she lost concentration for a moment. She imagined him at the centre of a crowd of girls. In a hall? A bar?

'It's changed my life really. I can see everything more clearly now. It gives you hope, doesn't it? When you realise how things could be so much better, so much fairer? And that you can do something about it.'

'I suppose it must.' *Life isn't fair*, thought Felix. But she'd never met anyone before who thought you could change the fact.

And then he just blurted it out. 'That's why I'm going to Spain.'

The word 'Spain' came out as a croak, so he repeated it quickly, with too much emphasis.

'Spain?' said Felix, uselessly.

He nodded.

'To fight. *No pasarán*. You know,' he said. And watched for a reaction.

'Spain. That's . . .' She fumbled with her thoughts. 'That's brave. Very brave.'

'You're not going to try and talk me out of going?'

'Should I?' she said, wishing she knew more. *Is that what he wants me to do?*

Spain always seemed so far away. She had never really thought about its civil war till she saw the banners today. 'Surely you're not going right now, are you?'

'A few weeks, I reckon. But nobody knows yet . . . Not even my sister. It's best that way. Believe me, my parents would kill me if they knew.' He laughed and shook his head and Felix found herself laughing too, though she wanted to cry. 'I don't even know why I'm telling you. I just wanted you to know. Because if I wasn't going, I'd want to see you again. I really would. I can tell you that for nothing. I knew it right away.'

Felix thanked God she wasn't the blushing type.

'You really are feeling better?' she asked. 'Sometimes a blow to the head can—'

'Yes, yes, don't worry. I am in my right mind, honest I am. Never felt clearer about anything, in fact.' He shook his head. He started his speech. It was as if he had to tell someone. 'The thing is I've had it with demonstrations and petitions and collecting tins. I've done what I can but it's not enough, not any more. You can see it coming, all over Europe . . . it'll be here too before you know it.'

Nat's voice was low and urgent and he rocked slightly as he spoke. It frightened and fascinated Felix.

'Germany and Italy do what they like,' he went on. 'But when the Spanish government turns to us for help, what do we do? Oh dear! Oh no!' (He affected a posh accent.) 'We can't possibly sell arms to the wicked Reds. Not in our interests to encourage the Bolshies, is it?' That's what our government really thinks about democracy.'

She had never had a conversation like this before. She thought about what she'd seen today.

'It makes me sick.' Nat's voice began to shake. 'And now the Fascists in Spain are nearly at Madrid. But the bastards would be nowhere without Hitler and Mussolini. Anyone can see that!'

Felix was hypnotised by the gleam in his eyes and the tension in his throat. She looked at his white shirt, undone at the neck, and showing a fragile glimpse of hair. She thought about the hands that would scrub at the bloodstained collar, and iron it crisp again.

I must learn this face, before it's too late, she thought. *Learn it by heart.*

Heavy eyebrows sloped in a way that gave a hint of irony to everything he said, and made his strong high cheekbones less formidable. Dark hair, pale skin. She could hardly be the first to fall for a face like that. Yet he didn't seem very aware of his charm. Hadn't he noticed the way the waitress looked at him when they came in? Maybe that was part of the attraction, this indifference.

'Does your boss know you're leaving?' she asked. *Did he even have a job?*

'Does my boss know? God forbid! But he won't miss me.'

A troublemaker then. And proud of it. And what was he . . . seventeen? Eighteen? He couldn't be much older than her.

'And you? You're a probationer?' He was looking at her uniform. The kind of person who just knows things: one of those boys who absorbs facts like air. She liked that.

'Yes, I've been training since January. I'm hoping to be a theatre nurse. I really want to be a surgeon. One day, maybe.'

'You never know.'

Nat kept shifting in his seat, apologising when his foot brushed hers. He didn't take his eyes off her. It was as if he found her own stillness compelling.

'Shame you're not qualified. Spain needs surgeons. And nurses of course.'

'Well, I don't think . . . I couldn't possibly . . .'

'Never mind.' Nat put a hand on hers and shook his head, and let go too soon. Then he took a book and a pencil from his pocket. At first Felix thought he wanted to give her a reading list. The latest history of Spain. The Communist Manifesto? Well, it would make a change from anatomy text books, and general hygiene, and dressing techniques. Though what Neville would think if he knew . . .

'Look, how about I write to you?' he said. She wasn't expecting that. 'It won't be too often, mind you. I'm not so good with words, so don't get your hopes up. But just to know I can, if I get the chance . . . It'll make a difference.'

'To have a girl at home?' The words escaped with a self-mocking smile she hadn't intended. But Nat looked at her so seriously that her heart began to beat faster. And then she thought of the bundles of letters from her father that her mother still kept from the Great War. She stared back at him with a sober face.

'If you like.'

He pushed the book towards her, and offered her a flyleaf to write on. It was Jack London. *The Iron Heel*. A well-read copy. Felix decided Tredegar House was safer than her mother's address in Sydenham. Fewer questions at the nurses' home.

Her writing was rounded, smooth, clear and young.

'So nurses aren't like doctors then,' Nat joked.

'What do you mean?'

'I can read this.'

'Good.'

'Felix?'

'Felicity really, but my friends call me Felix. Always have. I've no idea why, really.'

'I like it . . . Felix Rose . . . I like it a lot. Now, don't move.'

Nat stared at Felix intently, eyes moving over her features. Then he licked the pencil stub and in a few swift lines he caught her heart-shaped face and her calm smile and the straightness of her nose. A strand of hair had escaped from its grip, she saw. She tucked it back behind her ear.

'Very clever. Very nice. You're good. Really,' she said. She meant it.

It crossed her mind that he might have a whole bookshelf

of paperbacks like this – a different girl's name, address and portrait in each. When she met his gaze again, she decided it couldn't be true.

'You don't mind, then?' he said quietly. 'Was that a liberty?'

'No. Of course not. Not at all.'

They talked a little longer, until Felix became too anxious about the time, and then they both rose from the banquette at the same time, and nearly bumped heads. Nat paid for the coffees. Outside they stood and shivered for a moment, uncertain what came next. Then Felix clenched her fist, and held it awkwardly, up by her ear.

'*No pasarán?*'

'*No pasarán*,' he replied firmly, returning her salute.

3

Neville answered the door. He looked her up and down.

'About time.'

Her brother stomped off down the hall. Felix sighed and followed. Home from home. The nurses-in-training were always treated like children at the hospital too. Pausing in front of the mahogany-framed mirror, she patted her hair automatically. At the coat stand she hung up her cape. Nat's blood had dried to brown on her apron, so she took that off too.

'We're in the kitchen, dear. I'll just put the kettle back on.' Her mother didn't sound cross, but that just made Felix feel more guilty.

Mrs Rose was still bending over the gas when Felix walked in. Its hiss stuttered into a roar and Neville stared pointedly at a plate of sandwiches. The crusts were drawing back to reveal ham darkening as it dried along its edges.

'I'll take that through now, shall I?' said Felix quickly. *Why didn't he put a damp tea towel over them?* she wondered crossly. *Did he want them to spoil?*

'In a minute, my dear.' Her mother offered a cheek which smelled of Pond's cold cream. 'Was it a very long operation? Or was it the trains? Sunday services aren't what they were, I'm afraid.'

'Actually I ran into . . .' Felix still couldn't quite work out what had just happened. A battle or a carnival? A victory celebration? Definitely an awakening.

Neville's tight lips alerted Mrs Rose.

'Felicity, your stocking is torn! And where's your apron? What would the Hospital think!'

Her mother didn't often reproach her out loud. Why would she need to, with Neville around? They exchanged glances, which Felix pretended not to notice. That didn't work.

'What on earth have you been doing?' he said, on cue.

A shadow darkened the frosted glass in the back door. George's entrance crowded the kitchen, and changed the mood.

'Hello, George,' said Felix, extra cheerily. 'Not at the race-track? Don't tell me the paper's actually given you a day off!'

Neville's friend laughed obligingly.

'Sort of. But no rest for the wicked.' He was in his shirtsleeves, wiping his hands on a black-smeared rag.

'So what's Neville got you doing this time?' Felix asked. She took the rag from him, ran the tap and offered George the soap dish, still carefully avoiding Neville's question. Good old George. Perfect timing.

'Just that blessed lawnmower. Neville was hoping to manage a final mow of the season, but it's been up to its old tricks, I'm afraid.'

She passed him the hand towel.

'Nothing you can't fix, though?' she said lightly.

'You know me!' said George. 'Take more than a machine to defeat me! But it's too dark now to get the mowing done. Let's hope the weather holds till next weekend.'

'We may be lucky, dear. It's been a lovely afternoon,' said Mrs Rose, locking the back door.

'Good thing Felix didn't get here earlier really. It was more of a job than I'd imagined. But isn't she looking in fine fettle?'

George quickly straightened his own hair, fair and dishevelled, with damp fingers. 'Different, somehow . . .'

He looked at her, as if he were trying to work something out.

'I'm so sorry, Mother,' said Felix. 'I honestly didn't mean to . . .'

'What a fool I am!' George struck his forehead with his hand, and went for another save. 'I should have warned you! Don't tell me you got caught up in that demonstration? The British Union of Fascists were marching today.'

'In the East End? Oh dear,' said Mrs Rose. 'I wish I'd known.'

'There was a lot of talk about it at the paper on Friday. I *am* sorry, Felix. I assumed you'd be safely back home by the time things got going.'

'Kettle's boiling, Mother,' said Neville.

'Mosley and his biff boys were promising quite a display, I heard,' George went on. 'A pretty provocative plan, wasn't it? Fascists marching through the East End like that. Asking for bloodshed.'

'Well, they didn't in the end. The Blackshirts had to turn back. They didn't have a hope of getting through. Far too many people. It was wonderful. And everyone was singing, and chanting like mad – *No pasarán! No pasarán!* You know: 'They shall not pass.' Like the Republicans in Spain. That's what people were saying. We won't let the Fascists through. Not in Madrid. Not in London. At first I thought—'

They were all staring at her.

'Never mind . . .' Her voice trailed away. 'I'll warm the teapot, Mother.'

Her back turned, she stood at the sink, swirling the water round thoughtfully.

After all that, she hadn't set eyes on a Blackshirt this

afternoon. They hadn't even got close. Usually you couldn't miss them. They were always hanging round Whitechapel these days: thuggish-looking men with brass-buckled belts and black boots. She saw their victims in the hospital often enough. When they weren't using their fists, the Fascists brandished their newspapers like weapons. 'Read all about the alien menace! European ghettoes pouring their dregs into our country!' Or simply: 'The Yids! The Yids! We've got to get rid of the Yids!'

Yids like Nat. Nat Kaplan.

Would he really write to her? And what on earth would she write back?

'The other business, George.' Neville interrupted her thoughts. 'Shall we talk about it next door? Felicity? Mother?'

'Just coming, dear.' Mrs Rose gently commandeered the teapot. 'You two go on through. Neville, isn't the sugar bowl a bit low? Could you possibly . . . ?'

In the sitting room, the table was set with the best china, and the coal in the hearth was made up, but not lit. George's jacket and tie were back on, his nails clean. Felix stood and fiddled with saucers and spoons, distracted.

'So. How are the "gee-gees", George? Keeping you busy?'

'Very, as a matter of fact.'

Felix still wasn't really listening. George's job as a racing correspondent didn't much interest her.

'Why don't you sit down?' he added, gently, moving a chair for her. 'You must be exhausted.'

'I am rather, now I come to think about it. And gasping for tea, aren't you?' Felix collapsed, and looked up at George, behind her. 'Oh, don't hover like that. You know you're at home here. I expect you could do with a rest yourself.'

George considered the options, and sat in the armchair opposite.

'Well, I'm awfully glad you're all right,' he said, and Felix wondered if he was checking her over for damage. A moment later they heard the rattle of the tray at the door and George sprang back to his feet. 'Here comes the tea now! Thank you so much, Mrs Rose, yes, just one sugar please. Ham? Lovely! Don't mind if I do.'

'Yes, please, Mother.' Felix took two sandwiches at once. 'I'm starving.'

Finally everyone had a cup and saucer in their hand and George looked at Neville, who nodded briefly.

'Well, as I was just saying, work is quite frantic.' George took another sip of tea. Coughed. 'Though something rather fun's just come up. I've been talking to Neville about it.'

Felix raised her eyebrows politely. He always saw the jolly side of things. You could say that for George.

'There's a French filly I've been following all season. Corrida, she's called. Beautiful chestnut. Quite stunning. A three-year-old.'

'Oh yes?' Felix stretched out her legs and battled a yawn. She tried to concentrate on George, but into the brief silence in her head crept the thought of Nat, and her exhaustion changed into a secretly buzzing excitement.

'She took the Hardwicke Stakes at Ascot, the Grand International at Ostend, Prix de President de la Republique . . . oh, all the big ones! Well, the long and the short of it is that her owner – Marcel Boussac – the textile millionaire . . .' He glanced at Neville. 'He promised me a story on her if she bagged the l'Arc de Triomphe, and what do you know? She's done it! This afternoon. Only just heard.'

'Really?' Why were they all looking at her?

'So now you can go to France to interview this horse?'

George flushed.

'Well, yes, in a manner of speaking. And Boussac of course. But wouldn't it be rather jolly if the three of us went across? The stables are just outside Paris. We can make a long weekend of it. Next month. After the Grand Prix de Marseille.'

'Paris?' That took her by surprise. Paris.

'You deserve a break, dear.' Mrs Rose nodded encouragingly. 'They work you so hard. Sister Macpherson is such a task-mistress.'

But I love my work, thought Felix. Hadn't it allowed her to escape from all this? And then she thought, *Paris! I'm going to Paris!*

'So you'll come?' George beamed at her.

'Of course she'll come!' said Neville.

4

One last chance. Nat counted the chimes from St Mary's and walked more briskly. He was earlier this time: he'd left the print shop a full hour before the whistle, without a word to his boss. What did it matter now? Whatever lecture Mr Williams might have waiting for him in the morning, Nat wouldn't be there to hear it.

Outside the London Hospital he stationed himself under a lamp post, stuck his satchel between his feet, and shook out his copy of the *Daily Worker.* He settled down to watch and wait.

When a gaggle of nurses came down the steps about ten minutes later, he stiffened, and tried not to stare. They didn't give him so much as a glance though. They were like a little flock of birds, he thought, as they swept by in formation, giggling and shrieking, capes swinging and white caps bobbing with the movements of their heads. They wore the same uniform as Felix, but she wasn't among them.

Nat stared at the newspaper again, but he couldn't read a line of it. Everything around him seemed magnified this evening. Every detail stood out. He couldn't concentrate on words.

He was due at Victoria in two hours' time. He'd put on his best suit for the journey, the one his father made for him for starting work. *Klaider machen dem mentshen,* his dad had muttered through the pins in his mouth as he knelt on the floor sorting out the trouser hem. Clothes make the man.

Three more probationers soon followed, more quietly. One looked over her shoulder, hesitating.

'Come on,' said her friend. 'She said not to wait. We'll keep her tea.'

Then they disappeared too.

He should have sent a note to the nurses' home. He was a fool to have left it to chance like this. If there'd been a YCL dance last Saturday . . . something he could have invited her to . . . He should have been braver. She'd given her address, hadn't she? That must mean something.

Tell no one, they'd instructed him. But he'd let the cat out of the bag already with her. It couldn't do any more harm to say goodbye. He had to say goodbye to *someone*.

Nat straightened his jacket and wondered if there was another way out. Maybe she'd slipped out through a side door. He walked across to the next corner, peered down the side of the hospital without success, and turned quickly back to his first sentry post.

And there she was by the railings, looking neater and crisper than before. Her face more guarded. Concentrating, and hurrying. He didn't move for a breath or two. He wanted to savour this. If she turned away, or was angry, or laughed at him, at least he'd still have this moment. Then he gathered his courage and stepped into her path.

'What are you thinking about?'

Felix stopped so abruptly that she almost overbalanced. She seemed shocked at first, and a little angry – like a girl getting ready to shake off a stranger. But then she looked around quickly and said softly, 'I thought you'd gone. Have you changed your mind?' And instantly he caught the hope in her voice.

'No. Tonight.' He watched her face freeze over.

'Oh.'

'Sorry,' he said. 'I've got to. It's all arranged.'

'I know. I know.' This time he thought perhaps she really did. No good going through it all over again. That wasn't how he wanted to spend these precious minutes. He touched her arm gently. 'So, what *were* you thinking about just then?'

'Do you really want to know?'

'Of course I do,' said Nat. He shifted slightly, so he could protect her from the jostle of passers-by. His shadow fell across her face.

'Well, as it happens, I'd just left my notebook in Histology and I went back to get it and I noticed a poster in the lab and how pretty the muscle fibres looked in cross-section – sort of pale pink and green and seaweedy – and the blood cells were rather lovely too . . .' An embarrassed smile twitched her lips, and she finished defiantly, looking right at him. 'And I was actually thinking they'd make rather a nice print for a summer frock.'

He laughed. He knew it. She wasn't half as serious as she looked. How he'd love to see her in something other than that old-fashioned uniform. He was right to come looking for her again.

'I'll be back from Spain soon, you know,' he said firmly. 'You'll see.'

'It'll be over by Christmas?' she said, stepping back, one hand gripping the railings behind her through her cloak. 'Isn't that what they always used to say?'

She kept surprising him with her worldliness. Such a slip of a thing, as his mother would say, but something about her was so sharp.

'Course it won't be Christmas, but it can't be too long. How

22

can it be? They say there are volunteers coming to help Spain from all over the world.'

Felix didn't say anything. She just kept looking over his face in that searching way she had. Then she reached up with cool fingers and ran them gently across the fading bruise above his eyebrow, softly tracing the edges of the scab in the middle. Tentatively, Nat closed his hand over hers.

'Sorry,' she said. 'Too cold? Or does it still hurt? I can't see how well it's healed in this light.'

Nat shook his head. He couldn't speak so he pressed her lovely fingers to his lips, and breathed in the lingering smell of disinfectant as though it were nectar. The scent of her skin, under the Lysol, was just as he'd remembered it too, though he hardly knew what exactly it was he remembered so well. A smell of humanity. A sweetness. It made his chest swell with an incredible and overwhelming warmth. He felt even taller than usual, but perhaps that was because he had to bend his head so far to reach her upturned face. He couldn't think how he dared but neither could he stop himself. His arms were round her now, and he could feel her softness under the stiff crackle of starched apron. She still clutched the railings behind, giving strength to both of them.

They stood like that for a few long seconds, Nat labouring for breath, fighting his panic about everything that lay ahead. He wanted to ask her. Did she mind? He couldn't. He kissed her lips, as softly and as hard as he could.

And, almost immediately, Felix's head whipped round, and she shrank away.

'Nurse! Nurse Rose, is it?' The voice was harsh and Scottish and it was practised in humiliation. 'For shame! I thought better of *you*.'

Nat turned to confront a stout woman with a face like lard

and the long dark dress and gleaming white cuffs of a hospital sister. Looking through him and his protests as if he were invisible, she addressed herself entirely to Felix.

'In my office. Fifteen minutes.'

What have I done?

What else could *I do?*

He can't look down. Nat walks away from the ravine with two questions repeating themselves in turn. No answers. His ears are still ringing, and his limbs feel leaden, as if gravity has increased its force. Numbly, he kicks at the tracks, scuffing up the compressed snow, spreading the stains further when he meant to cover them up. Alizarin crimson. Titanium white. He's making everything worse, he thinks.

He doesn't know it's pointless. The flat grey sky above has begun to release a new fall of snow, and nature will soon have done this work for him. Another hour, and there will be little left to betray him. And he will be far away. But all Nat can see is the hatred in Felix's face before she turned her back. The memory of her eyes grinds into him more piercingly than any shard or shrapnel could.

NOVEMBER 1936

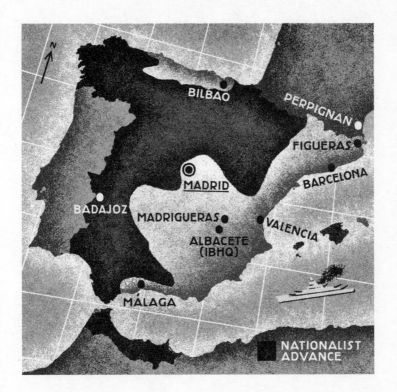

5

A fortnight later, Felix left for France on the boat train. Rain was forecast, Neville said. On board the ferry he shepherded Felix and George into the saloon, corralling them with their suitcases. It would be a long night. Then he went in search of coffee to go with the sandwiches Mrs Rose had wrapped up in greaseproof paper.

It was smoky and loud in the bowels of the boat. The rumbling under the floor began to get stronger.

'Would you excuse me?' she said, standing up. Felix couldn't bear to think she might miss the sight of herself leaving England for the first time. 'Just a touch queasy, I'm afraid. I may need a little air. Won't be long.'

'Shall I come with you? I should hate to think . . .' George looked helplessly at their luggage and over his shoulder for Neville.

'Oh no! Please don't worry. I'm afraid I'm a very poor sailor. Fresh air should do the trick, honestly.'

She was backing away as she spoke.

Felix loved the steepness of the stairs stretching her calves and the 'muster station' signs, and she felt quite heady with the tang of engine oil. Announcements boomed through the ship's tannoy in English and then again in slow pedantic French. Somewhere out of sight, instructions to the crew ricocheted around steel walls.

She arrived at the stern too late to see the gangway being raised. The widening expanse of dark water was choppy, and the fine spray on her face could have been sea or rain. There weren't many other passengers on deck; most were huddled in twos and threes.

Felix retrieved her headscarf from her mac and tied it on firmly. Her passport – crisp and new – was still safely in her pocket. She tucked herself into the lee of a tarpaulin-covered lifeboat, leant over the railing and swallowed great gulps of salty air, licking the taste off her lips. Slowly, the lights of Dover diminished. Without a moon, the cliffs looked quite grey.

She wondered if Nat had looked back at this moment, too. How unlucky they had been the night he left. So mortifying. She couldn't forget how Sister Macpherson had seen him silently off, while Felix just stood on the pavement as helpless as a baby. The memory still made her seethe with shame and fury.

Hearing footsteps, she squeezed herself further into the gap between lifeboat and rail. George might come looking for her, and she didn't want to be found.

She heard a match strike close by, and then an exhalation, the kind that follows the first draw on a cigarette. A cough. Not George, she decided, feeling reprieved. Too rough and low. But with the idea of his arrival – the thought of standing there alone on deck with George – a sudden realisation swept through her in a hot and prickly flush.

This trip was to be a finishing line. An end to months of hints and nudges and contriving. Her knuckles turned white as she gripped the railings. That was why Mother and Neville never let *her* fetch the coal, the hot water, the newspaper, whatever it was, when George was around. How could she have been so stupid? And just when she thought she'd almost got away.

Felix knew just what would happen now. She and George

would find themselves walking alone together . . . beside the
Seine . . . or by the Eiffel Tower . . . or . . . or . . . (she ran
out of suitable Parisian landmarks). And he would try to hold
her hand. And then . . . oh God. The terrible certainty of it all
made her dizzy with claustrophobia. She pictured the knowing
smile between friends when she and George returned to the
hotel. Neville's congratulations. His complacency. There would
be no discussion. And then George would introduce her to the
textile millionaire . . . as his fiancée.

'Looking your last on Albion?'

Felix started. Another man had joined the smoker, his face
also out of sight on the other side of the lifeboat.

'Ah bloody hope nae!' returned an older Scottish voice. 'But
it's nae Albion ah want t' see again, anywise.'

'No, I dare say it's not,' replied the newcomer. They were
clearly together, though hardly seemed an obvious pair. This
man sounded just like a doctor Felix knew slightly, a new arrival
at the hospital from Cambridge. 'Where are the others, anyway?
I thought we were supposed to stick together from now on.'

'You'll find them at the bar. Tempted t' hae a pint myself,
but ah want tae keep my wits abit me.'

'Quite right too. The last thing we need is anyone shooting
their mouth off before we've even reached Paris.'

'I'm wi' ye there. Tried tae tell 'em, but ye ken how it is.
Some folk don't like tae be told.'

Felix was glad she had kept in the shadows.

'Well, I'll retrieve them shortly. Got a light, by any chance?'

The matches were handed over. After a while, the conversation resumed.

'So, what's your previous experience? Ready for this?'

'Fifteen years in the Scots Guards. Four years on th' dole.
Aye. You could say I'm ready.'

31

'Good man. Good man.'

'You?'

'OTC at school. Officer Training Corps. Repton.' He cleared his throat. 'Haven't actually seen action yet. All rather theoretical, I'm afraid.' Felix noticed an awkwardness in his response.

Felix risked peering round the ropes and saw an angular young man in a gabardine coat, staring out to sea as he drew heavily on a cigarette. His gruffer companion wore a flat grey cap.

'Fred an' Ronnie met on the boxing circuit, seemingly,' he said. 'Amateur welterweight champions, the pair of them. Good thing too.'

'Indeed.'

'Speak French, do you?' asked the older man.

'Yes, as a matter of fact I do.'

'Spanish?'

'Just a little. My Latin's not bad, of course.'

'Your *Latin*?' Felix could almost hear the Scotsman's eyebrows rising, but he made no comment. After a short silence he said: 'So, woulds you mind tellin' me th' plan? For when we get to Paris? Or is that nae allowed?'

'To be honest, I'm not entirely sure of the details, though I hear it's all very efficient now the Soviets are on board.'

'Aye.'

'I believe we'll be met at the Gare du Nord. At the taxi rank. But that's all I know. Just have to take it from there, I suppose. And hope Madrid's still standing by the time we get there. It's not looking too good, is it?'

A silence fell. The wind picked up, and Felix began to shiver. The rest of the strangers' conversation was mostly drowned out. But she had already guessed where these men were heading: they were new recruits to the fight against Fascism. Like Nat, they were joining the International Brigades.

She was pleased to have put two and two together so quickly, though Felix still found it all rather confusing. She wasn't used to the idea of right-wing rebels, rising in arms against a left-wing Republican government. Wasn't it usually the other way round? And why did the Fascists in Spain call themselves Nationalists when they seemed intent on destroying the nation?

The spray turned decidedly to rain, and the men moved off. Bracing herself, Felix retraced her swaying steps to the saloon. Perhaps she'd have a chance to speak to them later. Would they think her very odd if she gave them a message for Nat? No, no, she couldn't possibly.

They sat with empty cups in front of them. Plotting? Neville's thumb and forefinger worked thoughtfully over his moustache. Checking to see if it had got any thicker, Felix always imagined. George looked more relaxed, his feet outstretched and his arms linked behind his head. They both rose as she approached.

'Your coffee's gone cold, Sis, but it can't be helped.'

'Never mind. Thanks for getting it.'

'Feeling better, Felix? Here. Let me move these bags for you.'

'Please don't worry. I'm fine.' Felix stepped over the luggage and they all sat down again.

The noise of the chugging engine filled their silence.

'I was just asking George about this horse we're going to meet on Monday,' said Neville. '*What* did you say it was called? Corridor? Funny kind of name.'

'Corre*e*da, actually,' corrected George. 'It means bullfight, I believe . . . in Spanish.'

33

'Spanish?' He finally had Felix's attention. 'Is it a Spanish horse?' she said. 'What's it doing racing when there's a war on? That doesn't seem right.'

'Oh no, no, she's French. But you know what racehorse names are like.'

'Ridiculous. Don't blame you for wanting to cover motor racing instead. Numbers are so much easier to remember,' said Neville. 'What was that other horse you were talking about? By Jingo? Something like that?'

George laughed his hearty laugh, and went on polishing the lenses of his binoculars. 'Yes, his sire's By Golly. I suppose Corrida's less absurd than many, when you think about it. It's got the right feel at least – speed, power, excitement!'

'Or murder, cruelty, bloodshed,' interrupted Felix.

Neville and George stared at her.

'The Fascists in Spain are using the bullrings to slaughter Republicans instead of bulls now,' she told them bluntly. 'Did you know that? 4,000 men dead in Badajoz. Think of it. The bullring was knee-deep in blood.'

'Calm down, Felix,' said George. 'You're upsetting yourself. What's all this about? Badda-where? I'm sure that can't be true. Why on earth would anyone do anything so beastly?'

'Because they're beasts!'

'Heavens. She'll be joining the Left Book Club next.' Neville caught George's eye, more amused than disapproving.

'I'll tell you something else. When the king left Spain five years ago lots of rich landowners in the south fled too. Do you know what the people did? They ploughed up the fighting bulls' pastures to grow crops. And they divided the animals between the peasants.' Felix was determined to make them listen. 'To eat, you see. To eat. Some of them had never tasted meat before. Imagine.'

'How very revolutionary!' George's laugh didn't hide his embarrassment. He didn't try to stop Felix talking again.

Neville had no qualms. 'Do spare us the lectures, Felicity. Self-righteousness is so unattractive in a girl. As I've told you before. Anyway, how on earth do you know all this? What makes you think it's even true?'

'Oh, I've been reading about Spain,' said Felix, a little defensively, thinking of her visits to Whitechapel Library. She'd managed to slip away quite a few times at the end of a shift, or sometimes in a tea break. Though often too tired to take much in, she was determined to be ready for the first letter that came from Nat. How else could she convince him she was worth another one? She wasn't just some silly little suburban ignoramus. 'Quite a lot. And talking to people. You know.'

They obviously didn't.

'Well, I'm surprised you've got time for all this stuff. Shouldn't you be working for your exams?' said Neville.

George tried a more placatory tack. 'There's not much we can do about Spain anyway. It's a civil war. None of our business, I'd say. And won't it all be over quite soon? Last thing I heard was that the government had fled Madrid.'

'Not much of a government then.' Neville clearly thought he'd had the final word.

Felix opened her mouth to contradict them both. *Germany doesn't think it's none of their business. Nor Italy.* And promptly shut it again. When was the last time she'd actually won an argument against Neville?

'Now, how about grabbing forty winks while we can?' he continued. 'George, why don't you let Felix use your coat as a pillow? Her mac's damp now and your coat's quite a bit thicker than mine.'

'Of course.' George quickly folded it up for her. It smelled of him – not unpleasantly. 'Next time we do this, we'll do it in style, I promise. Those sleeping cars really did look splendid, didn't they?'

Next time, Felix thought.

6

As the 'red train' pulled into Perpignan, to cheers and flowers and a loud French chorus of the Internationale, the ginger-haired boy next to Nat muttered something behind his hand.

'What?'

'I said, funny kind of secret,' the boy repeated.

It was, Nat agreed. After all the lurking at Victoria, and the messing around with coded matchboxes at the Lyon's Corner House. The black berets handed out in Paris. Not much of a disguise. More like markers of who they were and where they were going, Nat thought at the time. But he had played the game, kept quiet, admitted nothing. He couldn't believe his luck really. The Communist Party had started recruiting officially within weeks of his decision to go and fight. It made everything so much easier.

Just as they lurched across the Spanish border, the same boy started shouting from the back of the bus. 'I don't want to go. I've changed my mind.' His words came out in a kind of scream. 'Let me off! Please! I'm not going.'

Lights flickered on and off and men looked around in panic and dismay. Nat started to his feet, thinking irrationally that he could reason with him. The man in the seat behind the lad stood too. His efficient right hook knocked the protestor out cold. Nat sat down in a hurry.

And suddenly there they were, in Spain.

Figueras stank. And you'd think nothing could beat the stench and squalor of an East End tenement. With the first breath of human excrement, Nat gagged. The vast medieval fortress had a courtyard the size of Trafalgar Square, and it was covered. Nerves, or the food?

Ravenous from days and nights of nothing but French bread and chocolate, Nat arrived ready to kill for a cuppa. Others had been talking of beer for hours. Instead they sat down to red wine and rice. At least it looked more or less like rice. But it was black, and came in a strange sauce with bits in which looked like white rubber bands. Fishy. Nat knew his mother would be horrified – it certainly wasn't kosher.

Half a night's sleep in the dungeons, and the next morning the new recruits had orders to assemble at the drawbridge for their march to the train station. The view across the valley took Nat's breath away. The landscape was laid out like a painting, all golds and greens, umber, raw and burnt, and viridian. He wished he could get it on paper, and send that to Felix. Better than a letter. Though he wanted to be with her when she looked at it, to watch the expression in her eyes change. He wondered if she'd ever seen hills – mountains – like these. He certainly hadn't.

'*¿Bonito?*' A Republican Army guard was speaking. He caught Nat's eye, and nodded vigorously. 'Beautiful, yes? You like our country, comrade? *¿Le gusta?*'

'*Sí, sí.*' It was Nat's first chance to try out his book-learned Spanish. He felt a bit of a fool – stuttering and awkward. He'd never been one for play-acting, and this was almost worse. But he was determined to give it a go. What next? He tried to summon up the right page of his textbook. Then a useful phrase floated into his head. '*Moowee bonito, sí. Me gusta mucho.*'

The guard went on nodding, encouraging him. Nat thought something stronger was needed. You'd think he was at some kind of lah-di-dah tea party the way he was carrying on.

'¡Viva l'España!' he said. This produced the broadest of grins.

'¡Viva la Republica! ¡Viva la democracia!'

That was all right then.

All he really remembered after that was a blur of stations and slow trains, celebratory banquets and hard wooden-slatted benches. Cold nights and warm sunny days. There were other volunteers too, hundreds of them. They came from all over Europe, and filled carriage after carriage on the trains.

At Barcelona, a lively brass band greeted them on the station platform. '¡Alza la bandera revolucionaria!' the crowds sang. 'Raise the revolutionary flag!' The city's welcome caught at Nat's heart and his soul soared. This was what he'd come for.

All the hatless workers in Catalonia must have abandoned their tasks to greet these strangers. Staring with sleeplessness, the volunteers tried to rise to the occasion. Their march was hardly military, but each step was more in time. Music helped. So did the warmth of the crowds. How could you ever guess from the newsreels how colourful it would be?

'This all for us?' Nat heard one man ask his neighbour out of the corner of his mouth, indicating the gaudy array of flags and banners.

'You must be joking, comrade! Welcome to the revolution! Hadn't you heard? Barcelona belongs to the workers now. They're living the dream. Ain't it something?'

'And the red and black flags? What they all about then?'

'Anarchists.'

Political posters were plastered over every wall. Strong lines, blocks of colour – cadmium red and cobalt blue – intensely clean and bright against the faded brown advertisements for soap powder and stockings. Effective, thought Nat. One showed a beautiful young woman in overalls, a rifle on her shoulder, eyes fixed on an unseen horizon. A *miliciana*. Nat realised he was walking along with an enormous grin slap across his face.

They passed a café where children stood on tables to see them. A high voice shouted out in heavily accented English: 'Now we know we are not alone!'

7

'*Vous voulez un taxi? Un hotel? Messieurs? Mademoiselle? Permettez-moi!*'

At the Gare du Nord, a porter gripped the handle of Neville's suitcase. He had put it down so he could check the Paris guide-book, again.

'Certainly not. Give that back instantly!'

A tug of war ensued, which Neville won, with George's help. The porter shrugged and departed, leaving Neville stiff with offence.

'I say, why don't we just have some breakfast before we go any further?' George suggested. 'Give us a chance to sort ourselves out, eh?'

'Oh yes, do let's,' said Felix. 'Look, all those cafés over there . . . They look so lovely with all the tables on the pavement! Come on, Neville. And then, well, can we at least discuss the 'Paris by Night' tours we read about? Montmartre sounds heavenly.'

'Hmmm. I'm not sure about Montmartre. We'll have to be careful. They're very predatory, the Parisians, from what I've heard. Tourist prices for everything. They'll charge you an arm and a leg just to wash your hands if you don't watch out.'

As he spoke, Neville gazed at a smartly dressed American Express agent, standing by the columns a little way off. She had a neat circle of compatriots around her, all listening hard to her instructions about vouchers and charabancs. Felix hid a smile. Almost as much as she loved the indefinable Frenchness of it all – the jostling and the barging and the smells (*good gracious, the smells!*) – she secretly loved the fact that Neville did not feel at home. She had never seen him so ill at ease.

'Well, we can't stay here all day,' said George. 'We'll never see Paris.'

Felix picked up her case, and her chin moved forward.

'Not sure if those cafés are really suitable,' Neville fretted. 'It's far too cold to sit outside and I'd much rather get settled at the hotel. Now, let me just check . . .'

Felix moved off a few paces.

'The Hotel Cosmos, isn't it? Didn't you work out that the number seven would get us there quickest?' They were both poring over the bus map again. 'I don't think it's the right tube line. What do they call it here? *Le Metro*?'

Then she saw them. She was sure of it. The gabardine and the cap. And the two other men, both short and skinny but tough as anything (one with a broken nose) . . . they must be Fred and Ronnie. Every word of the conversation on deck came back to Felix. He'd extracted them from the bar after all. They didn't look too much the worse for wear.

Felix's heart began to hammer. She knew something was about to happen. Something huge. She could make it happen. In her pocket, her hand closed round her passport.

The four men were lining up at the taxi rank, looking around for some kind of sign, she supposed. Perhaps she was too. And this was it: her only chance. This time Felix didn't look back. Her suitcase banged uncomfortably at her legs, but she didn't run. She walked crisply and decisively towards the group of strangers, and slipped in behind them. Nobody noticed. It really wasn't like England at all.

There was so much hooting, and shouting, and brakes screeching, and movement, it was hard to make out what was going on. Felix kept her eyes on the traffic, her back to the station. Her whole body was alert and alive with excitement.

A bearded taxi driver swept in close to the pavement, and scanned the knotted crowd. As soon as he spotted the little English group, he put two fingers in his mouth. His piercing whistle got their attention.

'*Eh, camarades! Camarades! Ici! Venez vite! On y va.*'

'I reckon this is it,' said Fred, or maybe Ronnie. 'Come on.' The gabardine-dressed man waved and started forward. As his foot touched the running board, Felix reached his side.

'Oh please. I'm a nurse. Take me with you. I have to come now. They told me to find you.'

Without a flicker of doubt, the Scotsman took her case and put it in the front of the cab, in the space next to the driver. The others made way for her just as promptly. The glass slid back and the driver winked over his shoulder at Felix and gave her a most approving nod.

'*Bienvenus, mes camarades! Allons-y! Au Bureau des Syndicats!*'

The taxi roared through the city's broad streets and Felix knew that she'd escaped. They turned a sharp corner and she was thrown first against Ronnie, and then Fred. Or maybe the other way round. They steadied her between them.

'Thanks awfully.' Sitting up as straight as she could, she ground her feet to the floor of the taxi, and said brightly: 'They didn't mention I'd be joining you here then?'

All four men shook their heads, and their leader spoke.

'No, not a word. I suppose I should make sure you're not an infiltrator, but I think I'll leave that to the powers that be when we get to HQ.'

'Does she look like an infiltrator?' said the one on her left, scornful.

'You's all righ wi' us, hen.'

'Where's your uniform, ducky?' asked the one on her right. 'Where are you from?'

'London. The London Hospital. Whitechapel.'

'They've sent you on your own? A wee thing like you! Shame.'

The gabardine man let Felix off the hook. 'All right, all right. No need for the third degree. I'm sure they know what they're doing. I expect you're with Spanish Medical Aid, aren't you? Quite a few ambulances gone already, haven't they?'

'That's right.' She pretended to be better informed than she was. She was getting better and better at it. Then she remembered one of Sister Macpherson's favourite homilies. Attack is the best form of defence. (She'd been talking about germs.) So Felix started asking questions instead. Where were they from? What did they do? Normally, that was. But never why had they come.

The taxi crossed an enormous iron bridge over railway tracks, and then a smaller one over a wide and filthy canal, and pulled up in a wide sort of square. The Place du Combat, Felix noted, with a slight lurch. The driver gestured towards what looked like a bar. He wouldn't accept payment for the fare – just raised a clenched fist at the open window and sped off.

'Did he mean us to go in that café?' Felix asked, confused. At that moment a young man emerged from behind a green metal screen on the pavement nearby. She quickly looked away: he was still buttoning up his flies. That explained the stink of ancient urine.

She couldn't imagine what Neville would be making of Paris. What would he be doing now? Don't think about it. He's got George. Oh God, George. Poor George. He means so well. He

44

didn't deserve this. But at least she had saved him the humiliation of a refusal to his face. And nobody could ever accuse her of raising his hopes. She'd never been that kind of a girl.

'Over there? Yes, I think so. Can this really be the Trade Union HQ? I suppose it must be.'

The café was rough and ready and fairly large. So was its patron, who sized them up the moment they came in. Without a word, he thumbed at an unmarked door at the back. They trooped up the stairs without speaking. The office above contained a wall full of paint-chipped filing cabinets and three wooden desks, with mountains of paperwork on each. A loud conversation in a guttural tongue was taking place at the desk on the right, while railway tickets were counted and handed out to the left.

The middle desk was occupied by a heavy-browed woman. She studied them briefly, stabbed out her cigarette in an ashtray already close to capacity, and then leaned forward and stared hard at Felix.

'Sit down, my dear.' She was English. Her voice was rather grand and gravelly and very commanding, like a headmistress's. The others were still hovering, but the woman waved them towards one of her colleagues. 'Over there. He'll deal with you lot.'

Felix put down her case and scraped up a chair.

'And you are . . . ?'

Felix wasn't at all sure whether handshaking was done in Communist circles, but she couldn't help herself.

'Nurse Felicity Rose.' Her voice sounded several degrees calmer than she felt.

'Aha! Call me Rita. Do I know about you?'

Felix glanced at her taxi companions, but they seemed safely in conversation with the man at the other desk.

45

'No, actually, you don't, I'm afraid. It's been quite a recent decision – to volunteer that is. I don't believe I'll be on any records yet.'

That was something of an understatement.

'So you're not attached to any unit?'

'No, no, I'm not. Not yet, that is. Do you think that might be a problem?'

Felix sensed she was being weighed up. Whatever this test was, it made her determined to pass. Wasn't she going to ask her anything else? Her age, her training? Perhaps that came later.

'Not at all. Quite the reverse. Quite the reverse.' Rita repeated the words with a slow smile.

'Oh?' Felix's face retained its beautiful composure. So useful.

But inside it felt like that moment when you part with your coins at the bottom of the helter-skelter. You pick up your mat, and start to climb the stairs, and never quite know how things will look from the top. The world below looks slow and distant and small, workaday noises muffled and distorted. The pressure of the person behind forces you into the first slithering inches. Then momentum takes over.

Rita leaned forward. 'We've got a bit of a to-do on just now. You might just be the answer. London sent out a spanking new ambulance last week – absolutely marvellous, fully kitted out – and blow me, they haven't even made it to Chartres when one of the nurses goes down with appendicitis. Rotten luck for her. They came back to Paris right away – she's just been oper-ated on.'

'Oh dear . . .'

'Oh, don't worry, girl. She'll be right as rain soon enough. Well, no, in fact not soon enough for us of course. She won't be going anywhere in a hurry. We were about to send the vehicle off with an empty seat. Such a waste! But you'll do splendidly instead of Joan. Can you leave tonight?'

'Yes, that would suit me very well,' said Felix. *They'll never find me before then.* Then came an agonizing pang of guilt. 'Would it be possible to send a telegram . . . maybe get a message to someone? I just need to let my brother know.'

'In England?'

'No, no, he's in Paris. The Hotel Cosmos.'

'Don't you want to say goodbye? There's plenty of time.'

'Oh no, no, it's fine, really, we've done that,' she lied. 'It's just I promised to let him know exactly when I was going. So he doesn't keep the hotel room for me, you know, that kind of thing.'

Rita gave her a funny look. Subterfuge didn't bother her. Nor did much pass her by. 'Paper?'

'Yes, please. Thanks awfully.'

The older woman passed Felix a notepad and pencil. An envelope followed and then Rita busied herself tactfully, completing some sort of form which she finished off with a loud rubber stamp before moving on to the next in the pile. Felix sheltered behind the towering heap of papers.

There really wasn't much to say. Room for one more half-lie about being sorry. Well, she was. She didn't *want* to upset anyone. She thought about it just long enough for a horribly strong image of her mother to thrust itself into her head. (She was sitting at the kitchen table with a cup of tea and the mending.) Then she licked the envelope flap and stuck it down.

'Finished? Excellent. Well, I'll see it's delivered right away.'

'Oh no,' burst out Felix. 'Not right away, please. This evening will be fine, really.'

'I see.'

47

A phantom smile, the ghost of confederacy, and back to brusqueness and the paperwork.

It wasn't her business, all that sort of stuff. Rita just needed a nurse and she'd found one. This creature was far too young to have serious ties at home. No ring in sight. And there was something about her that Rita found reassuring, though she couldn't quite put her finger on it. She looked her over once more, in case she was missing something. Yes, this girl was certainly self-possessed. Hair on the long side, but she'd find that out for herself soon enough. It wasn't the usual way of going about things, but everything was happening so fast it was hard to say what *was* the usual way. Anyway, needs must. War's war.

8

That morning Nat woke to whitewashed walls splashed with cinnabar and Van Dyke brown and fountains of burnt alizarin. Then, with a jolt, he remembered. He was looking at bullet holes and bloodstains. These were barracks that had once belonged to the Guardia Civil, Spain's military police force. Holed-up Fascist sympathisers had refused to surrender a few months earlier. So the local militia executed them where they stood.

Albacete didn't look any better by daylight. In fact the whole place seemed grimmer than ever. It wasn't how he had imagined the International Brigade Headquarters, not at all. After breakfast the newcomers were herded through muddy streets into a bullring, sandy-floored. The milling men were slowly divided up.

Anyone who'd ever served in the cavalry to stand over there. Artillery over there. Motor mechanics sign up with that man. What next, Nat wondered? Electricians, then telephonists. Then what? It was hard to be sure. Orders were shouted in French, and translated into a dozen or more languages by anyone who thought they could. He wondered what they might call out that could apply to him. Printer? Lithographer? Hardly.

At last he was left with the largest group – the foot soldiers, he supposed. No . . . Infantry. That was the word. That's what he'd tell Felix. This was good. He was fed up with being singled out for his talent for art. It may have saved him at school, and saved him from tailoring too, but it was only a part of him, after all, and he didn't see why he had to be defined by it. He was just like all the others now. He nodded, and grinned. Shook hands. Compared notes.

Bubbles of laughter kept simmering up. This crowd was short on skills but not enthusiasm. Nat was beginning to enjoy the babble of different languages. He'd heard Lithuanian and Latvian and Polish and Russian in the East End all his life. Yiddish cut through borders of course, and it was reassuringly familiar here too, as well as useful. Quite a few Welsh voices rose and fell. And then there were strange versions of English . . . were these men Australian? Canadian? He wasn't sure. It wasn't quite like the films.

Nat preferred listening to talking just now. He would rather soak up the strangeness of it all than try to join in. He found himself searching the German Brigaders' faces for marks of experience. They seemed gaunter, wiser, harder than the rest. Shadowed. The Italians too. Or was that his imagination? These were men who had already lost the battle against Fascism in their own countries. He had no idea how many soldiers Hitler and Mussolini had sent to fight in Spain, but he knew it wasn't just one country's civil war. Nat thought about the hatred he'd seen on the faces of Blackshirts back in England, and the memory strengthened his resolve.

Then everyone was told to line up according to their language.

Eventually he reached the front of his queue. At the table sat a pockmarked man in a long leather coat. Nat took in the pistol in his belt, and the lines on his face. He seemed fierce at first, as he put out a hand for the papers issued in Paris. He checked them, and then double-checked Nat's age (now twenty-one – he'd managed to age another couple of years even since upping the truth in London). Nat watched his name appearing on his identity card. *República Española. Brigadas Internacionales*, he read upside down. *Carnet militar para appellidos: Kaplan. Nombre: Nat.*

'Political affiliation . . .'

'Young Communist League,' he offered. The man shook his head.

'*Anti-fascista*,' he wrote firmly, then looked Nat straight in the eye. 'Safer that way.'

Finally, the official handed him another folded card. 'And here's your pay book.'

'Pay book?' he said, amazed. 'But I'm a volunteer!'

'We all are, Sonny. But we're in the Republican Army now. It's only seven pesetas a day. Nothing to write home about. And you'll have a job to spend it most of the time.'

'Thank you. Sir. Comrade. Thank you very much.'

'OK. Next please. Move along.'

Sneaking a look back at the others, Nat saw a boy he recognised. Skinny. Ginger-haired. Bit of a putz. It was the boy from the bus and he was called Tommy. He looked a lot chirpier now. Nat shot him a quick encouraging smile, which he returned. Just a wobble then.

Back at the barracks, it was off to the storerooms for uniforms. Nat expected more lining up, more papers to show, things to tick off lists, but it was like a jumble sale in there. It made Petticoat Lane market look like Harrods. Heaps of mismatched clothing lay in tumbled piles, roughly sorted into coats, trousers and footwear. Men picked through them, and held garments against themselves, trying things for size. Some were laughing; some looked stony. Others were beginning to kvetch and grumble.

Nat spotted a thick woollen suit, remembered the snow he'd seen on the peaks of the Pyrenees, and made a grab for it. But he was too late, and the man who got there first wouldn't meet his eye. So he settled for a brown serge jacket and nearly matching trousers, the closest thing there was to a uniform. Boots seemed to be standard issue – strong enough, he hoped. Better than those rope-soled canvas things the Spaniards all seemed to wear, which didn't seem much like shoes to him. The clothes felt cool and slightly damp to the touch; they'd caught a chill from the cold stone floor.

In another storeroom, blankets were handed out. Each man showed the next: you had to roll them up like sausages, tie the ends together and wear them like a sash. Only possible because they were so thin. Next a groundsheet cape, rubberised and clammy. Finally a leather belt and cross straps, a bayonet frog and ammunition box, and a thin tin helmet, rather battered. It looked like something from the Great War.

Moving down the corridor, Nat saw it was time to give up his civvies. He handed over his jacket and felt the swinging weight of his book in its pocket.

'Half a mo.' He stepped aside to let the next man past, and rescued his Jack London and his pencils too. He certainly wasn't going to let those go. Was there time to look at the flyleaf? Just a glimpse of her face? Best not. The Spanish soldier clearly wanted his trousers too, and fast.

Nat hesitated. Goodbye, Dad.

'Waiting for a cloakroom ticket?' The laughing voice coming from the queue was familiar. London. Nat had spotted that open face before, right behind him in the line for identity cards. He knew his type, and he knew he meant well. 'It's not the Savoy, you know,' his new comrade continued. 'Believe me, you can kiss goodbye to them lot. Oh, I get it! It's a looking glass you're after!'

Nat grinned, and unbuttoned his trousers.

'Suits you!' The man rapped on Nat's helmet with his knuckles. 'Every inch a soldier! Stand up straight now. *Klaider machen dem mentshen*. Just don't expect that thing to stop a bullet, please God may it not have to. And if you think this lot's heavy, wait till you get your weapons and ammunition.' He winked. 'Though from what I hear, that could take some time.'

'So what now, then?' Nat asked. This man had a bouncy confidence about him that felt encouraging. Maybe he should stick with him.

'Follow me.' Just before turning, the man gave Nat another quick once over with crinkling eyes and stuck out his hand. 'I'm Bernie. Don't believe I've had the pleasure.'

Nat returned his hard squeeze.

'Nat. Pleased to meet you.'

A few steps later he heard Bernie murmur to himself. 'Twenty-one already? If you say so.'

Out in the sunshine, Nat blinked. Arriving? That was a joke. They were on the move again already. A crowd was forming, all newly kitted men, and a line of trucks was waiting for them, revving engines. Hadn't they already schlepped round half of Spain?

The British Battalion started to pile in.

'Next stop, Madrigueras,' said Bernie. 'Hold on tight.'

9

'It's Felix's writing, isn't it?' said George. 'What does she say?'

He was reliving that falling feeling at the Gare du Nord. He had turned to ask Felix what she thought, and found her gone. And just as he was despairing of ever finding her in the crowds, he had spotted her . . . at least, he thought he had. George and Neville argued all day about it, replaying the scene endlessly. Could it really have been Felix getting into that taxi with those strangers? Surely she was the kind of girl to put up a fight in a tight spot? George wanted Neville to go straight to the police. Neville didn't trust a French *gendarme* to sort anything out.

'Just tell me what's happened,' said George, wishing now he'd opened the envelope straight away himself, never mind the name on it.

Neville read so slowly he could have been translating from a foreign language.

Come on. Come on. 'Has she been kidnapped?' George asked. Stupid question. She'd hardly write her own ransom note. He felt the weight of the little box heavy in his pocket and despaired.

Neville still didn't answer. His whole body went limp and he let out a kind of moan.

'Oh God, why did I get her a passport? We could have come on a weekend ticket. There was no need. And she's only seventeen. I thought . . . I thought . . . No, we shouldn't have come at all.' Then he turned to George, looked at him with disgust and said: 'Why did you have to persuade me?'

George snapped. 'For God's sake shut up and tell me what she says!'

'She's gone to Spain. Red Spain. She's only volunteered as a nurse, the silly little bitch.'

George was rarely moved to violence, but he found his right hand had formed a hard fist. It took an enormous effort to hold it back with the other.

'Don't you ever speak about your sister like that again,' he said, very quietly.

Neville had shocked even himself. 'I'm sorry. I shouldn't have said that. Unforgivable.'

'Yes.'

'But how dare she? How dare she? Why the hell is it any business of hers what's going on in Spain? They can kill each other all they like without our help.' He paced the room, fingering his moustache. 'I was supposed to look after her. I promised Mother. What am I going to say to Mother?'

Like animals in a zoo, they circled each other, though there was barely room. The third time he passed the window, George stopped and struggled with the unfamiliar catch. He threw open the casement and the shutters. He didn't actually want to look at the ring again. It was nothing special really, not in itself: just a very simple solitaire, and not very many carats. But it had seemed just right for Felix. Without a word, he suddenly hurled the small red leather box down onto the street below, where it bounced faintly off the pavement and into the gutter.

'Damn. Damn. Damn.'

He couldn't get that image out of his head. Felix's navy coat disappearing into the taxi. Her bent head. She'd gone without a backward glance. If only he'd made his intentions clearer.

For a while, he stood hunched over the peeling ironwork, half-leaning out into the Paris evening. He breathed in the cold air, hoping for inspiration, or maybe consolation: he wasn't sure which. It dawned on him how much he'd come to take the Rose family for granted. George's first ever job, so soon after his mother's death, had been hard. What a difference it had made during those gloomy days in a strange city to have Neville at the office, showing him the ropes. His invitations home gave George the perfect excuse to disappear at weekends too. His heart would lighten each time he left the baby-sick smell of his older brother's house, and the noise and the mess and all those children, and set off for leafy Sydenham, where order reigned, and tea was always on time.

After he landed the job at the paper, his visits to Sydenham became even more frequent. It was round about then that Felix left home to start her nursing training and he started to think of her, well, like that. Quite a surprise, really. Had she changed? Grown up suddenly? He wasn't sure. But he knew she was nothing like the girls he met at work. You always knew exactly what was going on in their heads. Felix was so unpredictable. (Who would have thought she could care so much about Spain?) Was there such a thing as the quietly fiery type? Her face gave so little away. You wanted to look at it for hours, just in the hope you'd find some clue to her thoughts.

This was getting him nowhere. He turned back to the lit room, where Neville sat on the bed rereading the note with a terrible crumpled look on his face. George approached his friend, tentatively. He thought about putting a reassuring hand on his shoulder, and decided not to.

'Look, just give me a few minutes,' he said. 'I'll talk to the manager, see if I can put through a few phone calls. Might be able to come up with something. Track her down. Can I get you anything, in the meantime? How about a whisky?'

'Certainly not. I'm fine. You go.'

For once, Neville seemed content to put himself in George's hands.

George took the stairs two at a time, all four flights of them, his shoulder brushing against the flock wallpaper. He was panting a little when he got back. The ring was safely back in his pocket. It had missed a drain by a matter of inches.

'This is what we're going to do,' he announced. 'You get back to London and tell your mother not to worry about a thing. I'm going to fetch Felix back.'

'Pardon?'

'I'm going after her. To Spain.'

'You're not serious?'

'Absolutely serious.'

'Oh, George, this really is so good of you. If I can ever . . .'

The gratitude on Neville's face embarrassed George.

'No, no . . . It's nothing. I've squared it with the paper. Sports editor's not too cheery, but News is delighted. They've been pushing for months for a man in Spain they can trust. The editor's fed up to the back teeth with garish descriptions of the collapse of Madrid that turn out to be total fabrications, cobbled together in some café miles away. He's all for it.'

'She won't be hard to find, will she?' asked Neville, a little doubtfully. 'I mean, how many English nurses can there be in Spain?'

More than you think, George carefully didn't say. 'I'm sure I'll be able to find out where she's gone. I might even manage to catch up with her before she leaves France. You never know. The only trouble is . . .'

Neville wasn't listening. 'Maybe they won't let her into Spain!' he said. 'Isn't it against the non-intervention agreement?'

'Doesn't apply to humanitarian aid, I'm afraid.'

'What if they don't let *you* in?' Aghast again. 'Supposing they think *you're* off to fight?'

'Press card. I'll be fine. Don't worry.' George patted his breast pocket optimistically. He was pretty sure he was right.

'And you'll bring her straight back, won't you? As soon as you find her? She mustn't stay in Spain. She mustn't.'

'I'll wire you right away.'

Neville was reassured – enough, at least, to suggest they go out to eat. George decided not to confess just yet that he had to file his racehorse piece before he could set off for Spain. It didn't seem very valiant. Neville would take the news far better on a full stomach.

10

Felix stood on the dusty road, rereading the writing on the front of the ambulance and wishing she didn't have to get back into it quite so soon. She rolled the words round her tongue.

'*Medicamentos para los obreros de España.*'

The letters were hand painted in white capitals, bold against dark green paintwork. They got bigger and bigger until they reached the huge final 'A' of *España*. Each time she saw them, her heart beat a little faster. This was what she'd undertaken. Medicine for the workers of Spain. She was sure Nat would approve.

It had taken nearly a week to get through France, and as long again to crawl down the coast of Spain. Only when they reached Valencia could they safely head west, towards Madrid.

'Hop in!' said Kitty, when everyone had emerged from behind their bushes. Brisk and kind, she was returning to Spain with the full weight of experience behind her, and everyone respected her for that. 'If we press on, we should get there before dark. Look, I managed to get some oranges.'

Felix declined the fruit and concentrated on keeping the rest of her food down. Spanish roads were even worse than French ones. It wasn't a question of Charlie having to remember to drive on the right – he swerved to wherever he could see the fewest potholes. Wondering exactly what or where 'there' might be was quite out of the question. Felix was just glad she'd find out soon.

The vehicle was stuffed with so many boxes of supplies they could barely move. A folding operating table, sterilising equipment, instruments, drugs, and boxes and boxes of dressings. And disinfectant of course. The nostril-tingling smell of Lysol made Felix feel strangely at home. Knee to knee with Kitty again, she felt she'd known her new friend for ever.

As soon as they were all settled, Kitty's enquiring eyebrows appeared above the tortoiseshell frames of her spectacles and she asked, 'So who's ready for another Spanish lesson?'

John groaned. 'Oh, have pity, Kitty,' the doctor begged. 'I just can't take any more in.'

'There'll be no time for this kind of thing when we get to Tarancón. I know you think I'm a slave-driver – well, yes, I admit it. I am.' Kitty's energy was relentless. 'But it'll all make more sense soon, I promise. Once you're hearing it around you all the time. Though I suppose it depends where we all end up in the long run . . .'

'You're right. Now, where's my pen?'

Mr Smilie pronounced it 'pin', which made Felix smile. Their surgeon was from New Zealand. He was on a research trip to London when war broke out and he didn't plan to return home until Fascism was defeated in Spain.

Mr Smilie lived up to his name. They told him, and he just replied, 'Oh, call me Doug. We're all comrades here.'

He liked to learn his Spanish in inspiring phrases. Kitty was happy to supply them.

'¡*Primero ganar la guerra!* First win the war!' That was one of his favourites.

All through Catalonia and Valencia, and now in the hills of New Castile, they were welcomed with warmth. Every village they stopped at offered them food. Food and enthusiasm. Felix began to expect the women and children who came out to greet them. The only men they ever saw were ancient – tiny men, bowed and bent. They were the men who couldn't fight. At night, the medical team pulled over into a field or olive grove. They covered the ambulance with branches and leaves and slept on stretchers.

Felix's new companions were terrifyingly well-informed. Rather like Nat. Half of them wore spectacles and they all talked about the international proletariat and solidarity and justice, and sang songs she'd never heard before. 'Oh, I'm the man, the very fat man, who waters the workers' beer,' chorused Felix with the others, feeling more worldly with every verse. Then Kitty sang 'The Peat-Bog Soldiers', in German, while the rest of them beat time, and Charlie thumped the steering wheel.

'They sing it in the camps, in Germany. You know about the camps?' said Kitty.

'Camps?' Felix only knew about holiday camps.

'Work camps. Concentration camps. "Politicals" – subversives, that is – they got chucked in as soon as Hitler came to power.'

The others all knew of course.

'First it was communists and social democrats and trade unionists,' said John.

'Then it was gypsies and homosexuals,' added Kitty.

'Now they're sending the Jews.'

A squadron of German fighter planes flew overhead and Felix's last twinges of guilt about her mother and George were wiped out. *Aviones*, Kitty taught them. 'Listen out for the church bells. That's a warning. And they target ambulances, and hospitals, so don't imagine for a moment that a red cross will save you.'

After they had taken cover, Felix wrote her first letter home.

It had been forming in her head for days. The long drive left so much time to mull over things.

Now that I'm here I know. You see Spain in the newsreels, and it feels so far away, nothing to do with England. But that's not true. It couldn't be closer. Now I know this is a war that matters for everyone, all over the world.

Everything seemed so clear.

We're all involved. We can't let the Blackshirts win in England, and we can't let the Nationalists force their way into power here either. It's a fight for the only things really worth fighting for – everything I always used to take for granted, I suppose . . . like freedom, and elections, and being able to say what you think. I can't just close my eyes and pretend it's not happening. Fighting here is the only thing we can do right now to stop Fascist bombers flying over Lawrie Park Road next year, or the year after.

Or the tenements of Whitechapel and Stepney. Felix did not tell her mother the other reason why she'd come. She found it hard to admit to herself.

At last the ambulance swung through an archway and came to a stop. Charlie opened the doors at the back. They had just beaten the sunset.

'So this is it,' said Felix, staggering down the steps at the back of the ambulance, unlocking her stiff knees and stamping her feet – partly to relieve her pins and needles, partly because it was so cold outside. She tried to stamp away the sinking feeling too. It felt so grim here. What had she let herself in for?

Doug looked up at rusticated stone walls rising on three sides of the courtyard. 'Medieval, isn't it? Literally. What is this place?'

'It used to be a monastery,' said Kitty. 'It's a base hospital now. Takes the cases that can travel from the front. And local casualties of course. We're all five of us working here until further notice.'

Kitty bustled around hugging old friends, ticking off lists, showing off the new sterilisers, re-organising the storerooms. The others followed her, dazed, and trying not to show it.

'Come and inspect the wards now,' she said at last.

Felix hesitated. It was a stupid thought. But she couldn't block it out, and it made her heart throb in her throat. She pictured Nat lying there, his head on a crisp white pillowcase. She imagined a wavering smile of recognition. Running across to him, half-sobbing. *Don't be ridiculous*, she told herself. *This is life, not a fairy tale. Anyway, he'll be off training somewhere still. They couldn't possibly send men –* boys *– out to battle without teaching them how to fight.* She straightened her back and followed Kitty into the old refectory.

The operating tables stood where six months earlier monks had gathered for daily meals. A few curtains pulled across the corners of the room marked off the staff's sleeping quarters. The beds were in corridors and cells, neat and orderly, but defiantly out of place. Most were empty, waiting. Propped up in one bed, a child of about six or so was stroking a bandaged stump listlessly with one good hand. Its hair was cropped. Felix couldn't tell if it was a girl or boy.

'It's quiet now, much quieter than when I left,' said Kitty. 'The latest action's mostly been on the La Coruña road, they've just been telling me. It's a relief, I can tell you. Just random bombing round here for weeks now.'

'Just,' said Charlie, expressively, his eyes on the other occupied beds. They were nearly all civilian casualties in this room. The *practicantes* were settling them for the night, said Kitty. 'Medical students mostly. We've lost a lot of doctors to the other side.'

A small gaggle of white-aproned Spanish girls assembled,

summoned by one of Kitty's rapid-fire instructions. They shuffled together, whispering and giggling behind their hands, and eyed up the new volunteers.

'Aha, *las chicas*! Here they are!' Kitty greeted each one with kisses that knocked her spectacles askew. 'Meet the team . . . this place would be nowhere without this lot, I tell you. Washing, cooking . . . and you wouldn't believe how their nursing skills are coming along too. Felix, come and meet Teresa, and this is Maria, Amelia, Concepçion . . . and, come along, come along, now let me see . . .' Kitty's flow was cut short by the sight of a girl she didn't recognise. She hung back from the others, and they made no effort to encourage her forward.

'You're new here?' Kitty asked in Spanish, and the girl nodded, still looking at the floor.

'What's your name, dear?'

'Dolores.' She spoke in a husky whisper, and then, like an afterthought, darted her hand out to be shaken.

'Welcome, welcome. *Encantada* . . .' Kitty sped on in Spanish. 'Look! Fresh blood for us! Meet Mr Smilie, our new surgeon. And this is Dr John Phillips, from England . . . Charlie, our driver . . . Felicity . . . call her Felix . . .'

Felix smiled hard, exhausted but eager. This girl, Dolores, looked pitifully shy. Felix felt her own confidence grow in contrast. Maybe she could draw this *chica* out of herself a little, in time. They could learn how to manage everything together.

'*Salud*,' said Felix. She shook Dolores's hand, and didn't let go until she'd met her eye. Still not a smile.

After issuing orders to the girls, Kitty glanced again at Dolores and lowered her voice. 'Some of the local girls are finding all this awfully difficult. You have to be patient. It's just not what they've been brought up to do. They're not used to it. Simply no experience.'

'Of washing and cooking?' said Charlie bluntly.

'No, not that. It's the nursing.' Kitty's voice dropped to a whisper. 'Bodies,' she mouthed.

'Nobody's fond of corpses,' pointed out Mr Smilie.

'Oh, I didn't mean dead ones,' said Kitty. 'It's the wounded men. They don't like touching their bodies. Washing and so on. Say it's not proper. That's what they've been taught.'

Felix kept on smiling at Dolores. She felt uncomfortable discussing her in English like that, right in front of her. The girl must have realised, for she blushed, and walked away after the others.

'Weren't there nurses in Spain before the war?' Charlie asked. 'This country is even more medieval than I thought.'

'Oh, there were. But they were nuns, mostly. Now they're on the other side of course. With the Rebels. The Catholic Church has always been hand in glove with the Nationalists, you know. The clergy, at any rate. Too many centuries of running the show themselves to put up with a Republic.'

'The Bishops see this war as a holy crusade, I heard,' added Mr Smilie. 'Kill a Red and save your soul.'

'I suppose the last thing the *padres* want is social revolution,' said Charlie, eyebrows raised.

'Or women voting. Or peasants reading. That's why there's been such a backlash against the Church – how do you think we got this place?' said Kitty. 'But not to worry . . . times are changing, aren't they? Onwards and upwards. Workers of the world unite.'

Felix can't control her dreams. Perhaps it's the drugs they've given her. It feels a kind of madness. She's with Nat, always. Nowhere she quite recognises. Somewhere out of time. But they are alone and together at last. She's inhaling his outward breaths, intoxicating herself with the smell of his skin, dispelling the odour of death. He's turning her face to kiss her, pulling her towards him, and she's letting herself go, almost floating. She wants to fall. Finally, she feels safe.

She's wearing an enormous coat – it swamps her – and Nat has slipped his arms round her inside the coat so that it's wrapped round both of them. His hand explores the wing of her shoulder blade.

'Wait,' he says. 'I want to be closer. I want to feel you against me.' As he says this he's disentangling himself from her, moving away, and she can hardly bear this minute separation. 'You're so warm. I've missed you so much.' He unbuttons his jacket, and shrugs it off, never taking his eyes off her face.

And then she sees the gun and remembers everything.

NOVEMBER 1936–FEBRUARY 1937

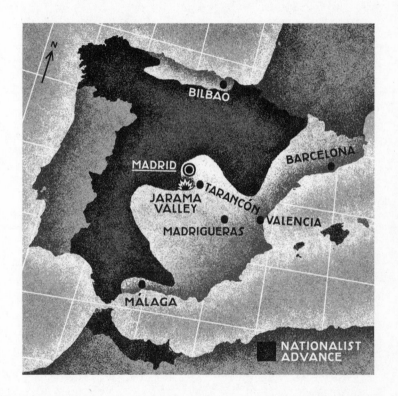

11

In Madrid, hunched at his dressing table in the Hotel Gran Vía, George's fingertips kept sticking to the keys of his typewriter. He turned up the collar of his overcoat, and blew into each fist as hard as he could, cradling each in turn with the opposite hand. It made little difference: the heat never seemed to get to the ends of his fingers.

If he didn't get a move on, there'd be nothing left to eat at the grill in the basement. For the past week it had been lentils, lentils, cauliflower and, on one good night, some ancient pickled sardines.

George swore quietly and backspaced laboriously. *Kerchunk, kerchunk, kerchunk.* The copy of his article was studded with dark XXXXXXXs where he'd typed over his mistakes. And every change of heart. He was writing an account of his visit that morning to Madrid's front lines. He wanted to capture the spirit of life in a city under siege. *No pasarán!* he thought it could be called. *Madrid stands firm against bombardment.*

He read through what he had written.

University City is just a tram ride away from the capital's centre. Trenches are carved out of the campus, a place so new it was still unfinished when war began. Now it is ruined. Exposed honeycombs of building tremble amid the rubble.

Now, how to get across this thing about the noise? It sounded so different when you got there, and everything was so much closer. George pushed his chair back from the dressing table, and stomped up and down the room, hoping to unfreeze his toes. Out loud, he tried different words for the sound of shells in close-up.

'Whining? Screaming?' A bit obvious. And too many other things were screaming. Sirens, children, rifle fire, animals. And sometimes, when it was really close, there was a kind of twanging sound when the shells fell and then it was more like a tube train just rushing towards you. It was terrifying.

He mustn't forget to mention the singing. The singing that so often greeted the shells amazed George. Had Felix heard the singing?

George's transformation from roving sports reporter to war correspondent had come as quite a shock to the system. He still wasn't sure he was up to the job. As for Felix . . . well, his 'investigations' into her whereabouts had been a total failure so far. No other word for it. So much for those blithe promises he'd made in Paris. Oh yes, very heroic he'd felt when he got on the plane. Deluded, that was how he felt now. Such arrogance! At least he had no witness to his failures. He'd write to Neville next week.

He looked into the coffee cup on the mantelpiece, but it held only dregs. George went back to the typewriter and resumed his syncopated hammering.

Here bullets are stopped by walls of books. For Spanish soldiers, as soon as the firing calms, daily lessons in literacy resume in trench schools up and down the front line. A short distance away, across a tiny strip of no-man's-land, if you are quiet, you can hear the laughter and curses of the enemy.

He frowned. So tricky to hit the right note. A French correspondent had been complaining in the bar the night before. Nothing *he* wrote from Madrid was printed these days. How had this war suddenly become old news? It felt so intense to him, so extraordinary, so unbelievable.

Flicking up the silver typewriter bar to release the carriage, George pulled out the last page and checked his watch. So late! His steps clattered down the marble stairs, and echoed into a near empty dining room. He *had* missed the food. Blast it. The vile smell of it followed him out of the hotel lobby, past the guards, and was lost in the smoky blackness of the street outside. On the threshold stood the concierge, frowning at the broken cobblestones and shattered glass left by the last shell.

'Very regrettable,' he kept saying, as though a heavy thunderstorm had disturbed his guests. 'Most regrettable. But not as bad as November. Last month was much worse.'

George stepped past. All clear now, thank God. And no fog tonight. A dash across the road, and into the towering mass of the Telefónica building. He reached the fourth floor, caught his breath and joined the other journalists waiting to hand in their copy.

'Hello, George.' It was Ilsa, one of the censors. He'd heard she'd come from Austria to help. Her plump face peered out from a mass of black hair. 'I'll look after this. I'm afraid it'll be a bit of a wait to file tonight. The Americans. Very wordy. Oh, any news of your . . . your friend's sister?

George didn't reply. Ilsa reached out and squeezed his arm, her sympathy quick and businesslike. 'Ah well. I'm sorry. Still, I do think that in a case like this no news is good news.'

'I dare say.'

Ilsa had a way of looking as though she knew more than you'd told her, and it embarrassed George.

'I asked again at the Casa de Medicina,' he told her as soon as his throat felt less choked. 'I think I've been to at least half the hospitals in Madrid already.'

'There are so many now. You have enquired at the new operating theatre at the Ritz Hotel?'

'Yesterday.'

'It's always possible she's travelling . . . working . . . under a different name. You've thought of that? Yes, I expect you have. Mmmm. And still no word from Albacete? No, it's never easy to get that kind of information from Brigade HQ.' Ilsa's face suddenly looked more hopeful. 'I could check the latest casualty lists for you . . .' she offered, and something inside George turned over. 'Just in case . . . ? They arrived a short time ago. I need to go through them anyway.'

'Really?' George managed to sound almost indifferent. 'Yes, please, yes, would you do that? Thank you. It's Felicity. Felicity Rose. She calls herself Felix.'

'Yes, I remember. Now, how about a coffee while you wait? The orderly is just going down to the canteen for Arturo.'

Arturo, the chief censor, sat at his usual place at the wide desk in concentrated silence. It was a huge room – it must have been made for conferences, with all those vast tables. Most of the windows were now blocked with sheets of cardboard and mattresses, suspended against shrapnel. Arturo had a brandy in one hand, a red pencil in the other. A cigarette hung out of his mouth, and a pile of typescripts waited in front of him. His gaunt face looked carved and grooved in the flickering candle-light. Behind him George spotted a camp bed with a tumble of blankets on top, pushed to one side. So he really did live here.

George retreated to the press room, and slumped into a chair to wait his turn. Typewriters clattered like castanets, blotting out the noises of the street. He got out his notebook and pretended to be writing a piece. *Felix. Felix. Where are you?* He wrote the words over and over again. He hated talking to the other correspondents. He could never quite shake off the feeling he was a fraud.

'George! How are you?'

'Francesca. You're back.'

For a moment he thought the American journalist was leaning in for a continental-style kiss. She often seemed to get closer than he was comfortable with. This time, luckily, she just pulled up a chair, swinging her shiny hair at him as she held out a silver cigarette case. She was so confident, so committed. Never a hint of fear in *her* eyes. He unfroze a little, and asked politely, 'Good interview?'

'Oh yes, some fabulous material on the political divisions emerging on the Republican side. Socialists and anarchists and all that jazz. Fascinating stuff. Horse's mouth, too. Planning to go to the Casa de Campo later tonight. Wanna come?'

'Maybe.' A lurch of terror, but luckily Francesca didn't notice. She was already dashing off her dispatch, as if it were a shopping list.

'Quite a few of us going,' she said without looking up. 'Should see some action.'

'I'll let you know.'

Ilsa reappeared, with a black coffee and his article. George could see that she hadn't yet initialled it.

'Anything wrong?'

'We don't like this.' It was a sentence about a young Spanish soldier. George had spotted him at the front because he had the shakes. Against the staggering resilience of his companions, the boy stood out, painfully, and this had moved George. 'Too critical. No good for morale. You know the rules. You understand the problem.'

He didn't exactly agree with Ilsa, but he did see her point.

'It's a war of words too, you know,' she had pointed out, the first time he filed a piece. 'I'm not asking you to lie.'

'Fine. I'll cut it. There.'

She signed it, and returned him the top copy.

'Is there a telephonist free now?'

'Over here. Oh, and no casualties listed of that name. Nothing like it.'

Relief and despair. George thanked Ilsa, and turned away quickly.

He handed his carbon copy to the switch control to monitor, and passed the number of his news desk in England across to the operator. After a few minutes she managed a connection, and handed him his receiver. The voice in London sounded weary, and a very long way away. London, George thought, longingly. Where the only fires on the street belonged to roast chestnut sellers and you could walk into a pub and know you were going to walk out again. A city without sandbags. But right now, it was also a city without Felix, and that was something he would change if it killed him.

'Hello, George. What have you got for us tonight, then? Something juicy, I hope.'

George began to read, without expression. He wanted his words to speak for themselves. Halfway through there was a prolonged bout of mortar fire, and he had to stop.

'Can't hear you, old chap. Can you speak up? Artillery, did you say? Yes, of course, awfully sorry, but you see I'm expecting another call very shortly. Paris. They've tracked down Mrs Simpson.'

George took a deep breath. 'Sorry. Nearly finished. AMID SO MUCH CONFUSION COMMA ONE THING IS CERTAIN STOP THE PEOPLE OF MADRID WILL DEFEND THEIR CITY UNTO DEATH STOP THERE IS TOO MUCH AT STAKE TO GIVE UP NOW STOP COPY ENDS.'

He realised he wanted to cry.

'*That's it, then?*'

'Yes. That's it. Anything wrong?'

'*Look, George. It's great stuff. Very . . . emotional. The thing is though McGinty has been asking for a different angle on the war. Need to move things on now. Haven't you got any red atrocities for us? Apparently* The New York Times *has been running eyewitness accounts of massacres – Nationalist prisoners, executed nuns, you know, that kind of thing.*'

'Eyewitness? *The New York Times*? Really? I don't think that can be possible . . .'

There was a click on the line, and then silence. George stood up, and a white wave of fury rushed through him. He scrunched up his script without a word.

'Atrocities,' he said, under his breath. 'You want more atrocities, do you?'

Instead of trudging back downstairs, he walked over to the lift. Perched in her corner, the lift operator was as chirpy as ever, until they passed the eighth floor, at which point she became pale and silent. At the thirteenth floor he got out. The top part of the building was all but abandoned. There was a lone observation post set up there, manned by a couple of artillerymen. Across a jagged hole in the parquet floor, through twisted steel girders exposed by a stray shell, they looked at George curiously.

The top of the Telefónica tower was the most exposed place in Madrid. But it was a good place to think. From here, the vertiginous pit of the Gran Vía directly below felt more distant than the fighting. Further away, you could see everything, laid out before you like a battle plan on a general's table. Towards the north, the craggy black outline of the mountains, the Sierra de Guadarrama. The gleaming arc of the Manzanares river brought the front line west and then south, sweeping closer and closer until it was in the city itself. Where George had been that morning. From time to time the ground on either side of the silver strip of water trembled, and the treetops of the Casa de Campo shuddered and swayed. First he saw it and heard it. Flashes in the sky like fireworks, a few puffs of pale smoke, the quickstep rattle of anti-aircraft guns. Then he felt it. The vibrations shimmered towards the Telefónica, till they arrived under his own feet like rumbling trains. It was time to go.

12

The early days of February brought with them a glimpse of spring, and the line was garlanded with white ribbons, drying. Fresh bandages, neatly rolled, were ready to go back on patients. Felix was doing the laundry with Dolores, though it wasn't really her job. She and Kitty had decided the best way to encourage the *chicas* in this lull between storms was to make it clear that nothing was beneath them either.

The sun was delicious. Felix and Dolores both stood for a moment, eyes closed, basking like cats.

'Heavenly, isn't it?'

Dolores nodded.

'I can't tell you how terrified I was when I started *my* training,' said Felix. 'The trouble you'd be in if you did the slightest thing wrong in the sluice room.' She must find some way to reassure her. 'And every ward had its own routine – just a bit different, you know – and you had to learn it in a flash, or else. You certainly couldn't think for yourself, not like you have to here. This place may be a bit rough and ready, but at least nobody tells you off for trying to make the best of things.' She rolled her eyes and tried to mimic one of Sister MacPherson's fierce Edinburgh reprimands. '"Nurse! Nurse! You are here to take orders, not take the initiative. Nobody's interested in what *you* thought best!"'

Felix was relieved to see Dolores smiling. She couldn't possibly understand all that Felix said, but she seemed to get the drift of it.

'Oh, that sister always made me feel such a worm,' she went on, reassured. 'Mind you, I do miss the lavatories. And I don't know if I'll ever get used to the rats . . .'

Alone with Felix, apart from the others, Dolores was beginning to look more relaxed. Yes, her slumped shoulders had definitely started to straighten. From time to time, Felix had even seen her joking quietly with a patient. Such a relief. If only the other *chicas* would be more friendly to her too. They all had homes to go to, near the hospital. Perhaps they couldn't imagine what it was like to be so far away.

Just a few more bandages to roll.

With her deft hands and instinctive neatness, Dolores had the makings of an excellent nurse. She was one of the best. And helping her made Felix feel so much more confident herself, a hundred times more competent and . . . *useful*. Dolores still didn't say much, but Felix wasn't usually a big talker herself. Nobody round here spoke of the past, if they could help it, or what they'd left behind them. It was hard not to wonder though.

'You must be lonely without your family,' Felix said, unable to stop herself. 'Oh, no, no, please forgive me, I didn't mean to . . .' Her mention of family had distorted Dolores's face, deforming her beautiful serenity; the anger in her eyes was undisguised.

'My family is dead.'

Muerta. In English the word felt harsh and final and clinical. In Spanish it sounded so much more painful, so full of mourning.

'I'm so sorry.' Felix put her hand on Dolores's shoulder, and felt it tense, and then relax. Shrugging her off, Dolores bent to pick up a bandage that had unfurled itself on the stones, and a curtain of black hair fell across her face. She crammed the bandage into her apron pocket. It was contaminated and would have to be washed again. Dolores clearly didn't want to talk about what had happened, and Felix knew better than to ask, or study her too closely. She had heard too many stories already to be hungry for more details. Schoolteachers paraded through village streets; men shot simply for wearing spectacles. A kind of vengeance Felix found impossible to grasp. 'Long live death!' was the cry of Franco's followers. '*¡Viva la muerte!*'

We'll be your family now. That was what she wanted to say to Dolores. She glanced at her again and recognised the guilt in her eyes. *I know that feeling*, Felix thought to herself, *a little*. When you've let your family down, hurt your own mother, and it was the last thing you wanted to do. You couldn't help it, I'm sure. It wasn't your fault, whatever happened.

'Come on,' she said instead. 'It's time to change the dressings. *Los vendajes.* Ready? We'll do it together.'

'*Sí.* Let's go. *Vamos.*'

The quickest way back to the wards was through the unused chapel. Felix went ahead, the basket in her arms. She never felt quite comfortable striding across its shadowy space as though it was any old corridor, and she guessed she wasn't alone. The *chicas* from the villages must have gone to Mass most of their lives. Old habits die hard.

A faint whiff of incense still seemed to cling to the damp stone walls. She knew exactly what Neville would have to say about that. *Bells and smells*, he'd scoff. In fact wasn't it Sunday again, already? He'd probably be at church in Sydenham right now, with her mother. Maybe George, too. Praying for her, no doubt.

She turned to say something to Dolores, something about

lunch. She wanted to change the subject, if only in her head.

Dolores had stopped. She was standing in front of the bare altar, her eyes shut, her head bowed. Her lips were moving softly as she made the sign of the cross.

13

At Madrigueras a mist of fine rain had been falling for six days. It was the kind that soaks you to the skin without you noticing. Not that this had dented Nat's spirits.

Three abreast, their platoon was off on another route march.

'We'll all be bloody good at marching, if nothing else,' muttered Bernie as they fell in. All those city boys were toughening up. Not a moan about blisters for days. Nat felt he could dig a foxhole to match the wiliest vixen's. He was stronger too. The muscles on his arms and chest were much more obvious, he noticed with satisfaction. He wondered if Felix would notice too, when he got back.

'Think they'll send us into battle with these things?' He heaved his replica wooden rifle back onto his shoulder. It wouldn't convince anyone.

'The front's the priority. Wherever that is.'

At the training camp, information like that was as sparse as ammunition.

Marching gave them too much time for thinking and Nat's thoughts always turned to Felix. He loved just saying her name in his head. Felicity Rose. Felix. He'd said he would write, but he'd sent nothing yet. What had he actually done so far? Nothing that sounded heroic. What would she think of his wooden gun? But he would get something on paper. Tonight. He must. She didn't know how she was keeping him going. He didn't want to lose her. He wasn't going to be in Spain for ever.

A pep talk that afternoon held Nat spellbound.

'Theirs not to make reply,

Theirs not to reason why,

Theirs but to do and die.'

Nat knew the next line. They had done 'The Charge of the Light Brigade' at school.

'Into the valley of Death

Rode the six hundred.'

The captain's eyes moved across the rows of silent men. 'Stirring stuff, eh?' A few nodded, enthusiastically. 'Except the thing is, it doesn't apply to us. We're a Brigade that's going into battle because we *do* reason why. That's why *I'm* here. That's why *you're* here. And in the end, that's what's going to make you a better fighter. Knowing what you're fighting for – and believing in it.'

The warmth of brotherhood flooded the room, and made Nat glow.

'Moving on. Some background. Yesterday we discussed the agrarian reforms undertaken by the Second Republic in Spain. Today we'll be looking at the kind of models the Soviet Union can offer. Let's start in the Ukraine. In the first five-year plan, grain output rose . . .'

There was a groan from the back of the hall. Nat didn't look round. A few volunteers struck him as short on political commitment. Maybe they were after a bit of adventure, or just wanted to get off the dole. Heavy drinkers, mostly, always in the village bars. Nat tried to steer clear of them.

But as the lecture went on, the protests got louder.

'Oh give it a rest, for Pete's sake!' came a voice from his

left. 'We've had enough of this bloody rubbish. What about some real training?'

'Yeah!' Others were joining in. 'We don't care about tractors. Just tell us when we're going to fight.'

'We want guns! We want guns!' began the chant.

What could you expect from an army recruited from born rebels? Men who never marched in step, on principle.

That night Nat had a dream: a nightmare, really. He was facing a huge line of Franco's Moroccan troops. Images from newsreels fed his sleep: white turbans, blank dark faces, nothing human about these dream soldiers. As he raised his gun to fire, Nat tried to move his trigger finger. He squeezed it gently, ready to take the kick, but nothing happened. Then he squeezed harder, and harder still, pulling at it viciously, then with despair. That was when he realised he had nothing but a wooden gun to fight with. He couldn't save Spain with a wooden gun.

A few days later, in the vast empty church that towered over Madrigueras, they sat down to eat. The midday meal was chickpeas, sinking in oil and garlic. ('Carbuncles again? You must be joking!') As the men made their way back to the parade ground, a truck pulled up, causing such a commotion that even the company officers hesitated.

Nat stared as the tarpaulins slid off their load. He felt the carbuncles inside him knot and plummet.

'What have they got in the back there?' he asked a broken-nosed man on his right.

'You're thinking what I'm thinking. About the size of coffins if you ask me,' replied Ronnie grimly. 'But why would they bring them here? Stacked up like that?'

'I don't know.'

Nat was even more shocked to see how they were handled.

With respect, yes, even with awe. But the men unloading the rough wooden boxes were looking positively cheerful. Were they hardened to death already?

The Political Commissar was approaching their captain. They conferred, the captain smiled, and suddenly the company was ordered to gather round.

'Oh no!' Nat said under his breath, when he saw they were prising open the lid of the first box. This was a macabre message.

The officer wore the expression of a father about to pick up his newborn son for the first time. He reached inside the nearest box. But there was no sign of a corpse. Instead sawdust and shavings and newspaper were cast aside and the man raised a gleaming rifle above his head.

A loud cheer rang out. At last. Real weapons. From Mexico. Or so the word went round. Those who knew about such things talked of Mosins and Remingtons and Lee Enfields. The rest tried to look knowledgeable.

They formed a line that was close to orderly.

Nat's hands closed on a rifle. He felt its weight, and inhaled the thick grease and newness of it. He stroked its steel muzzle, and fondled the bolt. Five rounds, he was told. And yes, there was the bayonet clip they'd learned about. He fingered an engraved hammer and sickle on the side. Mexico? Really? Putting the gun to his shoulder, he nuzzled into the hollow he'd made and held the coolness to his hot cheek. Checked the sights. Beautiful, he thought, and wondered at himself.

He caught the ginger-haired boy's eye. Tommy. He'd got over his nerves. He was OK, though he did go on a bit. They watched each other aiming their guns and tried to imagine firing them.

The weapons instructor was a gentle-looking man in his forties, who commanded attention by the softness of his voice. He'd once been a sculptor.

'Now just remember, comrades, without the bayonet on, the sights won't work. The guns will fire high. If you don't bear that in mind, not only will you be wasting ammo: you'll be putting yourself and others at risk. They may seem light, but they've got a real kick. If you're not prepared for it, you'll find yourself on the floor, not your enemy. So hold it tight against your shoulder or it'll break your arm.'

Nat hunched his shoulder harder. The rifle didn't seem light to him. On the instructor's order, the men lowered their guns.

'Bayonets ready? Good. I'm going to show you how they're attached. What else have you got to remember before you put them on?'

How close did you have to be to think about using a bayonet? Maybe it would be obvious. One of the old-timers spoke out from the back.

'Keep the barrel clean.'

'Precisely. Or you'll never get it off again. Look after your weapon and it'll look after you.'

As he talked, more trucks drew up. Men jumped out of the cabs with an air of urgency. The lecture was interrupted.

The Battalion commander had sent his adjutant, a wiry man with round horn-rimmed spectacles.

'Listen carefully. You'll be saying goodbye to Madrigueras tonight. I can't tell you when exactly. If you go to bed at all, it's got to be in full marching order, boots on, weapons ready.' He hesitated for a moment, and coughed. 'Perhaps I shouldn't tell you this now, but you'll find out soon enough. The Nationalists are close to cutting off the Madrid–Valencia road. If we don't turn 'em back, Madrid has had it.'

14

The convoy moved off at dusk, heading for the front. Three surgical teams. With so many vehicles, it wasn't safe to drive in daylight. Villagers joined cooks and *chicas* and patients well enough to walk and they all gave them a good send-off. A few hours previously, Mr Smilie and the Czech surgeon, Jiri Fiedler, had set off with a chauffeur and an electrician and a mission to locate a suitable place to set up the new hospital, close to the front line. Felix and Kitty looked down from the cab of a truck piled high with supplies, Dolores squeezed between them and the driver.

'I'm glad you decided to come,' Kitty told her. 'The more people we can rely on the better.'

Dolores nodded, and smiled briefly.

'It's going to be hard to find time to get more staff, or do more training when we get there. I don't want to frighten you, but it can get awfully busy. You know what they call these evacuation posts?'

'*Hospitales de Sangre,*' whispered Dolores.

'Does that mean what I think it does?' asked Felix. 'Blood hospital?'

'Yes,' said Kitty, staring into the darkness.

Without lights, the *camiones* couldn't move fast. The slowest truck went first, so they wouldn't be separated. They juddered past silent villages and over bomb-damaged bridges. Nobody said much. After a few hours, Felix thought she heard the crescendo hum of a motorbike. The convoy shuddered to a halt. Up ahead, a dispatch rider approached the *autochir*, the leading vehicle. The biker handed over some papers and sped off. The convoy set off again, slow and laborious. The road began to climb.

Felix was asleep, her head on Kitty's shoulder, when a shout from Mr Smilie roused her. There were torches ahead, bobbing circles of light that showed the shadowy outlines of buildings. Then their truck pulled into another courtyard – festooned with balconies, as though ready for a troop of Juliets to appear, thought Felix – and the unloading began.

'Here, bring the instruments through to the bar,' called Mr Smilie. 'We'll set up theatre there. There's water, after a fashion. And these counters are a good height for operating tables. Sterilisation that way. Dispensary over there.'

'Bar?' said Kitty, coming through with Felix and Dolores. 'What is this place?'

'It's the Alcaldía. Sort of town hall, I suppose you could say. Anyway, it was this or a baroque palace covered in saints and cupids. Very fancy. Very primitive. All I can tell you is that we're closer to Madrid, and closer to the fighting. Now follow me . . .'

'Electricity?' interrupted John, anxiously.

'Not yet. It's coming. Diego's working on it.' As if on cue, a few lights stuttered into life, and then flickered off again. 'Go on, go on . . . yes!'

It was enough to see something. Felix set down her box of swabs by the stone sink, and set off after the others to have a quick look around before getting her next load.

'Had a hell of a job to get them to let us in,' admitted Mr

Smilie. 'The watchman fella didn't like it at all. "Tell him he'll be arrested if he doesn't let us open up!" Jiri kept saying. I tried. But I couldn't remember the word for "arrested" – still can't. What is it, damn it? I think I said he'd be shot. Couldn't think what else to say. That got him down here quick enough. Anyway, he's been very helpful. Look!'

Three bare bulbs hung from the ceiling, shedding their yellow light on a huge empty hall. There was a small stage at one end, and a pile of wooden benches stacked at the other.

'Perfect!' said Kitty. 'We've got twenty-five mattresses, and no beds. These will do nicely. Shall we sort this room out, John?'

'When I've checked the plumbing.' John vanished, frowning.

'Felix, help me find the best place for triage – probably through there, by the looks of things. We'll need to be able to sort out the wounded as quickly as possible. It's going to be tough, I'm afraid, but it's all about priorities. I can talk you through it later, but I'm pretty sure Doug wants you in theatre.'

The lights flickered again and died.

15

The sun was just rising. The whole wide valley was deserted. Nat traced the narrow paths leading from the village up the hillside as far as he could follow them with his eye. He took in the olive groves, and the pines and swaying cypresses between them. The dawn light caught the leaves of the silvery oaks and made them shimmer. The sky was as blue as any he'd seen yet in Spain. Everything seemed intensely calm and clean.

From far away came the sound of tearing silk. Two droning waves of aircraft appeared from nowhere and machine-gun fire broke out above. Necks craned, the men debated. Were the German Heinkels 45s or 46s? Junkers, you oaf. The red markings? Yes, they must be the Republic's new Chatos. They'd heard about them. And just look at them turn! The business!

Nat found it all hard to take in. It was exciting of course. But unreal. The huge sky seemed like a gigantic cinema screen. It didn't seem possible actual men could be up there. Heads back, mesmerised, No. 1 Company of the British Battalion, XV International Brigade, watched the show. The Russian fighters seemed to be getting the better of things.

'So much for Hitler's bloody Luftwaffe,' said someone. 'Go back to Berlin!' another man yelled at the sky. Then a blast of whistles called them away from the distant dogfight. Marching orders. Heads down. Fall in.

Nat stood in his section, reassured by Bernie's broad back in front of him. Single file, they began to move, Nat near the back of the line. Each step released the scent of crushed thyme.

The hillside became steeper. A light frost dissolved under their feet, scorched away by the climbing sun. You wouldn't think it was only February. Sweat started to form on his back. Why hadn't they practised marching with such full packs before? Nat wanted to pee. Pints of coffee had woken them up all right, but it was having its effect now. His cartridge boxes banged against his hips.

A book bounced off a gorse bush, shaking drops from a sparkling cloak of spiderwebs. It fell open, face down, right into Nat's path. With a kind of joy he recognised its weight and spine and almost bent to pick it up: T. A. Jackson, *Dialectics: the Logic of Marxism*. It took him back, like an old man. He remembered a heated discussion at a study group in Stepney, an age ago.

As the march became a rocky scramble, books were discarded all around. A copy of Shakespeare's tragedies, a fair amount of philosophy. On they climbed. Slimmer volumes were jettisoned later: poetry mostly, less easily cast aside perhaps. *Look, Stranger!* Nat noticed. Its pink jacket was distinct against the pale white soil, W. H. Auden set clear in cream. Beton, wasn't it? That new German typeface. Very modern. Very clean.

He could feel his own Jack London still in his pocket. He wasn't going to give that up just yet. He'd manage. Or he'd tear out the drawing if he had to. Nat pulled his shoulder straps tighter.

'Not going to be a long battle then?' he panted out to Bernie, when he realised that volunteers were beginning to chuck down their overcoats too.

Bernie looked at them, but didn't answer.

'They'll have to come back for those,' said Nat. A couple of kitbags had been set down in the dappled shade of an olive tree, two blankets neatly folded on top of each.

Bernie grunted.

Another man interrupted. 'I heard we were back-up. Aren't we?' Nobody who could hear the question knew the answer.

Their line of men was quite strung out in places now, and the other three companies were out of sight. Nat had always imagined going up to the front line in stony silence, all focus on the job in hand. But it wasn't like that at all. He wanted it to be more serious, more momentous. Where was the background music? The mounting throb of guns?

The banter paused as they scrambled up a rocky escarpment, and renewed as the ground levelled out into a plateau, which they crossed. A core of veterans who'd spent the winter defending Madrid were getting to know the company's new recruits – some had only arrived at Madrigueras a week before. They didn't even know each others' names.

Scrub took over from olive groves. The distant firing became a fraction louder. Nat was aware of more dogfights, a long way off and up, and wondered if he was also hearing the thunder of heavy shelling. Then the flat land stopped abruptly and the ground fell away steeply into a dry flat valley, before rising again. Still he couldn't really work out where they were heading, or even exactly where the enemy was. They negotiated a kind of road – a mule track really, sunk into the ground like a ready-made trench. Down four feet. Through the puddles in the cart runnels. Up again.

Not so much talking now. Nat wasn't in the mood for it himself – he didn't have much breath to spare anyway – but it wasn't fear that stopped him. Not yet. He just felt a tremendous alertness, in mind and body, like a firework waiting for a match. He was ready.

They reached another rough ridge of hills. The next drop swept down towards the gorge of the Jarama river. Nat couldn't get a real sense of the lie of the land. Too many hills and broken ridges. Afterwards, he knew he could never draw what he'd seen, though he'd remember the colours, and the light. A rounded hill. Another, almost conical. And on the slope of the next, a white house, bright as a beacon.

A little way ahead, a runner was stumbling towards their new company commander, an Irishman called Conway. The lad seemed to be shouting out as he came closer, staggering on the rough rocks from time to time, then picking up speed. Conway looked round at his men, waved them on more urgently. They picked up their pace. Something was happening. Another messenger appeared, and the company's course changed again. The men headed for the middle hill. Their instructions came. *Hold it, at all costs. Don't leave till you're bloody told to.*

As soon as they reached the top they were in the thick of it. No time to think before bullets were whining past, one after another, faster than Nat could count. At first they seemed like birds whistling by. Was this artillery fire? He had no idea. And where did it all come from? The enemy was invisible and the noise ferocious. It blanked out sense. Gathering clouds of dust and smoke complicated every task.

He could make out the silhouettes of the men ahead of him, standing out against the ridge of the hill, right on the skyline. Then he saw his comrades falling, one after another. Like a line of milk bottles, hit by a misfired football.

Nat ran forward, half-crouching, fumbling with his rifle. Now what? Keep moving. He couldn't die before he'd fired a single shot for Spain. Not him. He remembered what someone had told him, weeks ago in Albacete: *It's the bullets you don't hear you should worry about.*

He made it to Bernie's prostrate figure; Bernie instantly reached out and pulled Nat down onto his belly. Then his hand came down on Nat's helmet so hard he found himself spitting and dribbling a mouthful of Spanish earth and saliva from the corner of his mouth. He ran his tongue round his teeth, trying to clear the dirt: how dry his throat was. Something was digging into his side. He was half-aware of Tommy, sprawled a few feet away, and struggling to sort out his rifle.

'Keep your head down till we've got some shelter,' Bernie yelled in Nat's ear, scrabbling at the ground with his bayonet. He whipped off his helmet and started using it as a shovel. 'Quick, get those stones in front of us. That's right. Build 'em up.'

It wasn't much of a parapet, but it was something.

At last he saw one. Had it imagined it? It seemed to vanish. No, there it was again. A scruffy figure, brown face, brown poncho, brown head cloth, bobbing up from a fold in the ground. Perhaps two hundred yards away. Gone again. Just one, as far as he could see. Nat had been anticipating a blood-curdling Moorish scream – *aren't they famous for their battle cries?* – not this silence. He trained his rifle to a spot just above a large boulder, gambling that was where the Moroccan soldier was heading. He'd be ready for him this time.

He wasn't. Neither was Tommy. He'd raised his head to fire and that was it. The bullet came straight into his left eye. Out through the back of his head. His right eye still stared, up at the blue sky, seeing nothing. Nat's panic was like quicksand. He couldn't move. He couldn't take his own eyes off Tommy's useless one. He wanted to crawl over and shut it for him. He started shifting, but Bernie held him back. The older man shook his head briefly, his eyes never leaving his rifle sights.

Much later Nat thought he should have checked Tommy's jacket. Had the boy's final letter ever got home? Tommy was always writing to his mum.

'Meet Franco's army of bloody Africa,' muttered Bernie, and took aim. A different Moor, somehow even closer, staggered and fell with his poncho billowing around him. 'Where the hell's our bleeding artillery?'

Nat's hands shook as he attached the bayonet as they'd been shown. Not so clean now. To begin with, he was shooting wild and high, even with it on. With his first round, he hit nothing. He pushed back his helmet, fingers sweat-slippery. He felt the chill of his sweat-soaked vest against his back. *Don't come any closer, don't come any closer, don't come any closer.*

Then he saw a man fall, and Nat knew it was by his bullet. His own body went as limp as his victim's. Another man appeared, moving up the hillside like a scuttling crab. Taut again, Nat took aim once more and fired, then ducked as a return of fire zinged over his head.

Bernie found a moment to shout at him: 'That's right. Keep at it. The best thing you can do for the Republic right now is survive. Watch it! At two o'clock!'

He and Bernie fired until their rifles were burning. Then, in turn, they unbuttoned their flies and peed on the barrels to cool them down.

Over and over again, Nat looked over the rocks to fire, and saw more Moroccans zigzagging up the hillside towards him. From time to time he dared a glimpse behind. *Where were their machine-gunners? What had happened to the Maxims?* All he saw were men of his own company thrown into contorted postures like dolls on a scrapheap, wounded or lifeless. Men he'd been drinking coffee with six hours earlier, men who'd made him laugh. So many men. Gone so suddenly. *We're lambs*, he thought, *lambs to the slaughter*.

There were no officers in sight now. Nobody to tell them what to do, where to go, how long to stay. What to think. Again and again, Nat had the sensation of watching a film. Somehow he was now both player and audience. The swearing never stopped. Guns jammed, over and over again. Someone Nat couldn't name helped himself to Tommy's rifle, using his corpse for cover while he emptied his cartridge boxes.

Time seemed to pass at two rates at once. Slow motion or triple speed? Nat couldn't tell. Once he clearly thought, *This is what enfilade means*, remembering a diagram on the blackboard at Madrigueras. Then: *There is nothing, nobody, on our right flank*.

16

Felix felt taut with purpose, almost elated. The light was fading, but she knew they were prepared. Gleaming instruments were sorted in their trays. Swabs. Gauze. Plaster. Waste buckets. All ready. The orderlies had their instructions. A last-minute hunt for a missing case of morphine had been successful. John and Kitty paced the reception room, checking, rechecking, counting. Saline. Glucose. Calcium chloride. All there. At the gateway they stood with cigarettes, ears cocked to the rumbling across the hills that sounded for all the world like a late summer storm brewing. In the courtyard, stretchers were lined up against the wall, like waiting sentries.

The first ambulance arrived at sunset. Four men were dumped in the courtyard. Two were already dead. The ambulance men grabbed fresh stretchers and drove back to the front, six miles away.

When the first soldier was carried into theatre, a black cross and a 'T' scrawled on his forehead to mark his pre-meds, Felix met the man's drifting eyes and took his calloused hand. A worker in the fields, she guessed. His bare arm was strong and sinewy and brown. '*Salud, camarada,*' she whispered, hiding her shock at the state of him. You didn't see wounds like this in Whitechapel. She held the mask over his face. Ethyl chloride. *Medicamentos para los obreros de España.*

'Hold it there. That's right.' Mr Smilie – Doug, she must remember to call him Doug – Doug knew it was only the second anaesthetic she had ever given and he talked her through it, calming her. Felix was glad this patient was Spanish, and wouldn't understand. She couldn't tell how old he was – old enough to be a father, easily. His hair was very black, receding a little at his forehead.

Felix counted, slowly, out loud. '*Uno, dos, tres . . .*'

The face behind the mask still had traces of mud on one side, where he had fallen. Only the wound area had been washed and shaved, prepped for surgery.

'He's off. So put him on the ether now. Watch the flow. That's perfect. Keep his chin forward, remember, don't let his tongue fall back. Ready. Dolores, you take over now. Can you manage? Keep it steady. Felix, scrub up, quick.'

She was already at the sink, sleeves rolled up to her elbows. Though the water was freezing, the routine's familiarity was reassuring. She needed reassurance. It was all she could do not to turn and run.

Mr Smilie kept talking. 'Look. Do you see? All the tissue damage behind the entry wound? We've got bone fragments in the musculature. Pass me the other forceps, yes, those small ones.'

She had them in her hand. And her hand was steady. And she knew her face would not betray her horror.

Mr Fiedler was operating on an abdominal case at the next counter, with the help of their only trained anaesthetist and two *practicantes* from Madrid. Felix was dimly aware of the other team – they sometimes bumped into each other on their way to the sink – but she tried to concentrate on their own patient.

Mr Smilie was quick, so quick. Just as well. 'More gauze. Here.'

It seemed only moments before Kitty rushed in. 'How much longer with this one? We've got an urgent chest case waiting. Category two.'

'Five more minutes.'

'They're arriving all the time now. We can't keep up. Do you still need Dolores or can we have her out with us?'

'We need her. Sorry. Nearly there.'

Operation followed operation. They simply could not sterilise the instruments fast enough. One tense-jawed face replaced another on the counter. Most were beyond speech. Others looked up at Felix as though they had seen a vision.

It was nearly dawn before Felix first left the theatre. She became suddenly desperate for air, as though she would die herself without it. On a nod from Mr Smilie, she staggered towards the courtyard.

Leaning on the doorjamb, Felix began to tremble. She couldn't go any further anyway: a body lay at her feet, blocking the way. She had nearly stumbled onto it. She bent to apologise, but as she put a hand on the man's arm, she could feel that it was already beginning to stiffen. From a little further off she heard a quiet groan. There were bodies everywhere.

'*Aquí, aquí . . . ayudarme.*'

She had never heard such desperation in a voice, but she could not move. *Here, over here . . . help me*, it went on calling. Perhaps drowning was like this. Felix felt herself sinking and the world blackening. For a terrifying moment she no longer knew how to make her lungs draw breath. Then a figure picked its way through the stretchers. Kitty was by her side, dry-eyed, solid. With a hand on each shoulder, she forced Felix to raise her head.

'You have to find the strength. It's in there somewhere. We need you.'

With an enormous effort, Felix drew herself up. 'I'm fine. Don't worry. You won't have to look after me too.'

'Good girl. I'll see you later. We may need your blood soon as well – are you Group IV, do you know? We've not nearly enough. It's desperate, truly desperate.'

As Felix turned to go back to the bar, an orderly clapped her on the back, and forced a hunk of bread and tinned meat into her hand.

'Eat,' he said.

During the next two days Felix slept for less than an hour – she took a blanket to the dispensary and lay there, where she knew she'd quickly be roused. There was no point in taking up bed space. Dolores found her soon enough, brought her a coffee, briefly took her place on the floor. The room was filling up with emptied boxes. They needed more supplies.

Then three things happened, one after another.

Felix found herself crouching on the floor, against the counter, her head clutched in both hands. The building shook with an explosion, short, violent and very close by. Shouting and screaming followed. An orderly came running in, gabbling in such rapid Spanish she had no hope of making sense of it. Mr Fiedler stopped cursing and slowed him down.

'No cause for alarm. Not much anyway. A hand grenade in the incinerator they think – no – not sabotage. An accident. An oversight. All soiled clothing to be searched thoroughly from now on before it's burned. That's an order.'

A short time later, a claxon hoot, and more shouting of a different kind: joyful and wild.

'Can I go and see?' asked Felix.

Released, she ran towards the noise. The wounded in the courtyard had been abandoned to the orderlies and guards. John and Kitty were both at the roadside, greeting the tall, balding driver of a small Renault truck. His neat navy boiler suit bore a Red Cross badge.

'An angel has arrived. Or a fairy godmother. Who knows?' Kitty's laughter had a manic edge. 'They've brought us blood, from Madrid. Pints of it. Who thought of that? Oh God, you don't know much we need this.'

'I think I do.' He was Canadian and triumphant, and his eyebrows rose like mountains.

'I love you . . . what is your name? Dr what? Dr Bethune. Dr Bethune, will you marry me?'

'Can you spare us any apparatus?' asked John. 'We've been surviving with two cannulas and a funnel.'

'I'll see what I can find. Oh, we've brought novocaine too. And an icebox.'

Unloading began, and Kitty fell on the racks of bottles like a vampire. Felix was about to get back to her post when John stopped her.

'Have you got a moment?'

'I have actually. We can't go on with the ops till the autoclave cycle's finished. I was just going to the cookhouse to get coffee for the others.'

'We've got a couple of new cases . . . the first from the British Battalion as a matter of fact. The news isn't good from that quarter, but that's another story. Let's focus on the task in hand.' John seemed to be telling himself. *Please, please not him*, Felix begged silently. They both quickened their steps. 'Bad shock. Exsanguinated. Borderline two or three. But they've no chance of surviving an operation without more blood. If you can help, we could get several transfusions going at once, what with the new equipment Bethune's brought. Can you cut down a vein?'

'In theory.' *If my hands could just keep still*. The British Battalion.

'Here, over here. No more space in triage.' He led the way, and they stopped to tell Dolores as they went. 'Can't get much out of them right now. I was hoping to find out what's been happening, but there's no chance of that.'

John took her to a small side room, off the main hall. It was piled with furniture and boxes cleared from elsewhere, but there was just enough floor space for a blood-soaked mattress. A man lay under a blanket. It wasn't Nat. This patient was broader, much older, as white as paper. Felix knelt and felt his pulse.

'Not much there . . .'

'Just you wait,' said John. 'I'll show you.'

They set up the transfusion together, opening their patient at the ankle. The vein was close to collapse, but they decided it would do under the circumstances. 'We're aiming at about seventy cc a minute. Give or take.' After a while John left Felix holding up the funnel, dripping citrated blood into the rubber tubing from a bottle that once contained wine.

It was almost peaceful here, after the operating theatre's frenzy. Felix's raised arm began to sway, and she forced her eyes open. Was it the light filtering through the window – *Red sun in the morning*, she fretted – or was he getting some colour back in his face? Yes, his lips were definitely less blue.

Her pocket watch was resting on the blanket, so that she could see it clearly. It fell to the floor with a clatter as her patient shifted his leg slightly. He let out a long sigh.

'You're in safe hands now,' murmured Felix, unsure if he'd hear. But his eyes opened, and looked at her.

The blood was nearly gone. She waited for the last drops to make their journey, removed the cannula, and bound up his ankle. She felt his pulse again. Much stronger.

'There. That's better.'

'I should say so.'

The rush of recognition made tears prick in her eyes. A London voice. Croaky, but clear enough. East End, she reckoned.

'Are they going to operate?' he continued.

'I expect so,' she replied, fighting for calm. 'You ought to be up to it very soon.'

'Where did they get me?'

Felix made a bit of a show of checking his casualty card, as if his wound was so slight you might not notice it. Bernard Solomon, she noted.

'Lower back.'

He grimaced. 'We weren't even in retreat. Just my luck. But it was bloody mayhem, I tell you.' He fell silent, then looked at her. 'Have you got a moment, love?'

'All the time in the world,'

'I'm dying for a cigarette. Could you help me?' He couldn't seem to move his arms, but he indicated his breast pocket with his eyes.

Felix remembered what Kitty had told Dolores. Never leave a dying man. She hadn't thought to wonder how you'd know. Anyway, this blood should do the trick. He'd be in theatre soon. They'd get him back on his feet. Felix knelt across the man, and gently drew out a tobacco pouch. Opening it, she caught a smell she used to know.

'That's not Spanish tobacco, is it?'

'No. Wills. My last from home. Been saving it for a special occasion. I reckon this counts, don't you?'

Felix couldn't confess now that she'd never rolled a cigarette in her life before. Most of the other English volunteers smoked whenever they could. She'd watched Charlie's ritual rolling, and she did her best to copy it now with this man's sole remaining paper. After several attempts, she thought she'd got it tight enough. Her mouth was very dry, but she managed to find just enough spit to stick it down. A few strands of stray tobacco hung from the end.

'Here you are.'

His lips parted obediently, cracking a slight crust of saliva that had formed at one corner. She put the cigarette in place, then found his lighter. The flame glowed blue. The man drew deeply, and a couple of tears came from nowhere, and edged down the sides of his face, finding the creases and wrinkles.

She took the cigarette away for a moment so he could exhale, and then let her hand rest on his.

'I don't know how many we've lost. Half the company, it felt.' He was finding it harder and harder to talk, but Felix couldn't stop him. 'Half the bleeding battalion gone, I should think . . . Wouldn't be here myself if it weren't for – we were stuck, you see, really stuck on a hill . . . so bare . . . couldn't see how we'd ever get back . . . Back to the sunken road. Just me and a pal. Nice lad . . . spirited. Clever, you know . . . About your age . . . Been with him since Albacete. A proper *mensch*. Came from the same neck of the woods as me, as a matter of fact . . .'

'Did he?' The thud of her heart grew faster. She remembered the feel of Nat's lips and the sound of his breathing.

'Stayed with me till the stretcher came, he did. Long wait . . . Believe me . . . And he didn't have to. "You should go," I told him. Did he listen to me? Hope he's doing all right now. No, I reckon he's the lucky type . . . he'll be all right, I reckon, please God.'

He began to ramble. Felix didn't really know what he was saying, but she nodded, and said, 'Yes,' and, 'Oh no,' and went on stroking his hand. It didn't seem right to ask the questions

103

she wanted to. He talked about the moon, how thin and wispy it had been. Gradually his speech petered out. Felix felt his pulse. Then his eyes opened again.

'That blood you gave me. Did me a world of good. Got any more where it came from?'

Before she could answer, Bernie's eyes closed. The last breath left his blood-filled lungs.

Despite herself, Felix began to sob. All she had seen in the past few days seemed to crush her at once. It wasn't just her hunger for Nat that was wearing her down. It was everything. She managed to stop herself when she saw Dolores, watching from the doorway.

He had been so quick at his task. Wasted no time. But he could still catch up with her. He'd find the right words to explain somehow.

Of course she's shocked. Who the hell wouldn't be? Right in front of her like that. There was no other way, of course. But still it was horrible. Horrible.

Nat breaks into a run. The ice-cold air tears at his throat as he breathes faster and faster. Passing the ruined house, he's confused by the tracks still visible in the swirling snow. Everything seems darker. He imagines a movement, and ducks inside. She'll be in there, waiting for him, needing the comfort that only he can give, surely she will. He can take her in his arms again. He can make it all right again. She's got to understand. War's war. She must know that by now. She must know that.

The building is empty.

MARCH 1937

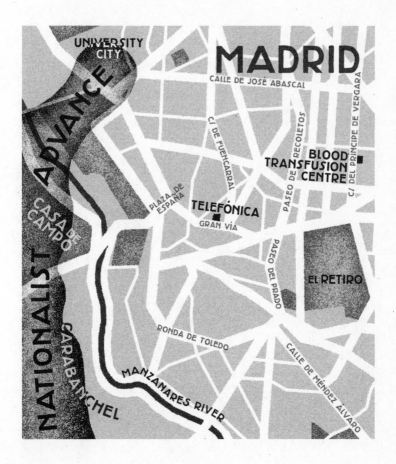

17

George was still waiting for a safe-conduct pass, and transport. He wanted to go the short distance south of the capital to the Jarama valley, to report on the state of play there. A few other journalists had already returned to the Telefónica bleak faced and disbelieving. Nearly two thirds of the battalion lost. And what had this suicidal bravery won? Stalemate. The two sides were dug in now, entrenched.

He wanted to go. And then again he didn't. If George stopped filing stories, his money would run out. But it left him so little time to look for Felix. He could never go back without her.

'Why don't I go to Valencia instead?' he asked Ilsa. Lots of correspondents had already left. The story in Madrid was over, they said. Valencia was the place to be now. And surely *someone* there must have run into a slight young nurse from Sydenham – a pretty nurse with long hair and lively eyes and a face so terribly, terribly young.

Unless she had gone south. Málaga had fallen to the Fascists. Refugees were dying on the roads, machine-gunned on their march. He'd heard there was no shortage of atrocities on the road from Málaga. Wasn't that what they wanted in London? Maybe . . .

'Forget it, George,' said Ilsa, sharply. 'You're stuck in Madrid till you get your pass. So go and write a story on the blood transfusion centre. The world should know about that too. It's going to help us win the war. It's a huge step forward.'

'Really?'

'Just wait. You'll see. It's on the Príncipe de Vergara. You can walk through the top of the park if you like . . . what's left of it. Just ask the way to Salamanca.'

'What about my pass?'

'It won't happen today. Not enough transport.' She waved him off irritably. 'Go on. Go and do something useful with yourself.'

'Wait. What's it called?'

'The *Instituto Hispano–Canadiense de Transfusión de Sangre*. Number thirty-six. You can't miss it. Go on, go.'

George wrote the details in his notebook, underlined the address, and set off, ears and eyes open to passing aircraft. He was less jittery these days. Better at hiding his fear. But you couldn't be too careful. This was a war that broke all the rules. George had never felt so powerless.

As he got closer, he realised the area was almost unscathed. He understood how it worked now: most of the city's Fascists had escaped, but their properties in the richer suburbs of Madrid remained. Franco did not like to bomb his own.

The first thing George saw was the queue, stretching down the boulevard. He was used to queues by this time: queues for bread, queues for water, queues for medical treatment. Women and children could be found waiting in line for hours, anywhere in the city. But this was different. Here the people of Madrid were queuing to give, not to receive. They were giving away their blood. It lifted his spirits. He began to whistle.

A woman in a colourful headscarf glanced at him and smiled, and began to hum along. What was that tune? He blushed, and faltered. Then others took it up. Good God! He knew what it was now. One of the Republican songs. *¡Ay, Carmela! ¡Ay, Carmela! ¡Deberemos resistir!* He didn't understand all the words, but his Spanish was improving enough to get the gist of it. *We must resist!* What would they take him for? But the tune was irresistible.

Time he made himself scarce.

18

Nat tried to join the end of the queue, but among so many women, he could hardly help sticking out. The sling on his arm didn't help. Like a white flag, wasn't it? The women immediately started to bustle him forward to the front of the line, treating him like the hero he didn't feel. Such a lot of fuss, he thought angrily, for a minor shrapnel wound.

It was only an upside-down kind of luck that found him here. His hand was healing well, but it would be another few weeks before he could fire a rifle again. On leave in Madrid, Nat gave himself over to guilt. It was hard not to brood, and Nat didn't even want to try to stop. Every time he thought about Bernie, the words of *Kaddish*, the Jewish prayer for the dead, crept into his head. *Oseh shalom bim'romav hu ya'aseh shalom aleinu v'al kol Yisroel* . . . He who maketh peace in His high places, may He make peace for us and for all Israel.

A number of rooms opened off the hallway, none of them looking much like laboratories. From one, a middle-aged woman emerged wiping her mouth with the back of her hand, calling back her thanks to whoever was inside. She looked pale but happy, and held a packet of rice to her chest. At the bottom of the staircase a nurse in a spotless uniform sat at a table, her white flowing headdress bowed over her paperwork. 'Next please,' she called out, glancing up at Nat only when she sensed his looming height in front of her.

'Can I help you?' she asked in Spanish, smiling broadly.

'I wanted to give,' said Nat, fumbling for the right words, holding out his good arm. '*Sangre*.'

'And are you on our donor list, *camarada*?'

The shell that caught his arm had also burst his eardrums. 'Sorry?'

She repeated the question, more loudly and slowly.

'No, this is my first time. Does it matter?'

'It depends. Will you be a regular donor?' She was staring at his uniform. 'Most people on our register come every three or four weeks.'

'I don't know,' he said truthfully. 'I'm not sure how long I'll be in Madrid. I'll come every time I can.'

'Well, you'll need to give me some details, and we'll take a sample, and then we can let you know.' She opened a file and began to fill in a form. 'Name?'

He answered her questions. Nationality: British. Marital status: single. Colour of iris. Colour of skin. No, no children, living or dead. No hereditary diseases that he knew of. No, he'd never had malaria. No (he flushed), not syphilis either. She rang a bell, and another nurse led him away to a room lined with refrigerators. Four long thin tables, with armrests at each side, served as couches.

The nurse helped Nat take his place on the only free bed. It was awkwardly high, when you only had one hand working. He swung his legs up, leaned back, and inspected the ceiling. A great many cherubs were looking down at him.

The nurse put a tourniquet on his uninjured arm, and showed him how to clench and unclench his fist. He hardly noticed when she found his vein with her needle.

The blood was flowing nicely into the syringe when he heard a deep Canadian voice. In strode a tall man with the most enormous bald forehead Nat had ever seen. A few paces behind him, a fair-haired young man was earnestly recording the Canadian's words in a notebook.

'So it's really just like delivering milk. Not half so easy to get containers of course – we can hardly do "rinse and return" on the battlefield. Though as it happens, milk bottles work very well.' Inspired by Nat's presence perhaps, he continued: 'My plan is for every soldier in the Republican Army to have a dog tag showing his blood type, eventually. That way we won't waste time, and we won't make mistakes. But for now, the great thing is to have got the blood moving. It's getting to where it's needed.'

'So the essential principle is to take the blood to the wounded, not the wounded to the blood?'

The man reminded Nat of a schoolboy, checking his facts with a charismatic headmaster. Not a show-off, but the swotty type who hates to get things wrong.

'Precisely. The difference is phenomenal. We're saving hundreds of lives this way.'

'Any real figures?'

'Hard to say exactly. I'll have to let you know. The recent breakthrough is training. You see, when it comes down to it, any fool can do a blood transfusion. Yes, of course I exaggerate . . .'

'I was just going to say—'

'Well, it hardly takes a surgeon. Their skills we need at the operating table. Training medical minions leaves us a lot more time to get on with the collecting, as well as the distribution and organisation. And of course training others. As it happens, we're expecting a couple of nurses here in a few hours' time to do just that. You can interview them if you want to hang around.'

The man with the notebook seemed to hesitate, nervous blue eyes flicking round the room.

'I'm not sure. You see . . .'

Oh make your mind up, thought Nat.

'Suit yourself. Now come this way, and I'll show you where we prepare the serums.'

Nat heard the conversation fade. Some journalist on a deadline. All right for him. He'd be back in London with his girlfriend in a few weeks' time, boasting about his next assignment.

The nurse withdrew the needle, pressed firmly on Nat's vein, and then stuck a plaster over the bead of blood that immediately began to form.

'Now you are entitled to a drink and some food. Just take this card to the counter in the room opposite. But you'll probably want to rest for a few minutes here. I haven't taken much this time – it's just for testing – but even that can affect some people. Ten minutes.'

Nat shook his head, and let her pull him to his feet. His ears immediately began to roar and pop, and a rushing sensation swept through his body. He was weaker than he thought. Even when he stopped swaying, nothing seemed any clearer. Worse, if anything.

A figure was forming, a girl. He knew that nose, that forehead, didn't he? Not this hair, cut short into a bob. There was not enough of it left for a dark strand to escape and fall across the cheek of this girl. He must be confused. Or deceived. His longing for Felix was doing him in. Playing tricks on him. It had become like a craving, an addiction. He felt half-crazy with the ache of it. Nat's vision blurred and the rushing in his head grew louder. He closed his eyes, staggered, and gripped the arm of the Spanish nurse to keep himself upright.

19

Felix took a deep breath and just stopped herself from running across the room and pushing the other nurse aside. She didn't know if she wanted to hit Nat or hug him. She felt she could knock him down, but not until she'd held him hard enough and close enough to know for certain it was him. She wanted to thank him just for being alive, and to punish him too, for all that he'd put her through.

You'd never have known, to look at her. She walked calmly towards him, through the silence of watching eyes.

'Nat? Nat!'

No response. The soldier just stared at her blankly.

'Is that you? Can't you hear me?'

Perhaps the strength of her yearning had made a fool of her. Felix stopped, just a few steps away, as a chill crept over her. She took another gulp of air. Blinked. Let out her breath. No, no, she wasn't wrong. She couldn't be wrong about this. He looked different, of course. Worn. Wounded – but not, she guessed, too seriously. Some of the light had left him. The optimism. But this was definitely Nat. There was no doubt about that.

She stood frozen, like a child caught in a game of grandmother's footsteps. He had seen her. She couldn't move. Why didn't he?

'Nat, it's me, it's Felix. I came.'

Still no response. Speak louder, more slowly.

'You see, I came. Like you said I should.'

Nat spoke at last, so quietly his voice got lost in the echoey whispers of the clinic. 'Felix! Blimey. It is you.'

'Yes, of course it's me.'

'Oh, Felix . . . you shouldn't be here. You shouldn't have come here.'

She felt the skin on her face prickle and tighten as the blood drained out of it.

'What do you mean?' Felix was dimly aware that Dolores and the other nurse were staring at them, unabashed. She didn't care what they heard. 'What do you mean I shouldn't have come? Of course I should. Spain needs more nurses. That's what you said. Don't you remember? I wouldn't be here if it weren't for you.'

'Of course I remember. I remember everything.'

At last he took a step towards her, and stood on his own. *I hardly know you*, she thought suddenly. And realised right away that it didn't matter.

'Coming here's the best thing I've ever done,' she said, holding out her hand.

'Was it?'

'Yes.' She let her hand hang.

They were inches apart now. There was less of him than she remembered. It was as if years had passed, not months. She stared at his bandage. Would he let her see what was behind it? The nurse from the blood transfusion centre coughed gently.

'Your coupon, comrade. You'll need this in the canteen.'

'Oh, yes. Thank you.'

'You'll be hearing from us very soon.' She turned to address Felix and Dolores. 'And you? You have come for the training, I think? We weren't expecting you so early.'

Felix recovered herself. Made herself look away from Nat.

'We got a lift in with a convoy, before dawn. We were lucky.'

'Good. The administrator will be with you shortly. You will wait? There is plenty of space for waiting. Second room on the left.'

The nurse was trying to move them all along. Another donor was in the doorway, ready to take Nat's place on the table. Others were getting up from their couches. Another conversation was starting up in the hall, echoing off the marble floor.

'The second Frigidaire? Again? Oh no . . . he thinks he can fix it? Let's hope so.'

'Yes. Unbearable for all that blood to go to waste. And it's group II.'

Felix became terribly aware of Nat's breathing. She knew he couldn't stop staring at her. And then she realised that Dolores was staring too, at both of them. She quickly broke the silence.

'Nat, let me introduce you to Dolores. We work together at one of the *Hospitales de Sangre*. Dolores, this is . . . this is a friend. Comrade Kaplan. From home. From London, you know. England.'

Dolores and Nat nodded gravely at one another. Oh, when would he speak again? And what had taken the life out of him like that?

And then, as though they were at a dance, and the band had stopped for a rest, they were moving off, all bunched together, out of this high-ceilinged room, and into another. And what was this he was saying to her, so seriously?

'How long will you be in Madrid?'

Felix felt Dolores's eyes on her, intent and careful.

'Just tonight,' said Felix. 'Then back to our team, and after that I believe we're moving on in a few days' time. I can't say for sure. They don't give us much notice. You know how it is.'

Her words came out quite casually at first, and then they began to wobble.

'Where are you staying now?'

Felix told him. Not the general area. The exact address, the number and street of their small hotel. She wished she had a phone number to give him too.

'Not too far from me then.'

Go on. He was looking at the floor now. Felix stared at the elaborate marble tiles equally hard, and observed the colours in their flecks. Go on. She would look at his face when he spoke again. Her foot twitched. She watched his boots shift. Go on.

'I'll take you out tonight.' This came out very quickly.

'In a blackout? Very funny,' she answered. Their smiles met and wavered.

'You'd be surprised.'

'Are you sure you don't want to take me to a meeting?' she said, remembering, filling the next silence.

'Well, I expect I can arrange something. If I have to.' Mock serious. 'There's always a meeting to go to.'

'You don't have to. Let's not go to a meeting.'

'OK. We won't. We'll have a meeting on our own.'

At exactly the same time, they both remembered Dolores. Felix couldn't tell how much she had understood. She had a look of intense concentration on her face, and was frowning slightly, waiting. Felix knew she couldn't abandon her in the middle of Madrid. They would have to put up with her silent gaze. Well. Maybe it wasn't such a bad thing. Her presence might stop them from being reckless. Felix felt reckless just at that moment, and the feeling made her nervous.

As if he understood, Nat turned to Dolores brightly – a little too brightly. 'I'll see you both at around nine. *A las nueve?*'

20

George emerged from the garage at the back of the building. He brushed the dust from his hands and knees with a sense of satisfaction. It *had* been worth coming. The Frigidaire was up and humming again, and he'd saved pints and pints of blood, in next to no time. The mobile generator in the van wasn't quite so straightforward – he would need to improvise a spare part. But he had an idea for that.

Oh yes, this was more like it. Lots of people could write a news story far better than he could. And lots of them were more willing to give the papers the kind of stories they wanted. But nobody, he thought with an uncharacteristic touch of arrogance, nobody could mend a machine more quickly.

He felt in his pocket for his notebook, planning to make a quick sketch to show exactly what was needed when he got to the ironmonger's. Bother! He must have left it on the floor of the storage room.

Turning briskly through the main front door he nearly knocked over a donor who was on his way out. George had noticed him earlier when he was being shown round: with his bandaged arm and serious expression, the Brigader made rather a poignant picture. A good intro to the piece. *Even the wounded are playing their part . . . etc . . . etc . . .*

George risked English. 'My apologies, old chap. Haven't hurt you, have I? Your arm all right?'

'Sorry?' He hadn't heard him.

'Did I hurt you? I didn't mean to. In a bit of a rush.'

'No, no. I'm fine.'

Relieved, George hurried on, wondering if he should offer to service some of the unit's other machinery while he was there. Regular maintenance, that was the thing. You couldn't expect these things to keep grinding on, day after day, not without a little tenderness. Machines were the same as anything else.

The notebook was just where he'd left it. He could hear the director's voice again. He hesitated on the threshold, listening at the half-closed door to judge his moment.

'I can't stress this more strongly. Accuracy in determining blood type is paramount. Could you translate that, please, Angela? I want to be quite sure that Dolores understands.'

He couldn't just barge in.

'Obviously, the standard serum makes it a hell of a lot easier, but it's not essential. Just so long as you know the blood type of the donor, that is. What I'm going to show you now is the open slide method of compatibility testing . . .'

Definitely not the moment. He'd make his offer when he came back later.

Walking back past the queues of waiting donors, his stride regained its spring for the first time in months. Really, these women were simply marvellous. Such courage, and – the thought came into his head before he knew it – so beautiful, so many of them, despite the pinched look that hunger lent. He grinned at them cheerily and remembered Ilsa's stories about the early days. When the siege began, the women of Madrid forced their fleeing menfolk back to the front. Told them to put up barricades. Even grandmothers waited on their balconies with pans of boiling water to greet the Fascists. Incredible.

Oh look, there was that young man again. He was giving his food coupon to a barefooted girl with a baby on her hip. She ran off right away, as if he might change his mind. George gave him a wave. Good chap, he thought. Every little helps.

21

And then Dolores did what Felix was least expecting.

'I'm very tired.' She yawned. 'It's been a long day. But very interesting. So much to learn.'

Felix checked her watch again. It was 8.37 p.m. At last.

'I have a headache too,' said Dolores. 'Do you mind if I stay here?'

Would she *mind*? Felix wanted to throw her arms round her. But Dolores was already pulling back the thin cover on the bed they would have to share that night, and inspecting the sheets. Felix couldn't quite decide if there was disapproval in her voice. Perhaps Dolores thought her shameless – rushing off like that with Nat, without a thought. Perhaps she was.

'You're quite sure you'll be all right here on your own?' Felix began picking stray hairs from her hairbrush, like petals from a daisy. *She will. She won't. She will. She won't.* 'I can stay if you like. I don't have to go out.'

Except I do. I really do.

Dolores shook her head, and plumped the bolster. 'I don't want to go. I will look at my notes from this afternoon. I don't want to make any mistakes. It's complicated, this blood thing. I didn't know.'

'You have to be careful,' Felix agreed.

'Very careful.'

Felix walked towards the window to hide her delight. She was already imagining Nat coming round the corner, glimpsing the top of his head, seeing him before he saw her this time. Would the pressure of her gaze make him look up? But she couldn't open the shutters, not without switching off the light. It was still early. He wouldn't be there yet. Would he?

Felix turned to remind Dolores about the lights. She was starting to unpack the small leather bag she'd brought with her to Madrid. An amber-beaded rosary slithered to the floor. Dolores scooped it up, hastily, without looking up, and Felix pretended not to notice. Just as she hadn't commented on a ghostly ochre outline on the wallpaper: it was obvious that a crucifix had recently been removed. With reluctance or relief? Another of those things it might be better not to know.

Nothing was straightforward in Spain, Felix thought, for the hundredth time. As far as she was concerned, church had always simply been a place she went with her family on Sunday mornings, if she really had to. Here it meant so much more: a building, a refuge, but also a terrible tyranny . . . something like an empire, even. Felix found this entangled mess of politics and religion as impossible to sort out in her head as it seemed to be in reality. The more she discovered about both sides, Nationalist and Republican, and all the different allegiances they contained, the more confusing everything became. So she had taken a decision: concentrate on the job she had come to do. That was straightforward enough.

Now she simply excused herself and walked back down the tall, narrow corridor to the communal bathroom at the end. Not the cleanest, but it had running water. Glorious to wash from head to toe. By herself. On the chipped tiled wall, there was a mirror, age-spotted, but serviceable. It had been weeks since Felix had seen herself. With the corner of a towel, she rubbed away the condensation on the glass.

She could see why it had taken Nat so long to recognise her. Bread soup and dysentery had taken their toll. Her cheekbones stuck out more and there was room for a jersey now under her nurse's uniform. At least she wasn't in her dungarees. Her haircut made her look very different too. Practical, but hardly stylish, despite Kitty's best efforts. She was sure it made her look older. She ran the brush through it.

No need for lipstick – her lips were permanently bright red, chapped by wind and cold. Felix had a little pot of petroleum jelly, a present from Kitty, and she fingered some on to make her lips gleam. Then she pinched her cheeks to relieve their pallor. She overdid it. Now she looked feverish, like a TB patient. Though come to think of it, this yellow light hinted at jaundice. Struck by mild hysteria, Felix laughed out loud at herself, and her reflection laughed back, just as artificial, and the laughter rang off the tiles.

It was already nine, just. She put her head round the door of the bedroom to say goodbye.

'Don't wait up. I'll try not to wake you.'

'Enjoy yourself. Don't worry about me.' Dolores was already getting ready for bed. Felix knew she liked privacy to change, and quickly withdrew.

There was a very small reception area downstairs. It was empty. To judge by the food smells and the clattering of cutlery, the hotel staff were all eating their supper. Felix sat down on the narrow upholstered bench, kept still for about forty seconds, and then jumped up again.

They hadn't exactly agreed where to meet. Perhaps he was already outside, waiting, wondering where she'd got to. What if the bell was out of order? No, it couldn't be. It had been working that morning. Determined to be decisive, Felix pulled open the door.

The pavement was empty. Far away, she could hear the echo of light artillery. It was very dark. Felix shivered. City darkness was more alarming than night in the countryside. You didn't expect to be able to see much in the middle of nowhere. Except when the moon was full of course, and then you didn't go out if you could help it. Not when there was a bomber's moon.

The sound of footsteps made her stand up straight and set her face ready to smile. But they faded before they reached her, turning off into a side street.

Felix's eyes began to see more details. A few bold posters. Washing on a balcony, gently billowing. She paced a little, experimentally, four steps in one direction, four in the other, stiffening her knees against their shaking. Again she listened. She could just catch the faint strumming of a guitar, invisible in some upstairs room. Horse hoofs somewhere, or maybe a donkey. A siren. It was funny how there were no other animals on the streets of Madrid. In any other city, this was the kind of night you'd expect to encounter a cat on the prowl, or hear the howl of a dog. Maybe a rat rummaging in the gutter.

Like a bad conscience, the imagined voice of Neville came into her head. What was she thinking of? Waiting alone on a street corner at night, in a foreign city, in a war, waiting for a boy who was little more than a stranger to her? How naïve could she get? Even George wouldn't find an excuse for this, she decided, and you could usually rely on him. A belated surge of affection caught her by surprise. Coming back from the clinic that afternoon she'd glimpsed a man in the distance she'd almost taken for George: he had just the same purposeful walk and mess of sandy hair. She had nearly called out his name. How idiotic. As if! When she got back to London she'd have to find some way of making it up to him. Felix didn't want to rake over old coals – and it would be easy to embarrass George with apologies, so she'd have to be careful – but she must let him know she was sorry. Sorry for disappointing him, at any rate. Not sorry for going.

Nat's voice finally broke into her thoughts.

'Not late, am I? I got lost. Streets all blocked. A place doesn't look the same here two days running.'

His head was cocked forward as he walked, as if he were making sure it was really her. His face and his sling gleamed whitely.

'It's fine,' she called back, and his steps became louder and quicker. She felt stiff and self-conscious, and it seemed an age before he reached her.

He stopped a foot away. His expression was shadowed. She took heart from the jaunty angle of his beret. As he shifted his weight on his feet, she heard his leather jacket softly creaking. One sleeve hung loose and empty. She started towards him. Then held herself back.

'Your friend isn't with you?' he said.

'No. She wanted an early night.'

'Oh.' It was just a moment of awkwardness, which dissolved without an audience. 'That's good. Let's go then.'

Nat finally closed the space between them, and she let him link his good arm with hers. She even leaned against him a little as they walked. Their steps quickly found a rhythm.

'I can't believe this,' he said. 'Let's go somewhere I can look at you.'

22

The bar could have been chilly with its painted tiles and flagstones, but it was crammed with people, and warm with their body heat. They'd been lucky to spot another couple, just slipping away from these stools. It had been hard to know where to take her. Nat couldn't imagine her in an English pub, but everything was different in Spain.

He reached across the barrel that served for a table, and held the candle up to Felix's face. She was more lovely than he'd remembered. Far more. Felix turned her head, this way and that, like a film star posing for flashing cameras, while he absorbed the line of her jaw and neck.

'Convinced now? You don't think I'm an imposter any more? Or a Fascist spy? A fifth columnist?'

Shouting above the hubbub of the bar, she swished what was left of her hair, and he simply stared. He couldn't stop himself, though he knew his scrutiny was making her nervous. There was red in the brown of her hair, he saw now: Venetian red, or maybe terra rossa in the sunlight. It was the first time Nat had noticed the down on her face too, a faint and fascinating silveriness that ran into the hollow beneath her cheekbones and disappeared. The hollow seemed more pronounced now. He had to stop himself from running his finger down it.

'Do you?' she said, tailing her hand back and forth along

her collarbone, as if she could actually feel his gaze penetrating her skin.

'What? No. No, I never thought that.' He just couldn't stop staring. 'Mind yourself now. Don't set yourself on fire.'

'Put the candle down then . . . look, you're dripping wax everywhere.'

She scooped up a finger-full, warm and smooth, and rolled it between her fingers. The empty bottle that held the candle was draped in wax, like a stalagmite. You could hardly see the glass any more. Nat set it back down, and gazed at Felix through the halo of the flame. God, it was good to see her. She couldn't know how good.

No need to write now, he thought.

Her fingertips went on moulding the wax methodically. When she turned her hand palm up, he saw how the blue map of veins on the inside of her wrist faded into the pale skin of her forearm. The skin was so delicate just there. After a few seconds of silence, Felix frowned at him. 'What? . . . what *is* it?'

'I can't really say . . . sorry . . . didn't mean to make you feel uncomfortable.' He couldn't seem to say quite the right thing. 'Just . . . like I said before . . . I didn't think I'd ever see you again. And here you are. I keep wondering when I'll wake up.' He cupped his hand behind his ear to catch her reply through the ringing in his head.

'Don't you feel that a lot, here?'

'In Spain?'

'Yes.'

'I suppose I do.'

'Sometimes nothing seems quite real.' She looked a bit puzzled.

'Yes, I know.'

'But then again, what could be more real?'

'Exactly. You're exactly right.'

They looked at each other some more, relishing the understanding between them. It gave Nat a strange sensation. His chest seemed to be swelling up, filling with something warm. Floaty. Watch it. Watch it. Easy. A drink. That was what they needed. Would she be all right if he left her for a moment?

'Thirsty?' Nat looked around. More people had arrived. 'Wine or sherry?'

'Sherry?' She giggled. Like a girl, he thought. She is a girl. He loved the sound of her light girl's voice, hard though it was to hear. Men's voices were all the same. He'd had enough of men's voices.

'What are you laughing at?' he asked. He wanted to share everything, know everything about her.

'Oh, I don't know. I suppose I'd never thought about sherry coming from Spain before. It always makes me think of Christmas at home.'

'Makes you homesick, does it?' Nat was sympathetic.

'The opposite.' Her eyes widened, and she shook her head firmly, and frowned. 'Really, quite the opposite.'

'The opposite?'

'It makes me realise what I've escaped. The annual sherry ritual. So predictable. So irritating. So much fuss about nothing. Ghastly. In fact, I don't even know why I'm talking about it. Of all things . . .'

'I want to hear.' He leaned forward.

'Oh, don't get the wrong idea. It's not a proper ritual, not religious or anything. It's just that's when we always drink it. On Christmas Day, once a year. The sherry bottle comes out of the corner cupboard, after church and before lunch. Harvey's Bristol Cream. It's funny how it never seems to run out.'

If he concentrated on her lips, it was easier to hear. And her lips were so lovely. Shining.

'Neville, that's my brother, he always gets the glasses out – Waterford Crystal, don't you know? – and then wipes them all, terribly carefully, one by one . . .' (She was laughing – at her brother?) ' . . . as if they were, oh I don't know . . . the Crown Jewels, or the Holy Grail or something. I mean they're just sherry glasses. Cut-glass sherry glasses, for God's sake. Six of them altogether. Not that we need six. I think they must have been a wedding present. To my parents, that is.'

Her eyes softened, and withdrew from the Madrid barroom. What was she remembering?

'And . . . ?' He wanted to get her back. He wanted to know everything he could, as quickly as possible. He had so little to go on, and not much time. He wanted to know how to think about her, later.

'And last Christmas – no, of course, it was the year before – last year I was already here. The last few months have gone by so quickly. Anyway, the year before last, George joined us for Christmas for the first time. So there were four of us, which was better.'

'George?'

'He's my brother's friend. Well, a family friend now, really, you could say.' She seemed on the point of elaborating, but she checked herself. 'Yes, a family friend. He spends a lot of time with us now. Awfully kind. Very good to us all. A second son, as far as Mother's concerned. But that was his first Christmas with us. Though I suppose he must have been there last Christmas too . . .'

Again, Nat felt an urgent need to bring her back to the here and now. He wasn't interested in this George.

'And what happened?' he asked, too impatiently. Felix

seemed to shake herself a little, like a dog coming out of water. Then she looked straight at him again.

'Oh, nothing really. I don't know why I thought of it. I suppose because it all seems so irrelevant now. All that worrying about *things*.' Pausing briefly, she finished in a rush. 'What happened was that George tried to give me some sherry, and Neville wouldn't let him, because he said I was too young, and George thought I wasn't, and they had a kind of argument, except it wasn't really an argument, because they never have proper arguments, not shouting, or anything. It was more of a disagreement and I thought it was funny because they were both so quietly insistent and wouldn't give in and I didn't even like sherry anyway – I'd tried it in secret already, horrible stuff – and so I didn't care. But they gave me some in the end and of course I drank it all far too quickly and then I felt in a very silly mood, and kept laughing at Neville and he didn't like it at all. He was very cross with me.'

'I can't imagine anyone being cross with you,' said Nat. He couldn't really imagine a house with cut-glass sherry glasses either. And all the family arguments he'd ever known were conducted at top volume. With the neighbours joining in too, often enough. Through the walls.

'That sounds a bit soppy.'

She was teasing him, wasn't she?

'Sorry.' *You make me feel soppy*, he thought to himself, smiling, feeling schmaltzier than ever. He still hadn't managed to get to the bar, to get drinks, but when it came to it he didn't want to leave her even for that length of time. 'It's true.'

'Shall I tell you my diagnosis?'

'Mmmm.' He was back in Whitechapel, feeling her fingertips exploring the cut on his head, tingling, and remembering

132

the smell of her hair when she passed under his arm as he held the café door open. He was outside the hospital once more, about to kiss her, properly. He could hardly focus on what she was saying.

'Female deprivation. It's turned you soft.'

'Really?'

'It's very common, specially in the army. You might almost call it a syndrome.'

'See it a lot, do you?' It was becoming a huge effort to speak. He made himself concentrate on her eyes. But he was transfixed by her lips. Her teeth were lovely too. Not perfect, but the slight irregularity made them more interesting.

'Oh, an awful lot. It's terribly common in these parts. In its most extreme form, it can lead a man to propose to a complete stranger. We nurses have to have special training, to learn how to deal with it.'

'You do?' He wondered where this was leading. He wondered if they should leave the bar, and where else they *could* go.

'No, of course not. Though maybe we should. Really, I'm surprised you're so gullible!'

When she laughed again, it broke the strange spell he was under for a moment, and he laughed too. Nat loved being teased by her. It made him feel as if they'd known each other for ever. It had been the other way round, he reflected, the first time they met. He remembered her utter confusion when he talked about the Party. The Communist Party, he'd had to explain. She'd seemed such an innocent then. Although, in a way, she still did.

She reached round the barrel, and put a hand on his knee, pressing down on it firmly. He hadn't realised he was twitching again. It was a habit he didn't notice any more. He was always jiggling his foot. As if he was waiting for something, and couldn't bear to wait any longer.

'It's all right,' she said, so quietly that he saw rather than heard her words.

23

Felix removed her hand. She felt a little dizzy. Nat looked away, and began to feel in his jacket pocket. He took out a packet of cigarettes, Spanish ones. All the soldiers were issued with the same kind. He held the packet in his half-bandaged hand, and used the good one to take out a cigarette. Felix shook her head as he held out the packet to her. *Matches?* she panicked, hoping he wouldn't have to fumble it with one hand and need help, but luckily he leaned into the candle and took a light from that.

Her own hands were folded back in her lap. She sat and fretted. He looked so serious. Had she been too forward again? She shouldn't have touched him like that. She hadn't been able to help herself. And now the atmosphere had changed, just when it was all going so well. At least she thought it was. Was it too late? All she'd done was talk about herself – nerves, she supposed – and there was so much she wanted to ask him.

Then he exhaled, smiling.

'Don't look so worried!' he said lightly. 'I was just thinking. It's so hard to hear you with all these people around. Do you really fancy a drink? We could always just go for a walk . . . while the skies are still clear?'

'Oh yes, let's,' said Felix, standing up immediately.

Nat rose too, and straight away a voice called out: '¡*Los internacionales*! ¡*Benvenido a los internacionales*!' and they were pulled into the knot of people at the bar. Everyone plied them with drinks, clapped them on the back, thanked them profusely for coming to Madrid, and generally made them feel they'd saved the city from Franco without a helping hand. The barman thumped the counter and struck up a war song. 'Los Cuatro Generales'. The noise level rose.

Eventually they escaped, followed out by more thanks and cheers. The old man at the door checked the skies and pronounced the all-clear, then raised a clenched fist salute.

'This way,' said Nat.

Felix let him lead her around some wooden struts that were holding up a bomb-damaged building.

'I reckon we've got a couple more hours,' he said, taking her arm again. Her hip brushed against his leg.

'Until the bombardment begins?'

Nat nodded, and tightened his grip on her.

'They time it,' he said. 'It usually gets going just as the theatres and bars are shutting. When the streets are most crowded.'

They both looked up. Nothing but stars. From far away, the thin whip crack of rifle fire urged them on. From the west, a deep rumbling.

'The *dinamiteros*. They tunnel under the lines at night. Both sides.'

Felix and Nat walked on, watching where they walked, avoiding fallen masonry, alert to possible shelters. Watching how they talked too. All the time Felix kept wondering how she had survived all these months without seeing him. His presence felt like a drug to her now. She was addicted. She didn't know how she could ever bear to say goodbye again.

136

'So, now are you going to tell me why you came?' said Nat. 'And how?'

Felix gave him a version of what happened in Paris. She felt him shake his head, slowly. She knew he was admiring her, and it made her feel braver and stronger than before. Taller even. They moved steadily closer together as they felt their way through the darkness. She didn't ask too much about Jarama, and he didn't tell her. Instead they compared notes on food, and vermin, and swapped advice.

'My mother would die if she knew I had lice,' said Felix.

'Mine too. But that's the least of it. The food alone would make her weep. She's very *frum*, you see. Always used to make my dad wait up for me in the dark on Friday nights when I wasn't home in time. For lighting the *Shabbos* candles, you know.'

Felix nodded. She'd seen them in Whitechapel windows.

'He was meant to give me a good talking-to. Least those were Mum's orders. And first he'd always say I mustn't be late again. Like he had to. Job done. Then he'd say, "Your mother's your mother, so what can I do?" And then I'd know *he'd* forgiven me again, at least. He hated our rows, but he knew why they happened, even if she couldn't admit it. "The truth is heavy. So people don't like to carry it." That's what he'd always say. And then, just as I thought he was going to bed, he'd turn round and ask me exactly what everyone had been saying at the meeting I'd just come from.'

'And so you'd talk politics for the rest of the night?' Felix laughed, incredulous. She loved hearing about his family.

'Usually. I remember a question he asked me once – he'd heard it at the Workers Circle. He used to play chess there. And listen. "Was it true?" he said to me. "Did the rabbis and the rich people talk about God just to keep the poor in their place?"'

'What did you say?'

'"Yes," of course. Then I felt terrible, so I said, "Well, some-times." And then he said, "So I'll see you for synagogue for the morning."'

Nat couldn't see Felix's face, but he must have sensed her smile. 'You don't have to believe to be a Jew, you know.'

'I suppose not,' she said, wishing she knew more. She wondered if it mattered to him that she wasn't Jewish.

'I tell you another thing,' said Nat quickly, in a lighter voice. 'If my dad saw the cut of this jacket . . . ! He's a tailor – did I say? His dad was too. Made to measure.'

'Very smart. So did he make your suit? The one you were wearing when you came to say goodbye?' Felix had been surprised and delighted by the elegance of that suit. She'd never imagined a communist might dress like that.

'Yes. God knows where that is now! I was sorry to lose it, I can tell you.'

'Is he angry with you? For coming here? Does he write?'

'Not yet. My big sister does sometimes. Rachel. They're getting over it. She says.'

'That's good,' said Felix, wondering if the same were true in Sydenham. She still hadn't told them where to reach her. Only that she was safe. Perhaps it was time to relent.

Distracted, she stumbled on a broken paving stone, and Nat caught her before she fell. He moved his arm to her shoulders, and she felt his fingers brush against her hair. Before she could stop herself she tilted her head and rubbed it briefly against his hand, like a cat.

'Oh, how I wish I wasn't going back tomorrow,' she risked. He gave her an awkward one-armed hug. Once, twice. She was so close now she felt a kind of shudder run through him, and its ripples seemed to spread to her own body.

'Me too,' he said. 'And I wish I didn't have to stay. I hate it, you know. Being here, useless. And helpless. It's driving me crazy.'

'I know. You want to get back to the front.' They all did. It had shocked Felix at first. Then, in the first quiet spell at the hospital, she'd understood.

'I feel guilty, safe here.'

'Not exactly safe.' A louder explosion, not so far away that they couldn't feel it shake the pavement. He pulled her even nearer. She felt as light as air.

'Safer.'

'Maybe.' She shrugged. Everyone had picked up something of Madrid's fatalism. He stopped and she knew he was looking at her, curiously, trying to decipher her shadowed face.

'You like the danger, don't you?' he teased her, gently. 'Admit it.' Nat turned and took her face in his hand, stroking her cheek with his thumb, studying her as closely as the darkness allowed.

'No, no, of course I don't.' Felix was almost too embarrassed to enjoy the sensation, this warm weightlessness, as if every cell in her body were gently expanding. 'Not really.' She tried to look away, but he wouldn't let her. He'd seen through her.

'A bit of you . . . ?'

'Well, it's exciting,' she admitted, meeting his eyes again, at last. 'You know it is.'

'Life and death.'

That was it. He knew. 'It makes you feel so alive . . .'

' . . . A part of things . . . ?'

' . . . Here and now.'

Their lips were almost brushing as they spoke. Felix wasn't sure what would happen if she stopped speaking.

'Everything seems more important when there's so much at stake,' she said.

Everything. She kept silent at last, lips slightly parted. She'd said what she had to say.

'It is important,' he whispered, moving his hand to the back of her neck and then making it impossible for her to go on talking even if she wanted to.

Kissing Nat, here, in the dark, in Madrid, was more easy and delicious than Felix could have imagined. She'd always wondered if she'd know what to do. If it would be obvious that she didn't. If that would matter. At night sometimes she'd even tested her own lips against her own arm, felt their softness, as if it might somehow help when the time came. Her tongue greeted his, tentatively at first, and then more bravely. It even crossed her mind that he might think her more experienced than she was. Maybe that didn't matter either. He'd managed to shave since that afternoon, she noticed. She was glad.

As they came up for air, a half-sob escaped her.

'Felix?'

'It's all right,' she replied. 'Except my legs. I can barely stand. I don't know what it is.'

'Do you want to go back?'

'No, no,' she almost shouted. 'Not at all.'

'Here. Come here, then.'

He led her to a doorway, a great big one, with a great heavy door, and no sign of life behind it. In fact, half the building behind it was gone. They sat on the stone steps, huddled into the corner, and Felix wondered how it would feel to have both Nat's arms around her.

'This damned sling . . .' he said, at just that moment. 'Do I really need it just now?'

'Probably not,' Felix said, kneeling up so she could loosen it. An unprofessional stab of jealousy pierced her as she thought about the nurse who had tied the knot, and she had to stop herself from asking about her. She rubbed at the skin, feeling the indentation made by the sling. Then she stroked the bare nape of Nat's neck, where the short hairs became softer. His arms round her waist, he buried his face in her jersey with a groan.

'We can't . . .' whispered Felix, not even sure what she meant. 'We can't . . .' She heard the clip-clop of a mule coming up the cobbles, and froze. Then the echoing hoofs passed and retreated, and she let herself breathe out again. She slid her fingers under Nat's collar and enjoyed the smoothness she found there. Nat was trembling again. Was he in pain, or simply aching inside as much she was? She didn't know if she wanted to protect him, or be sheltered herself. She cradled his bowed head against her and felt the heat of his breath penetrate the wool and warm her skin.

He said something in a muffled voice. She caught the word 'taste' and tilted his head towards hers with terrifying courage, dropping into his lap. Gradually they both became more daring. But they did not have long. A familiar noise above forced them to break off and look up. A humming moan rose quickly to a roar. Five planes in formation passed across the narrow strip of sky between the buildings. Felix closed her eyes. The bombers sped on. Then came the explosion. A siren started up.

'Carabanchel, I think. I don't know how much more that place can take,' said Nat, drawing back so he could listen. Felix felt bereft. 'There'll be more soon. Quick. Let's get you back.' He pulled her to her feet. Her legs seemed to be working again now.

More planes soon followed and they started to run, not looking up any more, just concentrating on finding the right turnings, and avoiding the holes in the roads. They must have been walking in circles all this time; the hotel was closer than

Felix realised. Nat almost pushed her inside. He didn't seem to trust himself to say goodbye. 'Go on. Quickly. Stay with Dolores.'

Felix wanted to hold onto him, to pull him in with her. How could she possibly let him go? Something inside her felt so stretched it hurt.

'What about you?' she said.

'I know where there's a *refugio*.'

He was backing away from her, looking over her shoulder at the receptionist, looking back over his shoulder at the sky. Another siren started somewhere, closer. The old lady on duty set down her knitting, to watch and to listen, doing her own sums about how far away the danger might be tonight.

'I wish . . .'

'Me too.'

'Will you . . . ?'

'I'll write,' he promised. 'I really will this time.' And the door shut between them.

The receptionist quickly bowed her head over her needles. Felix said goodnight. Climbing the stairs, dragging her feet, she could still taste Nat. She buried her face in her hands, and breathed in hungrily, wondering if the smell of him had rubbed off on her, if she could keep it for a little longer. Her palms smelled of soap and cigarette smoke and something else she couldn't quite recognise.

On the landing, she saw a line of light under their door. She turned the handle as quietly as she could, wondering if Dolores had fallen asleep with the lamps still on. But Dolores was still sitting up in bed. She started as Felix entered, and turned her papers face down on the cover.

'How was your evening?' she said.

'Lovely,' Felix replied slowly, thinking about it. Her throat felt blocked and achy. She didn't want to talk.

Dolores said nothing.

'Sorry . . . I didn't mean to stay out so late.' Felix sat on the bed and took off her shoes. Why was Dolores looking at her like that? As though she despised her.

'You look . . . tired. You shouldn't have waited up.' Felix rubbed her feet, sighing. Dolores could be tricky sometimes. Not surprising, really after all she must have been through. Everything in Spain had changed so fast. *She thinks I'm a slut. She can tell somehow. She knows what I've been doing, and what I'm thinking now. Catholic girls don't have thoughts like these. Or feelings like these. I'm sure they don't.* 'Are you still studying? You are so good.'

'I've finished now,' said Dolores, putting her papers away, lips tight.

It was too bad. Felix's chin came forward. She didn't care what Dolores thought. How could she possibly understand this? Felix knew she wasn't mistaken about Nat. He really wanted her, wanted her properly, in the right kind of way. He wasn't the kiss-me-quick type, she was certain. How could he be? And as for those girls at the nurses' home in London, they were wrong too, the way they always talked about men. Not to be trusted. Always playing the field. She remembered their warnings . . . a man would say anything to get a girl to . . . No, Nat was different – well, of course he was different – and he wasn't like that. They just didn't know.

Has this place fallen? Nat screams into the ear of the motorcyclist as they sweep into the main square together. His comrade half-turns, his hair whipping into both their eyes, and Nat can briefly see the panic rising as he mouths: No sé. *I don't know.*

There's no way to tell who holds each village now. In retreat, no stranger can be trusted. Best not to stop and see.

The joyful faces that once greeted every arrival of the Brigades are all gone. You might catch a child, whisking out of sight, too late, or ducking fearfully into a doorway at the approach of an engine. You might glimpse a figure in black behind a window, moving away. You couldn't expect a welcome. It's no use asking for food in times like these. The signs outside the houses make it quite clear. No hay pan. *There is no bread.*

How much petrol do we have? Gas?

No sé.

The bike swerves round a crater and Nat fastens his grip, smells fresh sweat on the man's neck, feels the strain in his thighs. Then he sees the ambulance ahead. It's a burned-out shell, on its side in a culvert, one blackened door hanging open, and no sign of life. Must have taken a direct hit. They can't stop. They can't check. There's no going back.

Oseh shalom bim'romav . . .

144

APRIL–SEPTEMBER 1937

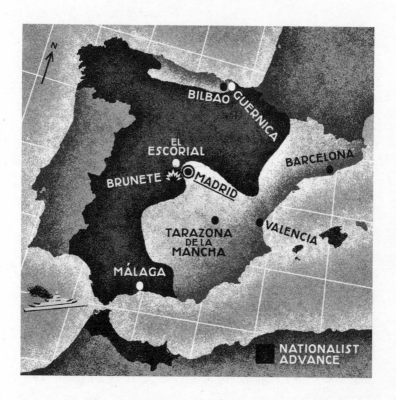

24

In April George's newspaper sent him to report on the rebel blockade of the Basque coast and he got away from Madrid at last. Bilbao was still a government stronghold. Getting there was tricky – the Basques were surrounded by Nationalists – but George arrived in time to see the first British merchant ship make it through. The dockside crowds were ecstatic.

There were only a few other correspondents in the city just then, old hands, the seasoned type, but they made George welcome enough, and he was grateful.

'Narrow escape this afternoon.' The Australian reporter gulped back some wine. It was a Monday evening and they were all eating together at the Hotel Torrontegui with the British captain and his daughter.

'You too?' said the Englishman from *The Times*.

'Six Heinkels. The machine guns were relentless.'

'They strafed us for a good fifteen minutes.'

'If we hadn't been near that bomb crater . . .'

'And the rebels still deny Hitler's helping them? Monstrous,' said George. It was unbelievable, how easily persuaded the papers were.

'You've seen this, haven't you?' *The Times* man passed across a leaflet. *Ultimo aviso*. Final warning. 'General Mola dropped hundreds of these at the beginning of the Nationalist campaign here. Go on. Keep it.'

'What does it say?' asked Captain Roberts.

'"I have decided to bring the war in the north of Spain to a rapid end . . . If your submission is not immediate, I will raze Biscay to the ground . . . I have the means to do it."'

They all fell silent. George looked up from the leaflet. The room was cold as well as bare, so he had an excuse for shivering.

'Let's hope the food convoys get here soon,' he said. And he'd thought Madrid was desperate.

The captain raised his water glass. A kind of toast. But at that moment a commotion on the stairs made the others pause. Some shouting, and a man sobbing. He burst into the dining room with searching, staring eyes, his face wet with tears.

'Guernica is destroyed,' he cried. 'They bombed and bombed and bombed.'

'Bloody swine!' Captain Roberts's fist thumped down on the table. The other correspondents were already on their feet.

'Coming, George?' That was the Australian, Noel. 'There'll be room, if you're not particular. The more witnesses the better. But we must make tracks.'

Some way out of Bilbao, George noticed the darkness through the windscreen giving way to a glorious pink light in the sky ahead. He nearly made a fool of himself. Surely it was too early for the dawn?

It wasn't the sun.

Five miles on, they reached the first group of refugees. They sat by the side of the road, lost in horror. Behind them, rosy clouds of smoke reflected the flames rising from the burning city. Ox cart after ox cart, piled high, came plodding towards

Bilbao. There were refugees on foot too, hardly moving. Noel saw a priest among them, and stopped the car.

'¿Qué pasa, Padre? What happened?'

George looked at the Father's blackened face and torn clothes and wondered if the man was capable of speech. Eventually the answer came: 'Aviones . . . bombas . . .' he whispered, still disbelieving. 'Muchos . . . muchos . . .'

They drove on. The hillsides around were dotted with light, fires, like tiny flickering candles.

When they arrived on the outskirts of Guernica it was clear that the man at the hotel had exaggerated nothing. The buildings of this town had walls made of fire. *How can I describe this?* George wound down the car window and all thoughts of his duty to his newspaper vanished. His face was swept with a heat so intense he could barely breathe. The smell was both sweet and putrid, sulphur and charred leather. He began to retch.

A group of Basque soldiers approached George and Noel as soon as they saw them. A few were sobbing openly, too much to speak, but the others made clear what was needed.

'Over there.' The soldier who spoke had a body in his arms, too charred and black to tell its age or sex. He gestured with his head towards the embers of a ruin, where a group of monks were at work.

George spent the next few hours helping to disentangle bodies from debris. His mind went blank and his body moved like an automaton. Nothing could blot out this taste and smell. He couldn't rid himself of the notion that he was consuming flesh each time he breathed in. Burnt human flesh. Stray particles seemed to stick to his skin and clothes, and form into grit on his tongue. From time to time, a hideous crumbling crash resounded, as another wooden building collapsed.

Why this place? Why now? George could make no sense of this. It was well back from the front line, he knew. The barracks and the factory outside the town had apparently not been touched. It was senseless, incomprehensible.

At around two in the morning, *The Times* correspondent came over to where George was working. 'I'm off. Tell Noel. I'll be back tomorrow. I need to think.'

'This is something new, isn't it?' said George, straightening his back, bracing his legs. He ran a filthy hand through his sweat-soaked hair, streaking his face.

'Yes. Unparalleled. In every way. But you know what it's about? Creating terror. Total terror. As simple as that.'

George nodded.

'They're determined to destroy civilian lives and civilian morale. And we've got to make that clear. You know you can telegraph from Bilbao, don't you? You won't need to worry about the censors there.'

'Right,' said George, ashamed that he had been too preoccupied to think about it before.

The Times man had been staring at the ground as he spoke, scuffing the smoking ashes with the heel of his boot, his mind apparently elsewhere. He stopped for a moment, and squatted down. 'Help me get this out.'

He'd uncovered part of a metal cylinder. Cursing the heat, they dug it out together. It was about the length of his forearm. The journalist held it gingerly, with a look of disgust, and rubbed at it with his jacket sleeve.

'Hmmm. Here's proof all right. Take a look.'

It was the stamp of the German imperial eagle, just visible in the shivering light of the burning buildings. And a date: 1936.

'I'll keep this, if you don't mind. See you tomorrow.'

He walked away, still searching the ground as he went, and

George turned back to his labours. Bit by bit in the course of the night, George pieced together what had happened. By dawn he had an idea of what he could write down. But he was no closer to understanding it.

Monday was always market day. Country folk gathered in Guernica from all the villages around. The aeroplanes were heard some time between four and five in the afternoon and the church bell began to ring the alarm. Clergymen kneeled and prayed, in cellars and dugouts, keeping the people calm. And in the open plaza too. Within five minutes the first plane flew overhead. Just one, circling low over the town, really low. It dropped six heavy bombs and a shower of grenades and departed. Five minutes later another arrived, and did the same. Three more soon followed – Junkers, one man thought. The militiamen's hospital was one of the first buildings struck, George heard. No, no English nurses there, they told him when he asked. Yes, they were sure. The Red nurses don't come much to Euskadi. That's what they call Basque country.

After that, the bombardment was steady, intense, and systematic. A relentless rhythm of heavy bombing and hand grenades. Craters twenty-five-foot deep. Then fighter planes, swooping in close with machine guns, killing people as they ran for shelter that was not shelter; finally more heavy bombs, and – most terrifying of all – thousands of firebombs, little ones, with bright yellow flames. They fell everywhere, a fiery downpour, until everything that could be was set alight. Everything was burning, burning like a town made of coals. Three hours later, when night fell, the German planes departed.

When dawn broke, and George had pulled fifteen blackened corpses from a mess of tiles and charcoaled rafters, and comforted some women mad with grief, and failed to console others, he knew he had to return to Bilbao to tell his story too. Driving back, drained of feeling, he saw carcasses of farmhouses on the hillside, their great stone ramps leading nowhere. Fields had been turned into slaughterhouses. Even sheep had been gunned down. Words tangled as George tried to form a cable in his head.

He would go to Bilbao to file this news, he decided. And then he would stop. He wasn't cut out for reporting this war. He wished he was. He'd thought for a good while that he might be. But he was wrong. He couldn't bear just to watch any more.

When he had finished in Bilbao, he would make his way to Valencia and offer himself to the Brigades. He could be a driver, a stretcher-bearer, a mechanic . . . he'd rather do anything than this. Anything was better than trying, and failing, to tell this story. And somewhere in his travels he might run into Felix yet. Then he would decide what to do about it. Though he couldn't help wondering what was the point of looking for her, if she didn't want to be found?

25

Felix spent most of the summer working at El Escorial, at the foot of the mountains north-west of Madrid. July was a nightmare: the battle of Brunete brought more casualties than anyone could have imagined. Later things were a little calmer, though no more certain. August was so hot that by early afternoon everyone just tried to sleep, patients and medics.

Sometimes Felix wandered down into the royal mausoleum simply to cool down. She loved to unlace the strings of her *alpargatas* and slip off the rope-soled shoes so she could feel the icy marble floor under her bare feet. It calmed her down. It emptied her mind.

She went there now, to prepare herself for reading her letters. Due ceremony, that was what she wanted to give them, though for different reasons. Facing the rows of gilded caskets, Felix stood for a moment and felt the rush of heat leave her head. Each scrolled golden cartouche opposite bore the name of a king of Spain. Her shoes made a slow pendulum as they swung silently from one hand. Fanned in the other, she held two envelopes. Felix stared at them, wondering which to open first.

Then she sat down, legs straight ahead, and hitched up her skirt. The floor worked its magic. The cold flooded from her calves up her thighs. Delicious agony.

Both letters had been opened before and resealed. She was

not the first to read them. That was what happened in wars. She knew that now.

Neville first, Felix decided. And then it would be over and done with. Seeing the Sydenham address at the top of the page gave her an unexpected pang.

Dear Felicity, she read. *Mother and I are very glad you've stopped being so silly and secretive about your forwarding address. We also have appreciated the fact that we are no longer entirely in the dark about your movements (it was certainly a relief to know you were alive) but it has been very hard for Mother. She wants to send you things, of course. She plans to write herself soon, but first she is keen to finish knitting you some gloves, as she hates to think of your fingers being cold. And yes, I did tell her that it would not be so cold in Spain now. And also that it was bound to be all over by next winter, one way or another. But she said, 'You never know.'*

Felix's strangled laugh bounced off the marble tombs. What had come over him? How had she got off so lightly?

She skimmed the next few paragraphs: about the cherry blossom in Crystal Palace Park, the silver wedding celebrations of the deputy director of Pearl Assurance, and Neville's hope that next door's wayward cat would not eat all the new goldfish in the garden pond.

Then she saw the word 'George'. What was this? Bother. The censor must have muddled the pages. She shuffled them back.

And I've been able to tell George where you are, finally. I suppose you still don't know he followed you to Spain? He spent months looking for you, with no success.

Felix couldn't believe this. George had been here too, all this time? Looking for her? And by now he'd be back in London – at the side of some racetrack, perhaps, binoculars in hand. Whistling cheerily, she hoped. She disapproved of his chivalry, but she had more than a soft spot for George and he deserved her thanks.

Neville was right. She had been silly. Horribly so. A selfish idiot in fact. Not for coming. But for cutting herself loose so completely. Just a few mysterious letters home so they knew she was still alive. Insisting – until the last one – that they leave her alone. She heard a quiet whimpering groan: she had made the noise herself.

Not like George to give up a search? Of course not. But perhaps if you'd given him a little more encouragement ~~instead of running off like that in Paris . . .~~ This is no time for recriminations. I'm sure you can guess how I feel about your behaviour.

Of course. But to be fair, George had never exactly made his feelings clear. Even now Felix couldn't be sure if her instincts about his Paris plans had been right.

Whatever it is about this war in Spain that's got you in its grip, it's captured George now too. I didn't quite understand his letter. Something about not standing by while evil takes over. Very excitable.

Felix felt all hot again.

George has resigned from the paper. It seems he's working as a mechanic, or a driver or something, for the International Brigades. I don't know more than that. Personally, I find the decision extraordinary. Mother says please to let her know if there's anything else you want.

She rolled over onto her stomach and laid her cheek flat against the coolness of the floor. Her pulse eventually slowed.

Dear God, she thought, *George is still here in Spain.* It was too much to take in.

As Felix puzzled over this news, she realised George's decision to stay was more in character than Neville seemed to think. George always was a decent sort: the upright type. A great one for doing the right thing. She must ask around. Perhaps someone here at El Escorial had come across George, and could give her news. Good for George. Who would have thought?

It was some time before Felix was ready to open the second letter. The tearing envelope was the loudest noise in the mausoleum, louder than her breathing. The paper was very thin – like tracing paper. No, it was lavatory paper. *Medicated with Izal*, according to the print along the edge. Must have been sent from England by some well-meaning Aid committee. If only they knew. But why so empty?

There were some random lines on one page, which could have been the outline of mountains. More lines, and some crosshatching on another. Rocks? Or the branches of trees perhaps. Each page, alone, looked like a half-formed idea. But layered, and held up to the shaft of light that cut across the room, an image took shape. Nat had turned the landscapes into her face. His name was at the bottom. With a date: 2nd August 1937. He had survived the battle at Brunete.

Bloodless with relief, her fingers accidentally released the papers. They fluttered to the floor, sliding away from her. She couldn't hold Nat so she held herself, wrapping her own arms around her own body. A hand round each shoulder, eyes shut, she hugged herself tightly while she tried to summon him back to her.

A breeze caught the fallen pages, a breeze from an opening door.

26

It was a big hospital: well-organised, but still overflowing with casualties from Brunete. The neighbouring graveyards were full too. When George arrived nobody knew quite where Felix had got to. Several orderlies and a few of the walking wounded shook their heads when he asked. And then a softly spoken *chica* overheard his question – his Spanish was still slow and loud – and she directed him to the mausoleum.

'*Gracias, señorita,*' he said. '*Muy gentil.*'

Rifle on knees, an armed guard in overalls lolled on a velvet-upholstered chair near the entrance to the royal tombs. He acknowledged George's presence with his eyebrows, inspected his papers, but made no effort to stop or question him further.

And there she was. At last. George had wondered for months if he'd even recognise her. Now he wondered how he could ever have imagined he might not. God, she was beautiful. What a girl! And there she stood, more real than ever. Real in a way that made him ache, and looking at him with utter amazement in her eyes. Her hands uncrossed and fell to her sides.

'Here, let me . . .' George bent to pick up the scattered papers. They seemed to be eluding Felix. He overcame the urge to look at them closely.

'Thank you. Thank you.' Felix snatched them back, far too eagerly. They were clearly precious. Then she tucked the pages quickly away into a pocket, without glancing at them again. She looked startled, in a caught-in-the-act kind of way. Another girl might have blushed. George coughed, so that he could turn away.

His heart had just frozen in mid-leap. He knew exactly what this meant. A wasted journey. The end of everything. The chill of the mausoleum reached his bones.

'So,' she said. 'You're here. Well, obviously you are.'

'And about time! It's taken me long enough to find you,' said George. Jovial, that's what he would be. Keep things jovial. But the cramped feeling he had got used to carrying about in the pit of his stomach took a firmer grip.

Felix's face had become unreadable again, guarded. He kept thinking about the taxi in Paris.

'Not that I'm blaming you,' he added quickly. 'Don't get me wrong.'

He smiled, very determined to be nice, whatever it took. But how strange. It had never even occurred to him that she might be in love with someone else. Not in a million years. So much had happened since Paris, and what could he know about any of it? His smile faltered slightly. Get a grip. *Damn. Damn. Damn.*

'I think you probably should,' said Felix. 'And *I* wouldn't blame *you*.' She was about to launch into something . . . An apology. Or a confession perhaps. But George was too tired to deal with anything like that. Every muscle in his body felt weak at once. He wanted to lie down and sleep and blot everything out.

'Shhh,' he said, putting his hands up, defensively. He was tempted to block his ears. 'Let's not. What's done is done. Best let bygones be bygones.' *Although* . . . and a train of thought began that did not take him in a useful direction. He put the brakes on it, before it got too far.

'That's very good of you, George, I must say.'

She was looking at him so warmly that he began to crumble a little again.

'And Neville told me . . . you're working with us now,' she said. 'You decided to stay in Spain. That's wonderful. I'm so proud of you.'

George coughed, embarrassed now.

'Well, after a certain point it just seemed the obvious thing to do. I couldn't ignore what I could see with my own eyes. It's different when it's all happening right in front of you, isn't it?'

'Yes, yes, of course. Of course it is. Completely different. I'm so glad you understand.'

'Actually, I wish I did,' said George. 'In some ways, the more I know, the less I do understand.'

He couldn't interpret her face. He thought he saw doubt, but maybe he was imagining it. She checked her watch.

'Do you have to go? On duty?' he asked.

'In a little while. Not just yet. Would you like me to show you round? There are several hospitals here. Oh, you probably know that already. You must have come for a reason. You're not just here for me?' She looked a little horrified.

'In El Escorial? No, don't worry. I'm picking up the bug hatcher.'

Felix began to scratch. 'I hate that name.'

George shrugged, half-smiling.

'Oh well, the delousing machinery if you like. And the portable showers. Mostly I'm at the *auto-parque* workshop these days – repairs, refits, anything that's needed really. It's been busy since Brunete. So much to do right now . . . well, you don't have to imagine. But they needed a *chófer* for this so I volunteered to drive. I fancied a change . . . fresh air. And I'd just

159

got a letter from Neville. He told me where you were. So it was a chance to finish what I'd started.'

Felix frowned.

'Tracking you down.' George couldn't quite look at her. 'That's all I meant. God knows, it's taken me long enough.' He stared at her bare feet – dark with sun or dirt? The remains of winter chilblains. 'Pretty useless, really.' He was suddenly finding it difficult to talk again.

'Oh.' A pause. 'Sorry. Thank you. That was my fault. I really am sorry.'

'Well. Never mind that now. Tell me how you are . . . that kind of thing. How are the kitchens round here? Could you "organise" us some coffee?'

Felix made a face. Anything hard to get had to be 'organised'. 'I'll try. Let me get my shoes back on and then I'll go and see if I can get away for a bit longer.' She sat down and he watched from a distance and longed to run his hand down her extended leg, soothe her bones and tie the laces round her ankle. He watched, and waited, and then pulled her to her feet. She smiled – that smile she had that always felt like a reward, or a prize or something.

'Come on,' she said. 'I don't suppose you came to spend the afternoon in a mausoleum, anyway.'

'I don't mind what we do. Just happy to be with you.' He shouldn't have said that. Idiot. Idiot. Anger rose. He nearly kicked the doorframe as he turned round to hide his shame.

A few minutes later they were blinking in the glare of the afternoon. She pushed the hair away from her face, and squinted at him.

'Look at you, all brown and blonde. The sun suits you!'

'Look at you . . .' he said, lamely, feeling his stubble, feeling self-conscious. 'You've changed too.' Yes, come on, keep it breezy.

That's the idea, remember. 'Go on then. Show me where you work. I'd like to see.'

'The wards are still packed. It's been so awful. Though we've just sent a great many patients off to convalescent hospitals on the coast. The only ones left here now are the men who can't be moved. But there are far more of them than we'd like.'

'I'm sure.' After Brunete, George had repaired – or rather reassembled – at least four ambulances. He'd seen the state of them, and he knew what had happened to their drivers. You couldn't weld human bodies with an acetylene torch.

As they crossed a vast courtyard, he saw Felix struggling to frame a question. He waited. There was only so much help he was prepared to give her.

'All this time. They haven't needed you in London?' she asked in the end.

'No. I've quit the paper.'

'Completely? You've given up your job?'

'Yes.'

She bit her lip. 'Was that my fault?'

George thought about this. 'That's not how I see it.'

'Oh . . . And are you writing at all now?'

'Just a diary. When I can. You know how it is. And I've done some bits and pieces for wall newspapers.'

Felix nodded, looked at the ground. George imagined her searching the Brigaders' makeshift noticeboards for her lover's name on the casualty lists, but never noticing his own byline. *Stop feeling sorry for yourself.* He couldn't, and it made him cruel.

'Obituaries, mostly, as it happens,' he went on. 'But I sold my typewriter after Guernica.'

'Oh. You were at Guernica?' Felix had gone white at this news. 'Oh God, I heard . . . is that why . . . ?'

'Yes.' George cut her off. He returned to Guernica too often

161

in his dreams to talk about it in daylight. 'Now I wish I'd kept the machine for the Brigade. It could have been useful.'

'Never mind.'

'Actually I did think of doing a piece for the Brigade news-paper – you know, the *Volunteer for Liberty*? Something about the drivers. Do you ever see it?'

'Sometimes.'

'I don't know what to make of it.'

'What do you mean?' asked Felix.

'Are we really winning? I can't tell. Was Brunete really a victory? It seems incredible. It felt like a disaster.'

'Of course we're winning. We've got to be. Every day of fighting weakens Fascism.'

George looked hard at Felix, and his lips tightened. She meant it.

'Mmmm. That's what they say. I hope they're right.' So much for keeping things jovial, he thought to himself. He'd never dared have such a dark conversation with anyone before. He felt safe with Felix, he supposed.

'Oh, do write that piece,' she said. 'The drivers are so impor-tant.'

'Yes, of course. Of course. That's not why I'm hesitating.'

'So . . . ?' Felix was looking at him with a confused expres-sion. He looked around. There was nobody within earshot, but he moved a little nearer all the same. And then he wished he hadn't had to, because he felt himself losing control again. Could she feel it? It was like silk rubbing together. If he came too much closer, there'd surely be sparks.

'Difficult to explain. It's just I find that kind of thing quite hard to do. All that morale-raising stuff, you know?' (*Did she?*) George ran his hand through his hair. His scalp was tingling. 'You read it and cheer. It's great. We're all marvellous. Everyone

162

is so brave. And that's true, isn't it? I know that's true. And then you read between the lines. And how do you know what to believe?'

She didn't answer. So he kept going.

'You never see the casualty figures. But you have a pretty good idea of just how many trips the ambulances have made. And you've cleaned the blood off them. And worse. Over and over again.'

Yes, she did know what he was talking about.

'It's been hell, hasn't it?' She put a sympathetic hand on his arm, and George made himself just keep walking, strolling on, one foot after the other, though the light pressure of her finger tips just below his rolled-up sleeves seemed to burn his bare skin.

George hated to think what Felix had been through, what was still to come. She still looked so innocent. Such a child. Quite unaware of the effect she was having on him. She couldn't possibly have guessed what he'd had planned for Paris. For a moment he considered abandoning everything, then and there. What chance he could persuade her to come home with him? Right now? He opened his mouth, and shut it just as quickly.

He could guess her answer. *And wait for the war to follow us to England? No, thank you.*

And then George remembered the envelope in Felix's pocket. It must be burning a hole. Her hand kept returning to it as they walked, checking it was still there, safe and sound. She couldn't help herself.

'But it's important to keep up morale, isn't it?' continued Felix. 'I mean, without that . . .'

'I know. Morale is crucial. It's just not my strong point. I'm not convincing.'

'Do you know, I'm not sure we should even be talking like this. It doesn't help. What if . . . ?'

'Fine. We haven't had this conversation.' He trusted her not to tell. That wasn't her way. She was far too busy seeing the good in people to think of the bad. Anyone else would say he was a defeatist. That's what they called you now if you expressed the slightest doubt about victory. That wouldn't do at all. These days, in fact, it was positively dangerous. You never knew who might report you, if you didn't toe the Party line.

'Really? OK. Look, through here . . . this is my ward.'

Bed after bed. High windows. Acres of floor. Blue and white tiles. All very crisp and clean after the black grease and filthy overalls of the vehicle workshop. A slightly older nurse with spectacles and a clipboard spotted Felix and began to stride over. She didn't look happy.

'There you are, Felix. Good. Can I have a word?'

Felix seemed taken aback. 'Will you excuse me please, George?'

He stepped aside, and the two women lowered their voices. But in the quiet of the ward, heads turned towards him and away from the patients, their words were still quite audible.

'What is it, Kitty?'

'I thought you'd trained Dolores to do the cross-matching.'

'For blood groups? Of course I did. She's been doing it for weeks now. I've been very impressed.'

'Well, I'm not. She's rushing the slide test. You can't get accurate results like that.'

'Oh, hell. Are you sure? She always seems so careful to me. Maybe she's tired.'

'We're all under strain, but tiredness is no excuse. Men's lives are at stake. You know what could happen if Group II types get mislabelled as Group IV.'

'Obviously.'

'You've got to supervise her more closely until she's proved her competence again. To my satisfaction. Discipline, Felix, discipline.'

'Yes, yes, of course. I'll speak to Dolores right away. Make sure she's really understood.'

'No damage done this time, but it was bloody lucky I was there.'

The other nurse turned on her heel, and set off down the corridor on a fresh mission. George saw Felix pass her hand across her face, which had turned a shade of grey. He felt for her. He hadn't understood its substance, but he could recognise a drubbing when he overheard one.

'George, I'm terribly sorry. Something's come up. Are you going back right away? Might we meet again in a little while? We barely seem to have scratched the surface . . . so much to talk about.'

'I'm not sure.' Just at that moment George wanted to get away completely. There was a limit to how much longer he could go on being nice and calm when, underneath it all, he just wanted to break something. But as he spoke he saw the disappointment in her eyes. 'I'll see what I can manage. How long everything takes. I'll do my best, Felix. Can I . . . ?'

'Oh, no, don't worry. I'm fine.' And then, unusually, her face seemed to cave in. 'It's just something that I'm not looking forward to terribly. Someone I have to talk to. She's very shy. Nervous, you know. But she's been trying so hard, I can tell. Really keen to get everything just right. And *I've* worked so hard to build up her confidence, and I'm awfully afraid of criticising her now . . . such a setback. You know what a difference it makes in a team for everyone to be utterly reliable.'

27

The summer was almost at an end, and Nat was sent for more training. It turned out he was 'officer material'.

On the gunnery course, Nat encountered his first Russian in Spain, a hero of the Revolution. Not that 'Pablo' discussed his origins. Discussion wasn't his style. Nor was Pablo his real name. He didn't speak a word of Spanish, and when he yelled at them to reload their machine guns more quickly he barked something that sounded like: 'Beestro-eye! Beestro-eye!' They got faster, fast.

Trench technique was taught by an American. Mark the earth before digging. Make sure a trench on a ridge can't be seen against the skyline. Throw the earth towards the enemy, not behind you. Clear every single rock because a bullet that hits rock is never just one bullet's worth of danger. A proper trench is built in zigzags, irregular, not more than eight feet long: a hand grenade or mortar shell in a straight trench can kill dozens of men, instead of only four or five.

Yes, that all made sense.

Two Sundays into training, there was a concert party. Nat was leaning against a tree, rereading his third letter from Felix, when the sound truck's speakers whistled and howled into life. (The last time he heard them they were blaring propaganda across the enemy trenches during a stalemate.) After a few crackling false starts, a rumba began to blare across the dusty square. Black-shawled villagers and freshly washed military men gathered around its edge, toes tapping.

Nat looked up. These evenings were always fun. You could end up dancing with anyone, and they'd rarely be female. He began to smile now as a leather-clad dispatch rider sidled up to issue an invitation to a giant of a sergeant major. Very bold. He'd join in himself in a little while, but Nat couldn't resist lingering a few minutes longer over his letter.

It was just like Felix, he realised, with the pleasure of recognition. Grave and serious for great stretches – and then it was a job to take in the technical details: something about median nerves and tying off an ulnar artery in a recent operation? Anyway, it had been a triumph! – and then suddenly, unexpectedly (just like that time in the bar in Madrid when her hand gently stilled his trembling knee and a painful joy had stopped him in his tracks), her tone would change. A few lines sent the blood rushing to Nat's head:

At the end of surgery, each time we finish, I look at my patient's face. And I think how very glad I am it isn't you lying there. And I picture you with your limbs whole and hale and hearty. If I imagine you whole hard enough, I hope I can keep you that way.

And then she was straight back to more medical stuff, debridement or something, whatever that was.

How should he respond? He found it so hard to put his own feelings into words. Reading the letter let him hear her voice in his head, and it made him feel quite desperate for her. He'd just have to send more pictures. She said nothing about meeting again, and neither could he. It was too uncertain. But he'd use his pencil to show her how he felt.

On the back of the last page, Felix's writing became a scrawl. *It's taken days to write this. Ridiculously long. Always in little snatches of time. I thought it was finished. Now something terrible's happened. I'm so sorry to burden you. But writing gets it off my chest, and I'm afraid to tell Kitty, though I know I should.*

Nat read faster, stumbling over her words.

We lost another patient today – well, that's nothing new. But this man was in with a chance. I'm sure he was. There was something odd about the way he went downhill so suddenly. I don't quite understand it. But I'm terrified it was my fault. I believe it was haemolytic shock, although it's awfully hard to tell. I don't know why Dolores didn't tell me his temperature had gone up almost as soon as the transfusion started – I'd left her to finish the procedure while I dealt with something else. I'm always telling her to watch out for that. Too many things going on at once. That's the trouble. You know how it is. I mustn't blame her, I really mustn't. My responsibility.

Oh Felix.

The man suddenly had a raging fever and started to vomit like mad. That was yesterday. And now he's dead.

We can't find out why. No autopsy facilities here. And there's talk of moving on again soon. Sorry. Sorry. Sometimes I can't bear it. Another poor widow, and four more orphans for Spain. They were all girls. He told me. Enough now. Stay safe, until I see you again.

The letter made Nat want to throw his arms around Felix, tell her not to worry, and hold her so close that their bodies merged. He wanted to stroke her shorn hair, and reassure her that she'd done the best she could, and of course it wasn't her fault, and she was a wonderful nurse and one day in the better and fairer world they were fighting for she could be a wonderful surgeon too, if that's what she still wanted.

He remembered the day they first met, when he swung her in the air after Cable Street, and how they'd lost and found each other again. Their parting at the café. The first time his lips had brushed hers, outside the hospital, with trams rattling by, and everyone going home for their tea. Before the Sister interrupted. He longed to take up where they'd left off in Madrid, in the air raid, when he couldn't even kiss her goodbye with that hag of a receptionist just kept staring and staring. And he could see Felix had wanted him to.

Nat gave himself over to thinking about kissing Felix properly. With no bandages in the way, no intrusions. Kissing for as long as they wanted, with nothing and nobody to rush them. He thought about exploring every inch of her, skin against skin, and time and space and warmth to take as long as they both needed. If she noticed his inexperience, she would forgive it, because it would be another thing they shared. He shut his eyes for a moment. He could almost see her now, almost feel her.

The low voice of Seneca Digges broke in: 'Brother, might I have the pleasure of the next dance?' Seneca made a deep bow, and winked at Nat. 'You was a long way away just then and no mistake.'

'Not any more, damn you.' They both laughed. 'Well, if you're the best thing on offer, I don't mind if I do.'

They set off round the square in a stately waltz.

'So you got a sweetheart waiting for you,' said Seneca, a black American from Chicago, now a lieutenant.

'Not exactly waiting,' said Nat proudly. 'She's hard at work, here, in Spain. She's a nurse.'

Seneca let out a low whistle.

'Oh, boy,' he said. 'You got it bad.'

The next record on the gramophone was a conga. Everyone got sweaty, snaking round the square. It was followed by some Bach choral music. At any rate, so Nat and Seneca were informed by an old Etonian called Rupert who joined them for a cigarette in the pause between dances. He wrote poetry and edited the wall newspaper at the training camp. By the time the Bach was over, he'd persuaded Nat to do some sketches for the display.

'Are you a cartoonist too?' Rupert asked.

'Not really. Why?'

'Just wondered. Cartoons are always good for morale. Have to be the right sort of course. Had some trouble a few months ago with some bad elements in that respect. Trotskyists no doubt. Thought they could make a joke about Stalin and get away with it.'

'And they couldn't?' Nat looked to Seneca for support. Had he not heard? He was examining his boots with great intensity. Defiantly, Nat repeated his question. 'So you can't make a joke about Stalin round here?'

'Certainly not.' Rupert gave Nat a very odd look, and wandered off.

He probably shouldn't have pushed it. You had to be so careful these days. There was so much whispering. Talk of spies even, and certain kinds of letters never reaching home. And then you heard stuff about denunciations, and court martials, and prison, and probably worse. God forbid those rumours were true.

Nat didn't know what to believe. A lot of stories were probably put about by 'bad elements', deliberately. Trying to stir up trouble. Anything was possible. What about the fifth column the Fascists boasted they had in Madrid – all those unidentifiable traitors secretly working for the enemy? There was just no way of telling. Nat felt his skin tighten round his skull.

'Do you ever get the feeling that you're being watched, by someone you can't see?' he asked Seneca, who had continued to stare firmly at the ground throughout the conversation with Rupert. He let out a non-committal grunt, and wandered away.

The speakers clicked off. Two very old men moved into the silence in the centre of the square. One had a guitar; the other began to clap his hands. Their rhythms were strange and compelling. When the singer opened his mouth, the hairs on the back of Nat's neck stood to attention. The words meant little, but the music's unexpected breaks and sudden turns pulled and twisted him until he was ready to weep.

Then Seneca spoke to him again, tugging him away from the crowd.

'Nat, listen to this. There's a guy in town with a pair of Belgian Brownings for sale. Nine millimetre. What do you reckon? Don't an officer need a pistol? That's what everyone says round here.'

Blood pools inside the body on the rocks, blood forced downwards now by gravity alone. With no heartbeat left to pump it through the veins, no oxygen left to circulate, the colour of the skin begins to change in patches. The flesh stays soft. Down at the bottom of the ravine, close to the stream, it is too cold for limbs to stiffen into rigor mortis, though they will freeze eventually. A light snowfall covers the surface of this corpse with no discrimination . . . hair, coat, face, mouth, legs, boots. Eyes that still stare. Snow is not fastidious. Nor does it last.

JANUARY–MARCH 1938

N

BILBAO

MAS
DE LAS
MATAS

MADRID ◎

BARCELONA

TERUEL

VALENCIA

MÁLAGA

NATIONALIST
ADVANCE

28

Just when Felix needed to stock up on sleep, it eluded her. For lack of beds, she and Kitty were sharing an attic mattress. Without waking, Kitty muttered something and rolled over, taking their blanket and her body warmth with her.

Waiting. Waiting. Everyone on edge. And nights were haunted by longing.

They were in a new part of Spain, Aragon – Anarchist territory – and had commandeered the house of a lawyer who'd long ago fled. Christmas – extra chocolate and cigarette rations all round – had been and gone, and the latest victory celebrated hard. Spanish soldiers had taken back the town of Teruel, the toe of a foot-shaped slice of Fascist territory kicking at Republican Spain.

The weather gave some breathing space: Franco's air force was grounded by snow. The International Brigades were on standby. Felix knew the British must be close. Surely Nat must have finished his training by now? If rumour was right, his company would need him soon enough.

Felix gritted her teeth and gave up the struggle to sleep. She was hopelessly wide awake now. She might as well get up, and keep moving. The uncurtained square of window glass in the roof was lightening to grey anyway. Felix had been watching it for hours. It would soon be time to take over from Dolores.

She rolled off the mattress. On hands and knees, she felt for a tinderbox, and managed not to knock over the candle stub. It was jammed into an empty condensed milk tin, which warmed her hands a little once the flame was lit. No need to get dressed, as she was wearing all her clothes already – a horsehide coat and ski pants 'organised' by Kitty on their way here a few weeks earlier. No water which wasn't frozen, so no hope of splashing her face.

She laced her boots and felt her way downstairs, wondering how the night had passed in the ward. Her breath made clouds. Felix moved quietly, not wanting to disturb the patients. There weren't too many here just then. Mostly flu cases.

Dolores was at the bedside of their only borderline patient, Ramón, a scout caught in crossfire during the street fighting at Teruel a few weeks earlier. He bore everything with immense fortitude, but he had lost a great deal of blood before making it to theatre. Abdominals – belly cases – they were always tricky. There was talk of another transfusion, if he didn't improve soon.

Doug must have given the go-ahead, for Dolores was preparing Ramón already. He had a cannula in his arm, and was managing to flirt quietly, despite his weakness. Felix hovered in the doorway, invisible to them both. Watching silently, she ticked off a mental checklist. She was always alert to accidents now. It was so easy to make a mistake when you were exhausted. Dolores asked Ramón to look away for a moment, and Felix smiled to herself. After what he must have seen . . . Then her smile froze.

Dolores had attached the tubing and was holding up the flask of blood. Gravity would speed the blood on its journey into Ramón's veins. At that moment the sun made it over the horizon, and a strong ray of light suddenly streamed through the window behind the nurse. Lit up from behind, the glass glowed. But not the rich ruby red Felix expected, the colour of Spanish wine. This was darker, much darker, almost brown. No trick of the light, she was sure. Something was wrong. Why hadn't Dolores noticed?

She darted towards her, crashing into the end of a metal cot so violently that the sleeping soldier in it woke with a shout of terror. Felix stumbled and caught at the flask. She felt an unexpected heat as it slipped from her grasp. Both nurses cried out. Glass shards exploded across the flagstones. A pint of blood splashed in all directions, flecking against sheets, walls, floor, legs, everywhere. It puddled at Felix's feet.

'*¡Qué pérdida!*' said Dolores. 'What a waste!'

What could she mean? That blood was already wasted. It was hot. It was damaged. She knew that. Felix stared at Dolores, and goose pimples crept up her neck and across her scalp. She couldn't say anything here. Not in front of the patients. A terrible lapse of judgment, another one. Every cork-stoppered bottle from the blood bank came labelled with a warning to check its colour. If it was not red, it was spoiled, couldn't be used. It was a simple test. This flask had somehow become contaminated, ruined. Why was it so hot?

'My fault,' Felix stuttered after a silence that seemed to last for hours. 'I'll clear it up. Do we have more blood?'

Dolores shook her head. 'It was the last.' She looked desperate, and began to roll up her left sleeve.

'What are you doing?'

'I will give him my own blood.'

'No, no.' Felix had to whisper. 'You know you are the wrong type for Ramón. You tested him yourself, didn't you? What are you thinking of? Fetch the mop. I'll ask Doug what we should do now. Where's he gone anyway?'

'No! No! Please don't! He is asleep.'

177

But the patients were all awake, watching everything. Be normal. Be normal.

'Good morning! Good morning! How are we all today? Sorry about that, Ramón. Here, let me feel your pulse . . .'

Felix beamed at Ramón. 'Excellent!' And it was. He was so much better than yesterday. 'You're on the mend!'

'But Dolores said . . .'

'Really? Ah well. Things change so quickly, don't they? You're lucky! Really lucky!' She said the last words so lightly. She could not have meant them more.

Think. Think. Don't be hasty. Felix had rarely carried out the handover routine more chirpily. Inside, she could hardly contain her fear.

She had been inattentive. Too tired. Too little time. What else might she have missed? She tried to remember. After they left El Escorial . . . that man from Murcia, the major. Why had he taken such a turn for the worse? The chills, the restlessness, the sudden stupor. What had happened there?

Dolores came back with the bucket and mop. She shook her head when Felix tried to take them, and, with a blank face, she set to cleaning up the mess herself. From time to time, she murmured to herself . . . *qué pérdida*.

What a waste. All the work Felix had put into training the girl – her friend: gaining her confidence, building her up, working alongside each other for hour after hour. They had been like sisters to each other. Not the giggling, secret-sharing kind perhaps, but sharing something else, just as important. They had been through so much together. And now Dolores was cracking up.

Felix knew it happened – to soldiers as well as nurses. And she knew you couldn't always see the signs. But she had seen them, and failed to realise what they meant. She hadn't supervised her well enough. She had let her down. She'd have to tell someone now. Confess to Kitty. The prospect made her feel quite sick. If only George were here, she thought, surprising herself. He'd know how to handle this.

First she must talk properly to Dolores though. Find out exactly what she'd done. But the last time had made her so upset. Felix could not bear more tears and shame and self-recrimination. Still, it had to be done, and quickly. Where was she now?

A patient with a bandaged hand beckoned Felix over. He had shot himself on purpose – no disguising those powder burns on his palm – and he was for ever trying to make up for what he'd done.

He made her bend close to his face so he could whisper in her ear.

'She's gone out to empty the bucket. That's where she is.'

'Oh.' She tried to stand up, but he pulled her down again.

'Listen, I haven't finished. You need to watch that one, you know.'

Felix sighed. In recent months all kinds of tales had been flying round. Disgrace and fear made people say strange things. She didn't want to hear this.

'I saw her last night. She was shaking that blood flask. Hard, I mean. That's not right, is it? That's not what you do, is it? I notice things, you know. I've never seen anyone else do that.'

'Really?' said Felix, in a voice she hoped was neutral.

'And then I saw her open it—'

'Thanks for telling me.'

She headed for the door. There was movement upstairs. The others were getting up. The kitchen women would soon be here to make breakfast, and collect the washing. She must get Dolores out of the way while she worked things out. Kitty would be down in a few minutes. She could leave the patients safely till then.

That thought was knocked sideways when Felix stepped into the courtyard.

'A visitor. For you.' Dolores nodded a blank face over her shoulder. Felix was looking past her already.

It was the cold that took her breath away, surely? She steadied herself against the rough wall, not quite trusting her legs.

Nat seemed taller than ever, and older. Perhaps it was his clothes. A peaked cap replaced his beret and his boots were high black leather, laced up the front. There was a new strength and authority in his bearing too. Then he took his hands from his pockets and held them towards her, palms up, half-welcoming, half-questioning. Not entirely certain of his reception, but having a pretty good idea. His face echoed the gesture. His eyebrows were up to their old confusing tricks and she knew Nat was still Nat.

Without realising she'd moved, Felix was in his arms, tears she didn't know she'd shed freezing on her eyelashes. His neck smelled of wool and wood fires and paraffin and cigarettes. She could feel the strength of its pulse against her face.

'You're here!' she said into his skin. Her stiff coat felt like noisy armour. It was in the way. All their thick clothes were in the way. 'How did you manage it? I've been hoping and hoping . . .'

'So have I,' he said, drawing back, just a little, and looking at the light in her face. 'I managed to slip away for a few hours. Officer's perk. Not fair at all, but I can live with that. The company's still on standby, just about, but it won't be long now. Not long at all.'

'Then we'll be moving too,' said Felix, excited, relieved, terrified.

'We're waiting for water for the radiators. The drivers are

melting it now. I hoped I might find you here.' He looked at her again, laughed, and rolled his eyes. 'No, that's not true. I asked everywhere. I was desperate to see you.'

Felix was breathless with laughter too, the kind that is close to sobbing. 'I always think this. I can't believe you're real.'

'Try me.'

He pulled off his gloves and they stood holding both hands before them. They leaned back against each other's weight, testing the sensation, and Felix hungrily absorbed Nat's presence.

'I'm due some leave soon,' he said eventually. 'After this battle's over.'

'And?'

'I wanted to ask you. Could you get away too? I was wondering . . . any chance I could take you to Valencia? I've heard there's a hotel there and . . . oh God, I'm sorry, I don't know how to say this—'

'Oh stop. You'll have me running away here and now. I don't know. We'll have to see.' Time felt too short. She'd do anything he asked right now. Anything at all. Damn the consequences. 'I'll try. Of course I'll try. Yes. I'll come. Of course I'll come.' But it was hard to look him in the eye. 'Look at your hand!' She kissed it, greedily, all over. 'You can hardly see the scar! And how are your ears?' She stood on tiptoe, and knocked his hat askew as she whispered into one of them.

'Is that a medical question?'

'Sort of. No. Not exactly. I need to use them. Something's happened. I'm not sure what to do . . . But can you wait? Ten minutes? Fifteen?' Felix had never felt more reluctant to leave Nat. 'There's a conversation I need to have first. With Dolores. It really is terribly urgent. Then I'm all yours, I promise, for as long as we've got.'

She knew that wasn't quite true but surely she could wangle something, under the circumstances. Kitty would understand. Nat pulled her back towards him, put both arms around her again, and kissed the top of her head, smoothing down her hair. Warmth rushed through her. She wished they could stay like that for ever, stop everything. But she wrenched herself away. Wait till Valencia. There would be plenty of time in Valencia.

29

Nat watched the two girls walking away from the yard, towards the outskirts of the village. Dolores held herself stiffly, while Felix bent towards her. Once she tried to take the Spanish nurse's arm, but the other girl shrugged her off and shook her head. She seemed to be leading the way. Nat frowned. Some kind of argument. Talk about bad timing. He just hoped they wouldn't take too long to sort it out. He didn't have very long.

He paced the road outside and the snow creaked under his boots. They were all saying this was the worst winter Spain had seen in twenty years. He could believe it.

Ten minutes later the girls were out of sight. Why so far? Distracted, he guessed. They had both looked very agitated. Nat was sympathetic, up to a point. Cooped up like that with everyone, you had to stretch your legs after a while. He'd be driven mad by it too.

Another few minutes went by, and Nat began to curse quietly. His feet were freezing. Might as well walk up and meet them coming back. He'd get a little longer of Felix's company. Though he could do without Dolores, he thought irritably, and her blank staring eyes. He remembered the way they made him feel at the blood clinic in Madrid. Uncomfortable. Uncertain.

Five minutes brisk march and still he couldn't see them.

He quickened his step, and followed the girls' footprints up a track turning into the mountains, where peasants gathered the thorn trees for fuel, and grazed their animals in the summer. Why on earth had they bothered to come all this way?

The noise of his own feet in the snow masked every other sound, so Nat stopped to listen. His breath caught raspingly in his throat and burned his nostrils. Somewhere far below he heard the icy music of a stream. And then voices at last. Voices carry in snow.

He couldn't hear their words, but he caught the strength of emotion and it made him uneasy. Perhaps it was better to wait where he was for the moment, just out of sight. He didn't want to eavesdrop. This wasn't his business, not his argument.

A small stone building stood between him and the girls. It was roofless now: only three walls left, and these half-tumbled down. A shepherd's hut, he supposed. He could take shelter there, and keep out of sight until Felix was done. He walked towards it, assembling in his mind a version of the fantasy he'd been forming for months. This time the hut was newly built and whole, with a huge fire burning in its hearth, and a meal on the table, and a bed that actually had sheets, clean ones. He and Felix were alone, with all the time in the world and nobody else for miles around to look or listen or judge. And afterwards, when they were done, he planned to draw her properly. Paint her even. And every bit of her, this time. A warm, loving painting, it would be, in yellow ochre and raw sienna, with shadows of Prussian blue. He'd have her looking straight out at him, gently daring. That was her way. And he'd have to be quick, because he didn't want her to get cold, or be apart from her for too long.

Then Felix's voice changed. It had been pleading before. Now it was raised in disbelief, her words as clear as anything, her Spanish fluent and furious.

'On purpose? No . . . please no . . . I can't believe you could. You're no better than a murderer.'

Silence.

'You *are* a murderer.'

Asesina? Reaching the hut, Nat found himself staggering thigh-deep in drifted snow. Steady. Don't rush to conclusions. Surely he had misheard. He crouched beside the wall, by the remains of a window opening, and waited for Dolores's response.

Their backs were half-turned, their faces only partly visible. They stood perhaps twenty feet away. Her reply was cold and calm.

'In war, killing is not murder. It is war.'

30

'My God,' said Felix. 'My God, Dolores, whose side are you on?'

Dolores didn't answer.

'And what kind of a fool am I?' Felix whispered to herself, powerless to move, but still too shocked to feel real terror.

'An honest fool, of course.' Dolores's voice had the snap of icicles. Felix had never heard her sound so cold. 'Too honest to suspect me. For far longer than I could have hoped.'

Like a puppet, Felix kept shaking her head. Her eyes ached with staring. Dolores stared back at her. 'I saw the signs,' Felix said. 'I knew what you were doing. But I couldn't see it. And each time I just blamed myself.'

'That was exactly why I could risk it.'

'I thought . . . I thought it was the strain of it all . . . that you were cracking up. Making mistakes. I even tried to protect you.'

'Yes. I realised. Thank you.'

'But how could you? Blood . . . the best thing we have. The purest thing. And you – you turned it into poison. How *could* you?'

'If I tell you, you won't understand. You could never understand.' Dolores was looking at Felix with a mixture of pity and disgust. 'You think everything is so simple. Black, white. Right, wrong.'

'And?'

'It isn't. I wish it was.'

'Of course it is. At least some things are. Murder is wrong. You know that.'

'Is it really? Always?'

'Always.'

Why is she asking me this? Felix felt too stunned to make sense of any of this. She couldn't settle her thoughts; just when she needed to harness them, they refused to work for her. *I thought she was a Christian, for God's sake, a Catholic. How many times have I seen her pray, and said nothing, and let her alone?*

'Don't think this is something I ever wanted to do. But I had to. Just as you have to do what you have to do.'

'I don't understand.' Felix felt utterly helpless. She realised she was repeating the words, over and over again, standing there, shaking her head, looking at the girl she thought she knew so well. She had to concentrate. It was no good getting hysterical. Dolores's steady gaze was making her worse though.

'You are very conscientious, Felix,' she said. 'Many times I thought I would not get away with it.'

'*How* many times? Tell me. Exactly.' Felix tried to think and to remember. She needed details. She wanted to punish herself with the information. After all, she had let this happen.

Such a clever form of sabotage. So easy to arrange. So hard to detect.

A bad reaction to blood isn't always obvious. It can happen weeks after treatment, long after a patient has been sent to the rear. Dr Bethune had taught them that in Madrid. She remembered Dolores's amazement at the fact. Another patient came to mind, a country boy with a lovely smile and a bit of a squint. A rash had appeared at the site of the cannula. Felix had noticed in time to interrupt that transfusion, replacing it with a saline drip. She remembered wondering at the time how Dolores could have failed to notice. The luck of that man! But what about all the others she'd never know about?

'How many times?' Felix demanded again. Dolores's hand moved to her pocket, but Felix hardly noticed.

'I can't tell you,' said Dolores. 'I lost count. And I don't even know how successful I was each time. How could I tell? But it was always worth trying.'

Felix wondered if she had caught the sound of a distant plane. Right now, she would have welcomed the sound of *aviones*. She felt a terrible hunger for something utterly violent to happen, right now, something quite out of her control that would wipe out what she had to deal with. And herself with it.

The noise was just the wind. *Keep her talking*, thought Felix. *Don't stop talking.*

'Last night. This morning, I mean. You heated the blood to damage the cells, didn't you? That's why the flask felt hot.'

'Yes, today I did. I tried everything today. Because it was the last of the donor blood. And I knew we were moving on soon. Some places are harder than others. Here it's been easy.'

'So you lied about Doug. He didn't order that transfusion for Ramón.'

'Of course not,' Dolores agreed simply, taking a step towards Felix.

'But the other times . . . you haven't always heated it, have you? I'd have noticed. I'm sure I would have noticed.'

Felix moved back, slowly, taking her eyes off Dolores. Both hands were in her pockets now. She seemed to be feeling for something. Something that would explain? A letter, an order? Felix still couldn't imagine how Dolores had suddenly become her enemy.

'Sometimes I heat a flask and then return it to the fridge. When I've known I would be the first to use it. At El Escorial it was the labels. Two of the donors – one was a driver, one was a local woman – I simply recorded the wrong blood groups when they first came to us. You thought you were giving universal blood, but you weren't. But then Kitty noticed. Yes, you remember that. So I had to try something else.'

'What did you try?'

Another step forward. Another step back. For the first time Felix realised how far they had come. How alone she was.

'Just what you taught me. Or rather, everything you taught me not to do. I have added too much citrate to the blood, I have shaken it, I have exposed it to air and bacteria. Spat in it. I've even tried to freeze it. All the things Dr Bethune said could affect its safety. Yes, everything. And you kept reminding me. Thank you for that.'

Again, Felix wanted to hurt herself. This *was* her fault. All her fault.

'A bursting feeling,' Dolores continued. 'I remember that's what one man told me he felt. He didn't know what I had done, of course. I was sorry for him. I told him he was dying a hero. Don't think I wasn't kind to them. None of them had any idea. But I had to do what I could. I'd promised.'

'Promised . . . ? But how could you kill men who are fighting for justice?'

'Because I am fighting for justice too.' Dolores face lit up.

She wants *to confess*, thought Felix, confused. *She has been waiting for this moment. I will hear what she has to say. But I can't absolve her. I won't.*

'You asked me before whose side I am on. I'll tell you. My God. And my family. My own family. Not the politicians. Not

189

the bishops. Not an idea, or a theory, or a principle. Simply my own flesh and blood. Mine. And I always have been.'

'Your family? Who are they?'

'Nobodies . . . what did you think? No, we were just an ordinary family. My mother, me, my brother.'

Like my family. Just as I have always felt.

'Quite ordinary. At least, we were, until 1936.'

'And then?'

She raised her eyebrows. 'Felix, you know. The war changed everyone.'

Silence.

'Maybe, for these times, we are still ordinary,' Dolores said bitterly.

Look away, look away. Don't let her see your uncertainty. Felix stared up at a pale, colourless sky; the kind of sky that warns of more snow to come. She hoped by staring that her tears would not spill out, but it was no good so she scrunched her eyes to keep them in.

'Tell me what you mean. Tell me what happened,' said Felix. 'I've wanted to ask you for so long. I always thought . . . I always imagined . . . well, there's no point in telling you now.'

Dolores took a deep breath. She was underdressed and beginning to shake with cold, but her voice was surprisingly steady. It sounded like a story she had told herself many times.

'It was late July. A Sunday. My mother had gone to early Mass. I was at home studying. Everything was very quiet.

'Our village was not yet affected by the uprising against the government, the coup. We knew something about it of course. But not what might happen. And then a boy came to the door. His mother was a friend of my own mother's. He came to tell us. To warn us.'

'What about?'

'There had been a meeting, the night before. A vote. They had voted to burn the church.'

Everything was so complicated here, Felix despaired. This wasn't the first time she had heard of such a thing. Not had it surprised her. All through Spain she'd seen huge ornate churches towering over hovels. Unbelievable wealth and unimaginable poverty, side by side. She knew what a backlash of violence and hatred the power of the clergy had caused at the beginning of the war. The Red Terror. That's what they used to call it in the newspapers in England. Nuns murdered. Priests shot. Nothing organised about it. What was it Doug had muttered? Revenge is a kind of wild justice. Something like that. He liked to quote things.

'This was the first you knew of it?' The longer she could keep Dolores talking, the more time she would have to work out what to do.

'Of course. We didn't go to the meetings, my mother and I. Father Antonio always told us not to.'

'So what did you do?'

It was like picking a scab. You know it will bleed.

'I went to the church. As fast as I could, I ran to try to stop them, to reason with them, stop the burning. Father Antonio meant everything to my mother. And he was a good man. He looked after us after my father died. When my mother was in despair.'

Felix couldn't believe she had got everything so wrong.

'The bells kept on ringing. Ringing and ringing, ringing and ringing, more and more urgently as I ran faster and faster.'

Dolores was talking so fast; it was a struggle to keep up. Despite her rising terror, Felix found herself moving closer, concentrating with all her might on Dolores's rapidly moving lips, which were pale with cold.

'Oh, please slow down,' cried Felix.

'But I was already too late.'

Dolores stopped talking and stared into space, remembering. From far below, down in the valley, the sounds of straining engines reached them. Faint shouts and curses followed. A truck was stuck on the road they had been walking on. The convoy was starting to leave. Felix gasped. She'd been so caught up in Dolores's story that she had almost forgotten Nat was waiting for her. He would go. She would miss him. It was unbearable. And still she had no idea what to do.

Dolores didn't seem to notice Felix's reaction. She hardly seemed aware of where she was.

'Father Antonio refused to leave the church. My mother refused to leave him. He was trapped. They had poured petrol on the pews and he was cut off, in front of the altar. But he showed no fear. Even when the flames were at his feet, he didn't move. He shut his eyes, and he prayed. Until he couldn't speak.'

'And your mother?'

'It had been my mother ringing the bell, trying to get help. But just as I pushed open the church door, she ran into the fire, straight towards him. She thought she could rescue him. I hesitated – I was so frightened – I hesitated too long. The flames were everywhere. I doused my shawl in holy water and managed to pull her out. God was on my side. Someone helped me get her out into the plaza. Water was brought, a blanket. We wrapped her up. She spoke to me. And she made me promise. That I would avenge his death, and defend the Church. That was all. She did not live much longer. They were her last words.'

Her face hardened again.

'So what are you going to do now, Felix? Arrest me?'

She took a defiant step forward. She managed a slight swagger.

192

Felix briefly wondered if she might raise her hands in mock surrender. But no. Both hands stayed firmly in her pockets. What was it she had in there? A picture? Her mother? One hand seemed to be turning something over. What was she going to show her? Dolores's clenched jaw jutted out at an unfamiliar angle.

You might think that war would prepare you for sudden noises. But if anything, it sets you even more on edge. Dolores probably didn't hear it herself. A faint click and then an ear-splitting gunshot which shook the snow from the thorn bushes. It was Felix who screamed. Dolores simply twisted and crumpled.

Felix stared at the body in the snow. Her scream faded into a high-pitched whimper, like that of a dog, begging to be brought in from the cold.

31

The surge of euphoria at the perfection of his shot crashed instantly into self-disgust. On his knees, half-buried, Nat vomited into the snow, then staggered upright. Through the windowless gap in the wall, he glimpsed Felix, staring at the stone hut.

On the battlefield, faceless figures appear from nowhere. They are anonymous. You may not even see their eyes before you shoot. Further away, a movement in a landscape gives away a position. A glint of metal or a flash of glass. You fire and never see what happens. You convince yourself your enemy isn't human. Nat thought he had come to terms with killing.

But this was worse than anything he'd known before. His head told him he had performed his duty. That was his job, wasn't it? He had despatched a threat. But that was not how it felt. He had done something terrible and he knew it. He had acted on instinct, and instincts couldn't always be trusted. And this was not a battlefield.

His fingers felt clumsy and useless but he made them slide the safety catch back on. There was blood on his hand, where the trigger had nicked the delicate skin between his thumb and forefinger. Some five feet away the bullet case had made a neat hole in the snow.

He stumbled out into the open, the taste of bile on his tongue. Felix looked frailer than ever in her bulky coat. She was swaying slightly, or perhaps it was him. The thought that he had so nearly lost her had sent him off balance. Everything was out of kilter. He just needed to get over to her now, and take her in his arms again, and look after her properly. He'd work out what to do next after that. Thank God he had followed her. Thank God he had been there in time.

The short walk seemed to take hours. As he got closer, Nat registered a change of expression in Felix's face. Its unseeing gaze had shifted into hatred. Who could blame her after such a betrayal?

He tried to gather her stiff body into his own, to wipe out everything with an embrace, but she shook him off with a shudder.

'Don't.' Her hands were raised as if she was defending herself against him.

'Please, Felix. Your face . . .' He reached forward with one hand.

'What? What is it?'

She backed away, wiping her hand across her cheek. She felt something, inspected her palm. A tiny fleck of blood, smeared on her bare skin. She rubbed furiously, distorting her face. When Nat tried to help her, she turned away.

'Don't, I said.'

'It's all right. It's gone now,' he reassured her.

'No. It's not all right. It's not all right.'

Nat waited, arms open, willing her to look at him again. She wouldn't. When he tried to smile, his cold numb lips didn't work. They caught against his teeth, turning his smile into a grimace.

'Felix, I'm sorry. I had no choice.'

She looked down again at Dolores's twisted body, and he made himself look too. It was completely still. You didn't need a medic to tell you that life had left it. Vermilion seeped slowly into the snow around her head.

'No choice?' Felix said. Voice cold. Eyes wide. She looked straight at him. That was when he finally realised that her hatred was for him, not Dolores.

'She's a killer,' he said. 'She told you herself. You heard her.'

'Like you.'

'Yes, like me. But I didn't know what she was going to do next. I couldn't take the risk.'

'You didn't give her a chance.'

They had been whispering. As if they could be overheard. Nat raised his voice and shocked himself with its loudness.

'A chance to kill someone else?' *To kill you*, he was thinking. 'She's the enemy.'

'A chance for a trial.'

'A trial? You don't understand. That's what I've saved her from.' He spoke slowly, and patiently, convincing himself with his words.

'What on earth do you mean? Saved her from a fair trial?'

Nat stepped towards Felix, and again she stepped back, shaking her head. Again she rubbed at her face.

'Nothing. Except she'd never get a fair trial,' he said. 'You don't know what it's like now. There's no such thing, these days. How can there be, in times like these? And what would be the point, anyway? You know she's guilty. She told you herself.'

'So who made you judge and jury?'

'Felix, listen to me. Listen. It was the kindest thing I could have done for her.' *She doesn't realise what's happening in Spain*, he thought.

'*Kind?*' A fleck of spit caught her lower lip.

Again Nat tried to approach her, to wipe her clean, and again

Felix backed away, the back of her hand against her mouth. She began to retch herself.

'Please. Just listen to me,' he urged. 'Hear what I'm saying. You don't know what these "trials" are like. They're not about justice. Nothing like. Believe me. You can't imagine what Dolores would have gone through if we'd turned her in. A court martial? Under these circumstances? They'd have executed her for this. This way at least it's all over at once. It's done. She hasn't suffered.'

'You don't know that. You can't be so certain.'

Nat couldn't answer that. Perhaps Felix was right. And he knew that it had been the last thing on his mind when he pulled the trigger. He closed his eyes briefly. He simply didn't understand. How could this be happening, the two of them standing there, arguing with each other? You would think *he* was the enemy. All he had wanted was to protect Felix, and keep her safe.

'She could have gone to prison. There are prisoners of war, aren't there?' said Felix. 'That's how it works, doesn't it?'

'Sometimes. It's how it should work. But even when it does, that's just another kind of hell. Anyway, what about the evidence?'

'What do you mean?'

Her face was like a mask. She really didn't realise. It wasn't surprising, perhaps. He was only beginning to realise himself.

'I mean you'd have been called as witness, and then what? It would have been your word against hers? Don't you see? You're not a Party member. You could be an unreliable yourself. What then?'

'You think I'm unreliable?' Her voice rose harshly, in a way he'd never imagined it could. 'I don't believe this.'

'No, no. Stop it. That's not what I'm saying. Of course *I*

don't.' Oh why couldn't he make her understand? 'Of course not. But that's how things are going now. Without a political record of any kind . . . There's nothing on paper to prove your allegiance. You're not in the Party. These are dangerous times. Everyone's under suspicion. You must have noticed.'

She's not taking this in, Nat thought despairingly. *She doesn't realise what it's like now, what else I've saved her from. She thinks I'm patronising her.* 'People are disappearing, Felix. People you thought you could trust. And it's not clear where they're going. Or why.' *And all that aside, there's something else neither of us could have known until it was too late.* If Felix hadn't realised, how could Nat be the one to tell her?

Felix turned away from him and dropped to her knees. She bent over Dolores. The bullet had gone through her neck. The exit wound – what he could see of it – was a mess. Dolores's face half-nestled in the colouring snow. Her eyebrows were still raised, expectantly; one taunting dead eye was visible, waiting for Felix's answer.

Down in the valley a horn sounded, and Felix's head whipped round. A thin cheer went up, quickly swallowed by the rising grumble of a truck engine. Nat took a deep breath, but dared not try to touch her again.

'Felix, you've got to go. Now. Everyone's leaving. They'll be looking for you now. And they mustn't come up here. Let me deal with this.'

She stood up very slowly. Fury made her tremble, not fear. She hated him now, he was sure. She really hated him.

Forgive me before you leave me. Please, please forgive me. But get away. You must go. Quickly, get away. He couldn't say it out loud.

One last chance.

'Felix?'

Refusing to meet his eyes, she shook her head again. She walked quickly away from him and didn't once look back.

Nat wanted to bellow and howl and beat the ground and tear his clothes to shreds. He wanted the earth to stop turning and the heavens to crack open. He wanted to shout at Felix, call her back, physically force her to meet his eyes and then beg her to see things for what they were and not let her go until she did. But there was no time, and he didn't trust himself any more, and he couldn't take the risk. So he watched her go in silence.

Then he bent down, hooked his arms under Dolores's, and dragged her backwards towards the sound of the stream he had heard earlier. Smearing their tracks, Dolores's blood painted the snow. At the edge of the ravine, Nat inched sideways, holding his breath. It was a very long way down. They would be far away before she could be found, he was certain.

He knelt at Dolores's shoulder, twisted, and slid his hand over hers, into her coat pocket. He felt around her unresponsive fingers. They were empty. Angrily, he jerked her hand out of the pocket, felt again inside, and panicked when again he felt nothing. You fool. She's probably left-handed. You can't remember how she was standing. He grabbed roughly at her other arm, and pulled the hand out of her pocket on the other side. As he did so, Dolores's fingers released the silvery surgical blade they were clutching and it bounced on the rock with a harsh ringing sound. Then it hit another rock below, and another, and another, tinkling its way down to the bottom of the ravine, getting quieter and quieter, until there was complete silence.

Nat let out his breath, and got to his feet. He manoeuvred the body round, so that it lay crosswise to him on the rocky ledge. Sitting down for stability and strength, legs in front, hands

199

braced behind, he pushed with his feet, gently at first and then harder, until he felt the body lose resistance. Dolores slithered out of sight, and Nat's hopes went with her.

32

They couldn't wait any longer. Kitty's rage was rocking the ambulance. She had found Dolores's kitbag and packed it with the rest of the luggage.

'Where the hell is that girl? She knew we were on standby.'

'Calm down,' soothed Doug. 'Dolores can't be far away. By the way, do we have enough catgut?'

'Yes,' Kitty snapped.

'I can't see her anywhere,' said Felix miserably, returning to the ambulance. 'I can't think where else to look.' The knowledge she was hiding felt like granite inside her. It seemed to slow every movement she made.

From the cab, Charlie called out something.

'What was that?' said Kitty.

'I said, there'll be plenty of other vehicles coming after us. She'll just have to get a ride with one of those.'

'She's probably found somewhere quiet to sleep and conked out. I can't think where though. God knows, I've looked hard enough,' said Kitty. 'What lousy timing.'

'I reckon she needed a rest,' said Doug. 'She's been looking awful peaky, don't you think?'

He looked thoughtful. What else had he noticed? Felix avoided his eye.

Kitty grunted.

'Never mind,' said Doug. 'She'll catch up with us by sundown, I dare say. At least we can cram in the other autoclave now, the small one. Better there than here, I reckon. Run and get it, would you, Felix?'

Inside the sterilising room, Felix hesitated, taking longer than necessary to empty out the autoclave, pouring the tepid water into a basin. She washed her hands a second time, checked her face against the steriliser's shiny side, and double-checked her hands, and her clothes, and her boots, and then her face again.

Time to go. She could hardly move. Come on. Come on.

She heaved the autoclave up into the back of the ambulance, terrified of what she might hear next. *Didn't I see you going up the road with Dolores earlier, Felix? You must know where she's got to.* Had Ramón said something?

'Ride up front with me if you like,' said Charlie. 'You can watch the sky.'

A truck full of Brigaders passed as Felix climbed up, and she turned to look. She couldn't stop herself. They were singing of course. It was hard at the front, but so much harder to be away. Seeing a serious face under a peaked cap, Felix nearly called out. *Stop.* But it wasn't Nat. Of course it couldn't be.

The ambulance pulled off the verge, and joined the convoy. As the weather grew worse, vehicle after vehicle ground to a halt on the steepening road. From time to time, their own skidding tyres gave up too, and they all got out and pushed, sliding precious blankets under the wheels to help them grip. Occasionally they sang, as if the words might keep them warm. Cigarettes took the edge off hunger, and for the first time ever Felix was tempted.

The last six miles took the longest. Snow was drifting in the pass, and the windscreen kept icing over on the inside. Their route was lined with work-gangs, trying to keep open the artery that was this road. Among them walked the lightly wounded, heading away from Teruel, towards safety, hoping for a lift on a returning camion. In their handmade ponchos – just holes cut in blankets – they made Felix think of shipwrecked mariners or discoloured ghosts.

Eventually she heard Doug saying: 'This is it. Cuevas Labradas.'

Two other nurses came out to greet them.

'Good to see you. What have you got for us?' An Australian moved swiftly in to inspect the contents of the ambulance. 'Any blood?'

The other introduced herself as Unity. Perhaps it was her real name.

'The village women will be here to help shortly. They only come out of the caves when it gets dark. You can't blame them. They've had a rotten time.'

They'd never expected to find themselves so close to the front line, the nurses told them, but the front had come to them. The village had just been bombed and their little hospital was half-full already.

'So what do you do when the planes come? Where do you go?' asked Kitty. 'Any ditches?'

'Oh, we can't leave the patients. Anyway, there's nowhere *to* go. I try to find bowls, basins . . . that kind of thing.' Unity giggled and gestured towards a pile of enamel dishes on the floor in a corner. 'If you put them over the patients' faces, it does seem to help, somehow.'

They unpacked on autopilot. No time to think. Now the lights for the operating theatre could run off the ambulance's batteries, and they also had a few torches between them. Condensed milk tins were fashioned into lamps, their edges beaten into spouts to hold a wick, and filled with oil.

They knew the fighting was bad because the operating table was occupied all night. To keep the temperature from freezing, Kitty poured alcohol into basins, setting them at the patients' head and feet. *Whup!* They went up with a hollow-sounding flare, at the touch of a spark. Like an eternal flame. But these flames lasted no time at all.

Limbs were collected, to be buried later with corpses when there was time. Blankets were borrowed from the dead. It was heartbreaking to hear the cries of the wounded when they emerged from the ether and found they could still hear the noise of artillery. '*Evacuarme,*' they begged. Evacuate me.

Nobody had time to wonder about Dolores. Then it was morning and still nobody mentioned her name. Felix realised then that either people were there, or they weren't there. For whatever reason. But you didn't talk about it.

By daylight, she looked about her and thought Cuevas Labradas was the most miserable place she'd ever been. Just what she deserved. The mountains rose black and bare, formed from twisting folds of rock. The houses were carved from the rock face, barely even hovels. Doorways spewed rubble. Such poverty. Felix saw women and children barelegged, their limbs blue, as they headed back from the caves. No coats of course. Just black frocks and shawls. And fear.

No more stretchers now till darkness returned. Unity yawned, offered coffee (more condensed milk tins for cups) and tidied away some papers.

'We managed some reading classes a few weeks ago, believe it or not. *Luchamos en el campo. ¡Leed!*'

Felix forced a smile. She knew the slogan. She'd seen the posters. We are fighting illiteracy among the peasants. Read!

'*Para ser cultos, para ser fuertes, para ser humanos,*' she replied. Read! To be educated, to be strong, to be human.

33

George was sent to Teruel to check out a clinic. The chief medical officer had heard the Fascists left a lot behind when they fled. No point in it going to waste.

This had to be done at night. They crossed the viaduct safely and George wondered as usual why there were always dead horses on the streets. The moonlight caught their flanks, and his nostrils caught their stink. He had almost completely given up breathing through his nose.

The smell of carbolic acid at the clinic was still strong enough to penetrate his throat and tongue. George nodded at the machinery piled in the street outside, and asked the captain what he wanted.

'Let's have a look first. No point in taking rubbish.'

They shone their torches over it and felt with their hands, like racehorse trainers checking for spavins. There were several sterilisers, an operating table, and a complicated looking piece of apparatus George didn't recognise. Bullet holes had pierced the steel of the table repeatedly, but it could certainly still be used. One of the autoclaves was a goner.

'So they tried to take all this?' said George, heaving the table into the back of the car.

'This place was occupied by the Fascists pretty much to the bitter end, I'm told. Guess they were still hoping for transport.'

'This doesn't count as looting?' George turned for his next load.

'Certainly not. Spoils of war. Perfectly legit.'

'Inside?'

The captain nodded and led the way. There was a lifetime's work here. A scientist's library, a decent lab with microscopes, and burners, and rows of cages: canaries and white mice. And the front window had a perfect view across the viaduct. The back looked over the barracks of the Civil Guard, across the street – one of the last positions to fall. The windowsills were pocked with bullet holes, and empty cartridges were scattered on the floor, all shapes and sizes of them.

'I hear there are still some snipers around,' said George.

'It's possible. Entirely possible. I'd keep away from that window if I were you.'

'What are these?' George picked up a spent shell. Word was spreading of all sorts of strange new weapons they were using now, honed in the labs of Berlin. In the early days, George had heard stories of Fascist grenades arriving stuffed with messages of support from saboteurs, instead of gunpowder. Now the talk was all of infrared cameras on German planes, cameras that could see through camouflage, of double-calibre machine guns and new kinds of poison gas. Thermite bombs he'd already seen, at Guernica.

No answer from the captain, who was searching the next room.

The drivers were always on top of the latest rumours. An English doctor had used blood for the living taken from dead cavalry officers, still warm. They'd been smothered in a shelter. Horrible. Or was it? George wasn't sure. Another piece of gossip was doing the rounds just then. A nurse had been found. A nurse? A young Spanish woman, they thought, shot in the neck. Thrown down a ravine.

'Christ almighty, come and look at this. I don't believe it.'

George obeyed. Their feet smashed on glass. Someone had systematically destroyed a vast stock of serums.

'Anti-tetanus?'

'And anti-gangrene, by the looks of it. Too bad. It really is too bad. Keep your eyes peeled for morphine though. There may be some upstairs.'

They kept going up, and soon encountered a tangled mass of bandages. 'This is better. And look – there's plenty more over here – we'll have those.'

'Embroidered sheets too! Very fancy.'

'Very useful. We've got room?'

'Plenty. Anatomy books?'

'Certainly. I'll pick some out.'

But what to do with the canaries, still singing to be fed? On his fifth trip upstairs, George remembered a hunk of stale bread in his pocket. Carrying something around for hard times had become a habit. While the captain's back was turned, he crumbled it in his hand and dropped the mess in little pinches through the bars of the birds' cages. The mice too. On the sixth and final trip up he simply opened up their doors.

'Off you go. It's every mouse for himself.'

34

The rumour reached Felix. Kitty heard it from Unity, who'd been talking to Charlie.

'Could it have been Dolores? Have you heard where the body was found?' Kitty asked Felix.

'No, I haven't. Just that there was a body.'

'Charlie said it was at the bottom of a barranco. Near Mas de las Matas. Isn't that where you were working before? I'm sure that's what he told me,' said Unity.

'You're certain it was there?' Felix looked up sharply. Her skin felt clammy, guilt oozing from its pores. She kept remembering what George had said to her, months ago, at El Escorial. How do you know what to believe?

'How?' wondered Kitty. 'Why?'

'And did you hear there were two Brigaders caught trying to desert, not far from here? Maybe . . . Oh, do move over, Felix, you're hogging the stove.'

'Sorry.'

'British?'

'Yes. They were shot. Court-martialled first. Then shot. Executed that is. They had to be, didn't they? They had a map, you see. They were going to give it to the Fascists. That's what Charlie told me. They were traitors.'

Executed, thought Felix. *Executed*.

Kitty swirled her coffee thoughtfully. 'What if it was Dolores? What if she was trying to stop them?'

'I don't know,' said Felix. I *don't* know, she told herself.

'Or help them, come to that? Who knows? She was a dark horse,' said Kitty, shaking her head.

'Who?' asked Unity.

'A *chica* we worked with. She just disappeared one day. Just before we came here. You don't suppose she was a deserter too? Tell Unity about her, Felix, you knew her best.'

'I don't know what to say. I trusted Dolores.' *And I trusted him.*

'We all did. We all did. And maybe we weren't wrong.' Kitty's eyes squeezed tight shut, and her face briefly contorted into a grimace. She took her spectacles off and wiped them on her apron and Felix turned away. She didn't trust herself.

'I'm going to check dressings.'

Felix could feel Unity's stare boring into her back as she retreated. She thought she heard a sigh from Kitty.

So, Nat hadn't even buried her. But then, how could he, in that frozen earth? With all his men waiting, and another job to do? Had he checked her pockets? What had she been holding in there? Why had she gone on walking, walking, out of town? Leading her up, up, up the hillside. What if . . . ?

She couldn't let herself pursue these thoughts. And soon exhaustion made her like an ant, without thoughts. Scurrying, hurrying, fixed on the job in hand, whatever it was that needed to be done next. Above the anthill was the shadow of the enemy's great boot, coming closer and closer. The skies were rarely silent.

The Republicans could take Teruel, but they couldn't hold it. Courage and cunning were no match for the machinery of war.

The town fell back to Franco the day Felix went down with typhoid.

In her delirium, she couldn't tell what was real and what was not. Even afterwards, little was clear. The retreat was chaotic and her convalescence was slow. Felix spent much of it worrying what she might have said in her fever, and trying to remember what had really happened.

35

Her memories went something like this:

The feeling she would never be cold again. Which brought a kind of joy at first. Until Kitty brushed against her, and was horrified, and took her temperature and sent her to bed. Except there was no bed, because they were on the move again already. She was lying in an ambulance, and that was all wrong, wasn't it? And the sides felt so thin, and it was dark, so dark, and she didn't know where she was, but there seemed to be someone above her, and blood was dripping down onto her face, drop after drop. And everything was so loud, and shaking. Where was Dolores?

A train, and a tunnel. Trying to make herself invisible, trying not to cough. More dripping. Dissolving snow, and water running down smoke-blackened brickwork. A hundred pairs of labouring lungs, trying to breathe silently. It's too dark to see. The important thing is not to draw attention to oneself. She must get back to her hospital, back to her patients. But she doesn't know where they are. Still, she has her *salvoconducto*, safe in her hand. She has not lost her pass. Everything else has gone, but not her pass.

Nat has a gun. He is going to shoot me.

There is a truck, and planes, and a dead baby, silent in a shawl. Stories she has heard from others confuse her. Bombs disguised as chocolate boxes. A petrol station, exploding next to a café. Bodies in the air. A cliff and a limestone gorge. Blindfolds and rifles. Bodies falling through space. Was she there, or not?

The taste of betrayal.

Es la guerra. Mañana mas. That's war for you. More tomorrow.

There was always more. A train rattles through the night and through the day. It comes to a halt on the outskirts of a small town and Felix gathers the strength to raise herself onto one elbow. Through the gap between papers plastered over glass, she sees a fair-haired young man sitting in the shade of a truck, surrounded by children. It's George and he's showing them his binoculars, and how to use them. In their efforts to see, they cover one eye and then the other, and laugh as the images shrink and grow, blur and sharpen. With his help, the boys and girls keep turning the heavy field glasses round, peering at each other through different ends, waving delightedly. What is George doing? Oh . . . Felix realises. He's distracting the children from the work in the cemetery behind, where they are digging more graves. She knocks on the window. She must tell him where she is. He needs to know she is alive. She needs him to know. He is so kind. But he can't hear her – he is concentrating on the children – and the train is moving again.

Eventually, a proper hospital. Hot springs. Cold sponging. Lucidity and pain. No food. Peach blossom and bare earth. And finally another convoy. The last surprise is a whitewashed room. Through the shutters just above her head, a glint of light. Felix pulls herself up towards it, hanging onto the sill, heart slowly beating. And when she opens the shutters she is nearly blinded. The sea, the sparkling sea: from the mountains, they have come right across to the sea again. It is beautiful.

MAY 1938

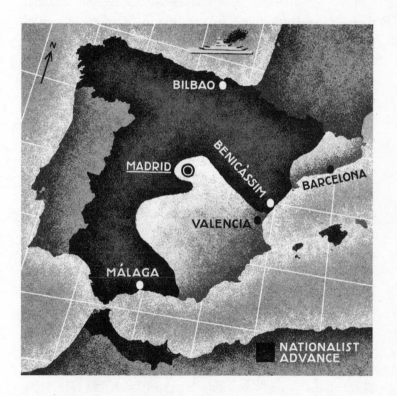

36

Beautiful, but not good. They are at the coast because their land is now divided. Franco has forced through Republican Spain. Hitler has marched into Austria. Nobody stopped them.

George tells Felix this, while he sits on the grey blanket on her bed at the convalescent hospital.

'Still here?' she says. He nods. She lies curled around the weight of him and stares at his khaki-covered knee.

'I saw you, you know. On my way here. I'm sure it was you. You were by a cemetery.'

'Maybe,' he agrees. His voice is choked. 'I've been all over.'

Then Felix reaches out a hand, and he takes it and squeezes it, and straightens it, and matches her fingertips with his own. It's as if he knows that all feeling has left every other part of her body. Just her fingertips are left. This is the first time in weeks that she's woken up glad to find herself still alive. She refuses to think about the other hand: the hand that draws pictures, and pulls triggers, and decides things.

'We've made it. So far,' George says.

Felix needs her hand back to shuffle up the bed so she can see him properly.

'Did you know I was here?' she asks, properly awake now, staring at him while she hugs her raised knees.

'Not exactly. I had a few days leave in Valencia, and some

215

other nurses begged me to bring them here. The cupid truck, they call it. I still always ask for you, wherever I go. Just in case. And for once I've struck gold. Looks like you have too. Not a bad spot, is it?'

Felix laughs. It's an alien sound and it takes her by surprise. Her body is beginning to feel lighter.

'It doesn't quite feel real, sometimes. It's lovely here. Everyone says so. Though I've barely left this villa.'

'I think you should make the most of it.'

'I suppose so.'

'There's no need to feel guilty.'

The silence that follows isn't awkward.

'Heard from home lately?' George asks, running his hand through his hair, just as he always used to.

'Mother sent me some chocolate a few days ago. I'm afraid it's gone now. Apparently Neville's had another promotion. Oh, and next door's cat's died.'

'Tragic,' says George, dryly.

'Not if you're a goldfish.'

'I suppose not.'

'Doesn't Neville write to you?'

'He did at first. Then he stopped.' George frowns.

Felix studies the corner of the blanket, where the stitching is becoming unravelled.

'Because of me?'

'He didn't say.'

'Just stopped?'

'Yes. I did wonder if everything was all right.'

'It seems to be.'

Neville's still angry then, thinks Felix. Of course he is. 'Mother says he's awfully busy at work. Quite high up now, you see.'

'Yes, of course.'

216

But George *doesn't blame me. Not for anything.*

'Thanks for coming,' she says quietly. For months now, it has been like living under water. A slow drowning. She is beginning to breathe air again.

'My pleasure.' George nods, smiling, a little stiffly, and Felix remembers how amusing she used to find his awkward formality.

37

They talk for about three hours. George gives Felix the barest details of the retreats: ambulances abandoned, nine drivers dead, four doctors. Three nurses and eight stretcher-bearers lost. He tells her names. He doesn't tell her about the time he edged along a road in the dark with no idea who held the hillside above. Nor how it felt to pull the pin on a Mills bomb and pitch it towards looming black shapes coming at you from shadows.

It is over now. The Battalion is getting its strength back. France has opened the border, and new Russian equipment is pouring in. Barcelona will never surrender.

George is worried that so much conversation will exhaust Felix, but she seems to gain energy by the minute. As the afternoon wears on, the light outside seems to liquify.

'You look like an angel, now,' George says, daringly. 'With rather a bad haircut.'

'Thanks,' says Felix. 'You're looking pretty luminous yourself.'

'I say, you don't feel up to a walk, do you? I haven't been on a beach since we went to Whitstable. Do you remember?'

'May Day bank holiday. 1936. Of course I remember.'

'I'd love to hear the sea again.'

'Me too.' It's odd, the way she says that. As though she'd never thought of it before. And there it is, the sea, right outside her window. She smiles suddenly. 'And, do you know, Neville was right about the oysters. I haven't had one since. But it was fun, wasn't it?' Felix slides her legs from under the covers. She pauses. 'I never thought I'd feel homesick. But just now I do. Do you ever want to pack your bags?'

George hesitates.

'Not much to pack . . . But yes, of course I'm tempted. I've come close, too.' Every time he moves a wounded man onto a stretcher and hears the grinding of shattered bones, George is tempted. 'But even if we wanted to, we couldn't go home now. You can't just change your mind about something like this. Not when you've promised.'

'I suppose not.'

'Remember what you said on the boat to France?'

Felix shakes her head, lowers her eyes.

'You said Fascism anywhere is a threat to people everywhere. I didn't believe you then,' said George. 'But now I do.'

Felix looks up. George resists the urge to drop to his knees and tell her that despite all he's just said, and the fact that he means every word of it, actually he would do anything for her: he would become a deserter today, abandon everything, do anything at all to make her happy. The urge becomes easier to resist when he realises that he already has made her happier, simply by coming. The dull deadness that frightened him so much when she first awoke is leaving her eyes.

'I reckon I can manage a slow stroll,' she says at last. 'Pass me those.'

George finds her *alpargatas*, and bends at her feet, tying up the strings. Businesslike, he thinks. That's the way. He steadies himself on the bedstead as he stands up. 'Have you got a dressing gown?'

'Don't fuss. It's so warm here.'

They join a small procession of ambling figures also dressed in striped pyjamas and heading for the sea. Some use crutches, many have casts and bandages. Lovely clean white bandages. They talk quietly, in lots of languages, calling out the occasional *salud!* George and Felix wander with them down to a path along the beach. It is lined with palm trees, and their fronds rustle in a way that makes George think suddenly of an ether machine.

'You can't beat Spain for sunsets,' says George, when the redness begins to spill out onto the waves on the horizon.

'Oh, let's take off our shoes and walk on the sand!'

'Come on then.' Instead of asking if it's sensible, in her state, George offers to carry her *alpargatas*. Bending his head over a knot in his own bootlace, he tries to work out how to extract the information he needs. He pulls Felix up to standing, and keeps hold of her arm as they sink into the sand, both breathless with the loveliness of it all.

Then he blunders into her laughter.

'I expect you've lost friends over here,' he says, and watches her face. Like cement, it sets.

'Yes. I have.'

George swallows the words: 'Anyone special?' Too crass. And the answer too obvious. She couldn't look like that for just anyone. He almost regrets asking.

'Sorry. We don't need to talk about it. But I'm sorry.'

He really is sorry. But he also has to hide a disturbing leap of relief.

Time to change the subject.

'Tell me, what's the food like here?'

She brightens. 'Heavenly. Real sugar. And fresh eggs.'

So George starts telling her about all the ways he knows of cooking eggs in Spain – in autoclaves and upside-down helmets and primus stoves of course. And how he once used an egg to mend a leaking radiator in a field ambulance.

They walk past men and women in groups and past solitary figures staring out at the Mediterranean sea. The sky becomes redder before it grows darker, and together they find the first star. Her shoes are strung around his neck, and Felix nestles into him as they walk, and all the time, with the hand he keeps in his right pocket, George turns over the ring he's been carrying since Paris. His insurance. He kept it because it was small and light and he knew that if he ever needed money to get away it could be useful. Also because he'd bought it, and he couldn't give up on what he'd bought it for. One day, he thinks, one day maybe she'll tease him for that.

While there is still light enough to see the simple jewel, he takes out the ring and shows it to Felix.

'Look. I brought something for you.'

He doesn't exactly expect her to throw her arms around him.

At first she doesn't say a word, or even look up. She just takes a deep breath. Her mouth quivers a little. She is deciding. Dear God, she is deciding. George keeps still. He actually steps away a pace. He wants to give her space to think. He loves her more than ever, but he is frightened of tipping her the wrong way with the strength of his love.

Finally she speaks, not quite meeting his eye.

'Well, look at us now. Sea, sunset, palm trees. Nothing could be more perfect. There can only be one answer, can't there?'

'You'll marry me?' He has to be clear. 'You really will?'

'When all this is really over. Yes. I'll marry you, George. Thank you for asking.'

JULY 1938

38

Even after night has fallen, heat rises from the dry earth with a force you can wade through. The river is cooler, almost cold. Nat feels its darkness swirl and eddy against his fingertips as he grips the side of the small boat, so low in the water that it sets his nerves jangling. He's never learned to swim. The Ebro is deep and broad, and its currents are strong.

Never have they felt so resolute. Buoyed with new recruits, mostly Spaniards, the company is fit and lean from marching. Rehearsals have been intense, and secretive. The new offensive will catch Franco by surprise, break through at last, distract him from Valencia, and the south.

Yes, they are ready.

They cross the river in near silence, six or seven to a boat. They aim upstream, against the flow, their course at an angle. Nat sits facing two local men, watching the steady movements of their dark hands on the oars. They barely make a splash. With the slightest shift of weight, the overladen boat lurches, Nat's stomach with it. Water tips over the gunwales and sloshes around their boots, but nobody speaks.

Nearly halfway across, the rebels' shells begin to fall – not close, for they are firing blind – but near enough to send small tidal waves to rock and pitch the boat. The rowers never falter. Nat huddles low with the other soldiers. Water slops in the bows.

The lowest of whistles comes from the far bank. A clunk of wood on steel. The oars are shipped and the boat glides to a halt, nosing into the reed bed. Nat is the first to jump ashore, wading at first and then enjoying the firmness under his feet, as he leads the scramble up the bank.

Now they are in Franco's territory. But they know they aren't alone, and that knowledge is sweet. For twenty miles along the river, on pontoon bridges and boats, Republican units are advancing – the polyglot Army of the Ebro. Nat feels again the glow of brotherhood that warmed him when he first arrived in Spain. Everything feels possible again, and black and white and simple. They just have to win the war. *Primero ganar la guerra*.

Nat counts men, double-checks his canteen is full, and takes a compass bearing. They are to head away from the curve of the river. Their instructions are to take the road to Corbera, flushing out opposition as they move west.

'Open order,' the sergeant calls out softly. The men are already stringing out. As the sky lightens, they become more visible. How quietly can they march?

Surrounded by such courage and confidence, Nat smiles. But his smile quickly dies. He can't stop brooding on what he's left unfinished. He knows he's failed Felix. At least, she thinks he's failed her, and that is just as bad. The last person in the world he wanted to let down, and yet he has, in the very instant he imagined the opposite. And then again, over and over again, ever since, with his silence. He never had managed to explain. He just couldn't bring himself to tell Felix that her friend was going to kill her. How could you put that on paper?

Just before Teruel fell to the Fascists, Nat looked hard for Felix, with no success. And then he'd tried to write. The chaos of the retreats quickly interrupted. And with it the numbness that struck them all. He'd never been any good with words,

226

even without censors to get in the way. This wasn't something he could draw, or paint. It was a pain he couldn't even put a colour to. The only way to sort it out was face to face, with time, plenty of time.

After this final push, after this was over, he'd get leave then, surely. It couldn't be too late. He would go and find her again and this time nothing would stop him. However long it took, wherever she was, he'd track her down and make her understand. In the end she would have to see why he couldn't risk being mistaken, and surely she would forgive him. And then they would go to Valencia at last, and have time together for everything. He just had to get through this next battle. And he was lucky, wasn't he? It didn't make sense to think that way, he knew, though everyone did it. Bullets with your number on, steel balls bouncing on a roulette wheel. Lottery tickets. Except you couldn't stop yourself. All he needed was a little more luck.

The river birds are awake. All around, conversations between machine guns are starting up too. At first, they take polite turns. Soon every weapon is talking at once.

39

'Can't you hear it?'

Felix strains her ears. Far away, across the Ebro, the shelling has begun.

'The breakfast bombs?'

'No. Listen.'

Closer to hand, very quietly at first, but getting slowly louder, comes the sound of singing, low singing. It has a kind of throbbing pulse, the tune familiar. Felix knows the words.

Si me quieres escribir, ya sabes mi paradero . . . if you want to write to me, you know where I am . . .

But this is a new version.

En el frente de Gandesa primera linea de fuego . . . On the Gandesa front, in the first line of fire.

They are going to Gandesa, on the other side of the Ebro.

'Shall we go up and see them off?' she says to Kitty. Lacking latrines, they're both squatting in a ditch at the edge of a field.

'Let's.'

They make their way to the road. The day before, the villagers of La Bisbal de Falset were mending the potholes with branches. Others bent with picks, widening hairpin bends without a word. Just the sound of steel on stone.

As they reach the verge, a huge open truck with a Russian number plate comes rumbling by. Kitty and Felix raise their hands, two solitary clenched fists. A sea of fists and smiles return their greeting.

'They look so young, don't they?' says Kitty.

'Fifteen? Sixteen?'

'*La quinta del biberón.*'

'The baby bottle brigade.'

The singing drifts away. Another truck is approaching.

'They don't know yet though. What it's going to be like, I mean,' says Felix.

'No, they don't know.'

All at once Felix feels terribly ancient as well as sad. She is also very itchy. She scratches at her wrist. 'These damned things. How I hate them.'

'At least you can see a louse to catch it.'

'And have the satisfaction of squeezing it to death. Every time I pop one between my fingernails I imagine it's one of Franco's generals. Or, even better, someone on the bloody Non-Intervention Committee in London.'

Kitty laughs. 'Who'd have thought anything could be worse than lice? But scabies! It's the utter limit!'

'Come on . . . let's get out the Lysol while there's still time.'

This hospital is in a cave. When Felix heard, she imagined a storybook kind of cave, where dragons lurk on piles of gold at the end of winding tunnels. Theirs is a great horizontal gash in the rock face of a hillside, an unhappy open mouth. But its roof is solid stone. And it won't be far from the fighting.

On uneven rocky floors the orderlies have done their best to recreate a ward, with staggered lines of camp beds on several levels. At one end is the food store, and the kitchen – a scrubbed wooden table and a vast cauldron bubbling on a fire, big enough to feed a coven of witches. A few stone walls, built like the terraces that step down to the valley below, offer more protection.

Kitty and Felix climb back up the stony path to the cave. In the olive grove, they pass the triage tent – the *equip* – and the transfusion lorry. A group of men in vests and dungarees are busy getting stretchers ready. Piles of wooden poles lie waiting to be fed through canvas. Trucks and ambulances nearby have bonnets up, and legs stick out from under chassis, as drivers carry out last-minute checks and repairs. The vehicles have a dead, hollow feel to them without their windscreens. Some have been smashed out by bombs, the others removed on purpose. The flash of sun on glass is an instant giveaway to the enemy air force. Even moonlight shows up a windscreen.

'Shall we just keep quiet about our engagement?' Felix suggested, during a snatched conversation with George when they first arrived. 'It makes things awkward for the others, don't you think?'

'Maybe.'

'I don't want them to feel uncomfortable around us. And I have to wash my hands so often. I'd worry about losing the ring. I could wear it on a string around my neck, if you like.'

'It might be safer that way,' said George. 'If that's really what you want to do . . .'

Felix knew he wanted to show her off. Make her promise more real by making it public.

'Everything's in limbo now. But it can't be much longer, can it? And then we can really celebrate.' She hated the sight of his disappointment, but she wasn't quite ready for celebrations.

They were unloading a new consignment of medical supplies, timing their journeys to meet back at the truck for another armful. Hidden by the big metal doors, she gave him a quick hug, only to pull away when they heard voices. Kitty and Doug were coming back for a second load, followed by some new volunteers from the nearest village. Spanish girls were rather shockable. Felix didn't want to get a reputation, she told herself. It made a good excuse.

But she is careful to offer George some small sign each day, something to make sure he doesn't feel neglected. Nothing that will attract attention. A quick squeeze on the arm is often all that can be managed. Once he grabbed a kiss in passing – but she turned her head, so her cheek took it, just by her ear. 'I can't wait for all this to be over,' he whispered. 'I can't wait.'

Last night she looked at him across a tin plate of beans and saw he really couldn't wait. At the end of the meal she whispered for him to meet her on the hillside above the cave. It was the least she could do, with the battle coming. No one need know. She waited in darkness, wondering, with her back against a tree, while, like a film score, the sound of cicadas built to a deafening crescendo. George loped towards her, unmistakeable, and Felix felt a rush of affection as she stepped forward to meet him. There was nothing to say. She kissed him with hard, fierce lips. She pushed herself against him. She waited for the hot, liquid feeling to flood through her. But the deadness wouldn't leave her body.

Felix finds George back at the cave, crouched over the generator with the maintenance engineer – a bespectacled American borrowed from the Abraham Lincoln Brigade.

She grins at both men, but looks longer at George. 'Getting close?'

'Definitely,' says George.

'Do you know what the plan is, later?'

'I'm to cross over with one of the field ambulances. It's light enough to go over the nearest pontoon. We're setting up a clearing post on the other side.'

Kitty has gone off to find the Lysol. Even so, with the American right at his side, there isn't much Felix can say to George.

'Good luck. You know I'll be thinking of you. Try and get some sleep today.'

'Will do. You too. I'll be fine. Don't worry. I'll see you later.'

The American is looking at them with interest. Felix is still in earshot when the ribbing begins.

'My, you've made a hit there! *She'll be thinking of you.* Crafty guy, aren't you? Who'd have thought?'

'Oh, Felix is an old friend. I used to work with her brother. In London.'

'Oh yeah?'

Felix hurries away. I'll be thinking of you. I'll be thinking of you. She hammers out the rhythm of the words with her teeth as she walks, jaw stiff with tension. It's clamped tight shut whenever she sleeps. She feels the ache in her molars and her face all day.

She *will* be thinking of George. She does love him, she's sure of it. He is very lovable. It's easy to imagine having breakfast with George every day. Going for walks, that kind of thing. Maybe they'd even have a car one day, when they got settled, and he'd spend Sundays fixing it up and they'd go for drives in Kent, with her mother, or to the races. She finds herself longing for all the things she once found so dull. As for the other stuff, it's probably just a question of time. This deadness inside her is because of her illness. It must be. After all, she's still not a hundred per cent. Once she's completely over it, everything's sure to feel better.

She'll try harder, for George's sake. Felix makes an effort to summon back the devoted blue eyes she's just been looking into. She stands with her own tight shut and thinks about last night, and his face moving closer, his lips meeting hers. She waits, testing herself. But all she can see is Nat, looking at her just as longingly.

'Oh, go away!' she says out loud, without meaning to.

'Who are you talking to?' calls Kitty from behind a sheet slung over a rope. She's making a great deal of noise as she slaps on disinfectant to keep the parasites at bay. 'Ye Gods, this stings even more than it stinks. Ah! Ow!'

'Just the flies. Hurry up!'

'Two minutes.'

Felix waits to purify herself.

40

On the other side of the river, spirits are high. They've driven Franco's forces from the steep hillsides outside Corbera. But everyone knows Fascist reinforcements will soon arrive and it's no surprise when the crash and boom of bombardment steps up a day later. The men scan the skies, and wonder if the German and Italian planes have got the trick of breeding. Nat sees fear rising in the eyes of lads who have not fought before, and he does his best to steady their nerves.

These rocky slopes give little reassurance. Trench strategy is out the window. Where they find earth, they quickly meet rock face beneath the soil.

'Stay with me when it starts, boys,' he tells them that evening. 'And don't be tempted to return fire too quickly. You'll be playing into their hands.'

Next day comes the order to take Hill 481.

'We take this hill, we get Gandesa,' says the captain, as they crouch in a *barranco*.

Orderly at first, they begin to crawl upward, darting from rock to rock, heads craned, ears cocked, listening, listening. There are too few trees. The terrain is scrubby, desperately exposed. Once Nat slips on scree. He hears the loose rock shift and start to roll and he holds his breath, imagining a cascade of stones falling on the next man, a kind of avalanche. He fears the fire it will draw and swears silently. He might just as well leap up and shout, 'Here we are! Over here! Come and get us!'

But nothing. Just the crunch and slide of boots on stone, and the swish swish of cloth against cloth, as legs move swiftly, unevenly. Crouching, as low as he can without grinding to a halt, feeling every step in his thighs, Nat looks up at the sheer rock above. A precipice. *Take that hill*, he thought. No mention of the concrete bunkers at the top, the barbed wire tangled round them, four feet high, the trenches that must be there, too, unseen from where Nat and his strung-out line of comrades lurk below.

In fact the first fire comes from the town, Gandesa. Machine-gunners – *high in the church tower perhaps?* Nat can't tell – firing from their flank, send up clods of earth and rock. Then he knows there must be Fascists holding fast to other heights around them. All at once, these other men, invisible in their bunkers, begin to fire in earnest. There's no hope of retaliating.

'Steve's hit!' Nat feels the cry in his chest. Steve is a Scouser, only a few months out of Liverpool. Nat likes him, though he hardly knows him. José, their first-aid man, is already inching his way towards Steve, bandages in a bag on his back. But Steve has been hit in the head, the back of his skull sliced off. He had no chance at all. He's dead before José gets close.

The fire is almost continuous the next day too. Impossible to move forward, impossible to retreat. They dig where they can, build up feeble parapets of loose rock, and wait in these shallow shelters. The ground cracks and splinters around them and they burn in the summer sun.

Nat's mouth is dry. Dry as dust, dry as sand, dry as bones. His limbs shake constantly. (Three or four a second, the shells fall.) Again and again, bile rises in his throat. He can't choke its sourness back.

His mind is blank, paralysed for as long as the shelling lasts. But in the pauses between fire, his thoughts bring reinforcements.

What is the enemy doing? Waiting for guns to cool. Reloading now. It will start again soon. Not long now.

In this silence the whine of flies grows as loud as *aviones*. They settle on excrement and wounds. They settle on Nat's face as though it is a corpse already. He twitches, shakes off the insects. Real planes are circling too. What are they doing? Why don't they drop their bombs? Come on, come on. Get it over with. Now's as good as later. No, the enemy must be too close. They don't want to hit their own. There they go, flying east, back to pound the river and the boats and the bridges.

Other thoughts leak from bowels and guts. *Just run away. Get out of here. Can't do this any more. I can't. I can't. Too much fear. Creeping through my body. My fear will get me.*

Night. They wait for news and hope for back-up. Men come, scrambling through the darkness. One has a vast reel of wire on his back, unspooling as he clambers up. With telephone contact, news filters through. Don't move. We've got Gandesa almost surrounded. They're waiting for us. Depending on us. Fresh ammunition? Food? Not much. The Fascists have opened the flood gates, you see. The Ebro is rising. Pontoons swept away, boats unmoored. Some mules on their way. A little water. Not enough. Cigarettes.

The wounded are dragged away.

Morning, almost. A fresh assault, their turn to lead. This is like running an abattoir, forcing these boys back up there, mute and passive as animals. A few try to turn and run. Nat sees one lad rooted to the spot with terror. The lieutenant brings out his pistol and the boy starts moving.

This time they get higher, close enough to meet grenades as well as machine-gun fire. The grenades come over the barbed wire in showers, rolling and bouncing down the hill like living creatures. One officer after another is wounded, and replaced. Nat frets, hoping his turn will not be soon. Talk about rising through the ranks. The attack comes to an abrupt end.

And once again, they are stuck. Nowhere to go till nightfall. Nat makes himself keep firing. Then he runs out of ammunition, and for an hour lies still.

Away from the stink of the trench, he smells the hillside herbs again. It brings back memories of Jarama, and the stilted letter he wrote to Bernie's wife after the battle. He should have done a better job of that. He'd make amends though, go and see her when he could. Somewhere off the Mile End Road, wasn't it? He would give her a picture he still has of Bernie.

He tries not to think about Felix. There's such a thing as tempting fate.

The sun is directly overhead. Less shadow should make things safer. Nat pushes himself up, just a fraction, trying to get a sense of things, where everybody is, who is left. Ronnie Evesham is a little to Nat's right. He's found a hollow of sorts, below some scrub. Ronnie catches Nat's eye, and gestures to him, mouthing the words: 'It's safer here. Come and join me.'

Stealthily, Nat begins to move. Like a baby who hasn't learned to crawl, he drags himself towards Ronnie on his forearms. A rock fragment digging into his kneecap nearly makes him cry out loud. Others crossed the Ebro with sticks of wood on strings around their necks, to bite on rather than scream. Too late now for that. Ronnie is signalling again. What is it? What does he want?

A blow to his side throws Nat on his back. The ground here is too steep to resist the momentum. Feeling no pain, he begins to roll, slithering and turning across the loose earth that must have come from Ronnie's hollow. Soil collects in his mouth. By the time a cluster of thorn bushes can halt Nat's progress, he has blacked out.

41

Felix opens her eyes to rough grey concrete a few feet from her face. She scrapes her eyelids back down over eyeballs so dry and dusty they seem to grind in their sockets. One minute more. One minute more, she tells herself, and then I will go back.

She's taken to sleeping in an underground pipe, just off the road. In the heat of the day, an hour or two on a cork mattress helps get her through the nights. She lies there, drowsing, one hand rubbing at her cheek.

Waking a second time, Felix recognises the hollow in her stomach as despair as much as hunger. *I'll just stay here and wait. It must be very near the end. Really, there can be no hope left.* Then she thinks of all her Spanish friends.

'While there's life there's hope.' Felix's sing-song taunt echoes back at her. Maybe tonight there'd be more news. Maybe this would be the breakthrough they were all hoping for. They would regain the ground they had lost. And George had got a message across with a stretcher-bearer a few days earlier. He'd be back soon himself perhaps. Then they could talk about things.

The realisation has been creeping up on her for days, like flu, making her skin crawl and her temperature soar. She gives into it finally with the relief that comes with giving in to illness.

There's no other choice left. No use fighting the truth. Felix is glad she said nothing before the battle: it would have been too cruel. Dangerous, even. But she can't put it off much longer. To go on saying nothing is as bad as lying, Felix tells herself, with sudden clarity. It simply isn't honest to pretend to feel things she can't make herself feel. Oh, maybe it would be different if she had never known Nat. If George was all she'd ever had. But even when she doesn't want to think about him, even while her mind is pushing Nat away, her body can't stop remembering him.

No, it's hopeless. George will be better off without her. *Anyone* would make him a truer wife than she could. She'll work out what to say that will hurt him least, and give him back his ring, and then they'll both be free. And he, at least, will have a chance of happiness.

She rolls herself onto her front and wriggles out. The sun hits her face instantly. As she walks, Felix looks at the sky. It's automatic. Five squadrons are curving in from the north, a great flock in V formations. Trimotors, she registers. Bombers, flanked by biplanes, four more Vs of three. Silver birds of prey. *If we had what they have, this war would be over by now. And I wouldn't be having to decide these things.*

The cave fills with patients as the skies fill with planes. The space is divided: one level for Republican soldiers, one for the rebels. The civilians from round about are taking it hard too. '¡*Curandera!*' they cry out, not knowing the word for doctor. '*Curandera, por favor, aquí, aquí* . . . Please, healer, over here.' Except for the mother who lies completely silent. Is she still a mother, with both her children dead and buried under rubble?

Winding round the beds, Felix assesses each patient for change. Kitty sits with a beautiful young man with golden skin and white-blond hair. From where Felix stands, he looks perfect, like a Norse god, not a scratch on him. But she knows he doesn't have much longer. Kitty strokes him, bending to catch his words. The man is a Finn, they think, though they can't be sure. He doesn't seem to understand Spanish or English, or French or German or Czech or Yiddish. But now he's trying to speak. And Felix sees from the way Kitty moves her head that still she can't understand him, and that he will die before they find someone who can.

An orderly tugs at her sleeve.

'Comrade Smilie wants you in theatre.'

It's for one of the prisoners of war, an Italian. Felix scrubs up quickly. Impossible to hate these men, however much you loathe their masters.

'Ah, there you are. We've got to amputate.' In English, with a patient who doesn't understand, Doug can be brutal. 'Gas gangrene. Out there too long. Like everyone else. Could be too far gone already. You distract him while I take his leg off.'

As soon as she comes close, the man grabs Felix's hand.

'*Per favore, signorina, per favore, me cantare una canzone della culla?*'

Felix doesn't understand. But the Spanish anaesthetist guesses the man's meaning.

'*¿Una canción de cuna?*' he asks.

'*Sí, sí,*' comes the response. His grip relaxes a fraction.

'He wants you to sing him a cradle song. Can you do that?'

Felix's mind empties. A cradle song? Then her mother's voice comes into her head, and her face becomes clearer too, and the nursery in Sydenham takes shape.

'Golden slumbers, kiss your eyes,
Smiles awake you when you rise,

241

Sleep pretty darling, do not cry,
And I will sing a lullaby.
Rock you,
Rock you,
Lullaby.'

Were there more verses? Felix can't remember. So she just sings that one, over and over again, close to the man's ear.

42

George is terribly tired. It is rather like drunkenness. No hiding it.

'Don't let me go to sleep, for pity's sake.'

'Right you are,' says Lou, the stretcher-bearer who sits in the front with him, watching the road and skies. The moon is close to full, making life both easier and more worrying. The front line keeps shifting. 'I'll keep talking. Just you try and stop me.'

'Ha, ha!' laughs George obligingly, wondering how much more he can stand. Not of Lou's chirpiness, which he finds impressive. Just, well, all this.

'I been thinking about a new invention. Might patent it when I get back home. A special clip, to keep your eyelids open. You could set it for different levels. Maybe just the one eye would do the trick in certain situations. What do you reckon?'

'Quite an idea. Attractive, even. You know, the wide-eyed look?'

'Oh yes, that's lovely in a woman, ain't it? Sort of startled?'

'Precisely. Actually, I can see this catching on . . .'

'You're telling me. Look at the call for it. Night shifts.'

'Train drivers. Nurses.'

'Think of the next war, mate. I quite fancy myself as a profiteer.' Lou's laughter breaks off before it gets going. He slaps the dashboard. 'Pull over, mate. Someone over there. Up there. I saw something move.'

George swings the ambulance across to the other verge, and listens for the usual calls. *Camilleros? Sanitarios?* Nothing. Not so much as a groan filters through the hum of cicadas. They both squint into the shadows.

'You stay with the meat wagon. I'll go have a look-see.'

Lou strides off the road and into the bushes. George imagines him tightening a fist on his grenade. He feels for his own small pistol. Then he calls to Bert, who has jumped down from the back and is starting to pull out the first stretcher.

'Not sure what we've got yet. Lou's gone to check.'

'Shall I go after him?'

George's nerves are returning. A pall of smoke has been rising all day, veiling the hill. They're expecting the worst night's haul yet.

'Yes. Go on. Watch yourself.'

George paces the road, breathing deeply, sending oxygen to his befuddled brain. The smell of rosemary makes him think of mutton and Sunday lunches. Eventually he hears muttering and grunting through the bushes, and the scrape of feet dragging on scree.

Bert and Lou emerge, a body slung between them. When the slope becomes more gentle they lay him down and go for the stretcher. A voice comes from another shape in the shadows.

'They sent me with him. I tried to carry him, on my back. I did my best. I couldn't keep going though. They'd got me too you see. I did my best. Guess it's over for me now. Guess I'm going home. Bloody useless. But look. Still got my machine gun. No ammo. But got my gun.'

'How many more up there?' George asks.

'Oh, a good few. A good few.'

244

Bert and Lou strap the unconscious man onto the stretcher, while George helps the other one into the back of the ambulance, and shines a torch over him. The bandage round his neck is black with blood.

There isn't much sign of life in the other fellow, but they slide him in all the same.

'I'll get these two as far as the river,' says George. 'Meet me back here?'

'We'll try,' says Lou stoutly. 'Cheerio.'

Lou and Bert set off back up the hillside with a second stretcher. George checks his passengers again. Neck-wound has fallen silent: in shock, most likely. George's cheek hovers over the other patient's mouth while he watches his chest for movement. He'll have to move fast with this one. It was always a hard call. Keep going and look for others, or make tracks with those you've got.

'Can you open your eyes?' He speaks clearly into the man's ear. No reaction. But he's definitely alive. It was worth a try. George is about to hurry back to the driving seat when something stops him, something he recognises about this soldier. He can't pin it down. Ah well, can hardly ask him now. But George is sure he's seen him somewhere before. Madrid, perhaps? Maybe that was it. That blood transfusion place.

The situation at the river is worse than he had expected. Most of the planks joining the boats have either been destroyed or swept away. Not a hope of walking over the pontoon now, let alone driving. There are injured men in the water, swimming from boat to boat.

George calls for help. A sloshing in the reeds, and a bare-chested man emerges and takes the other end of the stretcher.

245

Between them they sling it across a rowing boat, ready to tow across to the other side.

Thigh-deep in water near the bank, George hesitates, one hand still on the boat. He'd promised Felix.

'*Un momento, camarada,*' he says, pulling his pencil from his breast pocket. He scrawls a hasty note on the back of an envelope, writes her name, and sticks it inside the patient's jacket. This fellow's bound to end up on an operating table. Fingers crossed it'll be hers.

All well. See you soon. Chin up. George. x.

George makes six more trips to the battlefield during the night. He is back at the river at dawn when a new air raid begins. He quickly gets into the ambulance and drives away with the door still swinging on its hinges. In his far wing mirror, he catches sight of a great dark mass of water and debris bursting into the air, tinted red by the rising sun.

Through the window of his cockpit floor, the last departing Stuka pilot spots the movement of George's vehicle. He rolls into a lazy dive and releases his one remaining bomb.

George has already braked. He's on the running board when it hits him.

43

'Damn and blast,' Felix mutters, tears in her eyes. She's gashed her shin again on the corner of a metal bed. They're impossible to avoid in the dark. Blood trickles down. 'I'm coming. I'm coming.'

She doesn't look at the face of the man lying on the operating table under a gently swinging light bulb. The barber is in the way, shaving the wound area. And anyway, Felix has to sort out the instruments she's just collected from the steriliser, and lay out the swabs.

Doug radios down to the transfusion lorry to see how supplies are doing. He runs a hand over his bristly chin, as if thinking he wouldn't mind a shave himself.

'No good. They're completely out of bottled blood.'

He raises his eyebrows at her in a question that doesn't need asking.

The operating table is too high for Felix to plonk herself down on the ground as she usually does, legs outstretched, grateful for a break. Instead she manoeuvres a chair over with one crooked foot and sits with her arm extended. It's the first blood she's given so far that day. She's always happy to do it. Nothing else makes her feel so useful.

She closes her eyes. Doug finds the syringe, and asks for saline. She is just like a horse, Felix thinks. She can practically sleep standing up. But as the needle pierces her vein, she forces her lids open again. She can't miss this moment. It's the best bit. When you watch their faces change and life start up again. It makes you feel alive yourself.

This face is grey like all the others. She expected that. But not to know it. Not to cry out and make the others stare. Felix leaps up, cannula still in her arm. The chair clatters to the floor behind her, and Nat's eyelids flicker, but do not open.

'Steady on,' says Doug. The anaesthetist checks the two-way syringe and the double tube joining Felix to Nat. Still in place. He rescues the chair. 'Steady on.'

All the blood in her body seems to leave at once, in a great tidal wave. Felix feels giddy and light and terribly sick. She hears a voice.

'It's too much. She's going to pass out. Have you got her? Make her sit down. Get her tea. Plenty of sugar.'

'I'm fine,' she protests. 'Sorry. Sorry. I know him. That's all. I know him.'

Then she sees it happen. Nat's face begins to colour. She reaches for his neck with her free hand, holding three gentle fingers against a pulse that steadily gains in strength.

'Come on. Come on.'

She can will life back into him. She will *make* his pulse beat time with her own.

For fifteen minutes after the transfusion they chart Nat's vital signs. Felix finds it unbearable, the wait before Doug can get to work on him. When she feels the surgeon's eyes on her, she looks up, dreading the news.

'Well?'

'I can't say yet. Depends what we find. You know that. But let's get a move on. He's a good friend, is he? Are you really up to this, Felix?'

'Of course.'

Felix would rather be looking right into Nat's guts and know what is happening there than be anywhere else in the world.

Eventually, still working away, Doug speaks again through his mask. 'Right. You can see the picture. Bullet through upper left abdomen. At least it's not shrapnel. Splenic flexure torn and spleen nicked too, so I'll have to take that out. Resection and anastomosis first though.'

'No sign of sepsis.'

'No, it's looking good.' He gives her a quick exhausted smile, and doesn't look away. 'I'd say it was looking good.'

The cave begins to lighten. Felix goes back to the post-ops, Nat to recovery. She keeps watching him of course. She has to be there when he comes round.

Faintly, a few miles from their valley, the first air raid on the river is beginning. The cave's acoustics distort distance and direction, but still this doesn't sound close enough to worry about. Anyway, you can't worry about everything at once. It would kill you.

44

Felix has held the hands of more men than she can count in the past year and a half. But still the thought of taking Nat's again makes her shy.

They send for her when he opens his eyes. It's obvious that he doesn't trust what he sees.

'Felix?'

'Shhh . . . Yes . . . It's me.'

'Got to talk.'

'I know. Later. Plenty of time.'

'No. Can't wait.'

Felix wonders.

'I'm here,' she says.

Nat tries to close his fingers round hers, and she feels their roughness catch on her own. He makes an enormous effort to lift her hand, but can't yet manage it. So Felix takes up the weight of his hand under hers, and presses the back of her hand against his lips. They are warm and still soft, and after his kiss breaks she can feel his breath, uneven, against her skin. She rests her hand for a while on his chest, simply enjoying the fact of its rise and fall.

Nat drifts away again, no longer lucid. Felix sits and watches over him. He's gone for some time. It's just the anaesthetic. She's not worried. It's often like this. He'll be drowsy and confused from the morphine too. She sits and waits and a kind of serenity comes over her. They drift together.

His lips move.

'Nat?'

He looks at her, confused, eyebrows cocked. Trying to remember something.

'Dolores,' he says eventually. 'Dolores.'

Felix stiffens. She thought she was prepared. She'd known for hours this was coming. But now . . . she doesn't want to remember, ever again. If they could only pretend it had never happened. If only it hadn't. But that's impossible. The fact of Dolores will hang between them like a spectre for the rest of their lives. Pretending is no option. She looks behind her. The patient in the next bed is asleep, his breathing laboured, but comfortable enough. Nat's is the last bed. The candle next to it lights only rock face. Nobody will hear.

'I'm sorry,' he whispers. 'I couldn't see another way.'

She listens to his breathing, and thinks how to reply.

'I want to say everything's all right,' she says in the end. 'Or never mind . . . or something like that. But you know I can't. We have to go on minding, always, don't we? About all of this.'

She sees him sink slightly, deflate.

'But don't think I'm blaming you,' she adds quickly. 'What's the point in blame?'

Can he hear her?

Yes.

'So frightened,' he says. 'For you. I couldn't . . .'

'Yes.' She sighs. 'Me too . . .'

'She was going to—'

'To kill me?' she says calmly, and he nods, painfully, searching her face. 'I guessed that was what you thought. But you didn't know her . . . She couldn't, she would never—'

'No, Felix, she could. Dolores had a knife.'

Nat is becoming agitated, his words slurring. She must calm him down.

'A knife? No. Shhh . . .'

'A blade, a scalpel, then,' he says. 'Whatever you call it. Don't know. Surgical thing. In her hand. I found it. After.'

Felix feels the old chill return, the shaking. 'You're certain?'

Nat nods again, a tiny movement. She can see how painful it has been for him to tell her this. She knows by the way he watches her shiver as she turns the information over: the impossibility, and yet the possibility of it. She's been shying away from these thoughts for months, deliberately blocking both mind and memory at the last moment.

'She would have used it.'

'Don't tell me. Please.'

'Got to. She knew what she was doing. Promise you.'

Felix's sharp intake of breath resonates gently round their corner of the cave, and the man in the next bed lets out a deep sigh, stirs, and settles again. Felix kneels and lays her head on the pillow beside Nat's, and murmurs into his ear.

'Oh God. What would I have done? If you hadn't been there?'

She judged him so harshly, so quickly. She keeps remembering the words she used then. *Who made you judge and jury?* Who made her?

'I'm so sorry, Nat. So terribly, terribly sorry. I just couldn't bear what was happening. I couldn't bear what had happened. What I had let happen. I still can't.'

She feels him nod slightly. She knows she isn't quite making sense, any more than he can completely take it in. Telling her has exhausted him. She fumbles between words and ideas, falling between them. She can't find one solid place to stand. And she is so tired.

'I'm so tired,' she says. 'I'm sorry. I'm just so sorry.' Keep trying. She sits up, trying to gather her strength, and glances hopelessly round the rows and rows of beds in the cave, and hears the sounds of people in pain. 'This war. It's not right and wrong any more, is it? Just wrong and wrong.'

He looks up at her, eyes narrowed. As though trying to make her out through a mist, or a fog.

'Oh, I don't even mean that, quite,' she whispers, quickly. 'Don't tell anyone. Please don't. What do I mean? I don't know.'

No good. She can't work it all out now. They'll just have to go on talking, and go on remembering, until the pieces fit together properly, and they can make a new place to be. In time.

Nat's focus sharpens again, and his frown becomes a smile.

'Thought I'd ruined everything,' he murmurs. 'Thought I'd lost you.'

'No. Harder than you think. Go to sleep, my darling. I'll still be here.'

He sleeps. Felix wonders how much more time she can spare just to watch over him. It isn't fair. There is so much other work to do. She counts out his breaths. She tells herself she will go after the next ten, the next twenty . . . Eventually Felix looks up, hardly daring to believe her luck that nobody has summoned her yet. A *practicante* is coming towards her, holding out a torn and bloody envelope.

'It has your name on it,' he says. 'They found it in a jacket. It nearly got burned, but they were checking for ammunition. It is you, yes? Felix? Like *feliz* . . . the happy one?'

'That's me,' she says, taking George's note. She reads it with a complicated rush of relief, and glances at Nat.

He looks wonderfully peaceful now, his face smoothed out and still. Felix reaches across and touches his cheek with a kind of envy. She feels twisted up and hollowed out herself. Something is turning and tugging at her guts, trying to drag them out of her.

It really is no good. When George comes back, she'll simply explain everything. It will have to be a different kind of talk now. She can't just break it off, and leave him in the dark about all this. It had always been a mistake not to tell him about Dolores, never mind Nat. She'd been pretending to herself it wasn't necessary. Why hurt him more? But now it is finally time. She'll have to steel herself. George deserved to know everything. Though he won't think so much of her now, will he? This thought comes as a physical pain. She cherishes George's respect. It will hurt her to lose it. But at least he'll know just how much better off he is without her. And she's sure he'll keep their secret.

Then she hears Kitty's cry. 'Oh no. Oh no. Please no.'

Kitty stumbles towards her. The news has just come up from the olive grove. Kitty keeps staring at Felix, her eyes reflecting nothing. Then she falls to her knees in front of her, and buries her face deep in Felix's lap, spectacle frames digging into her thighs. Kitty's voice is muffled.

'Felix. Felix. They've got one of our field ambulances. A direct hit. They think it's George.'

Felix feels herself begin to float. There is nothing she can anchor herself to.

'George?' she falters, her hand moving to her throat. '*My* George?'

Somewhere in the valley below, an engine starts up. Another vehicle sets off towards the river.

APRIL 1939

LONDON

The registrar was running late. Wedding parties were backing up in the waiting room and beginning to overflow onto the pavement, risking early collision with other people's confetti and newly-weds celebrating on the steps. There were just two chairs left in the corner, with hard shiny leather seats. Felix sat down next to her mother and wished it felt a bit less like waiting for the dentist.

'Don't bite your lip, dear. You'll lose your lipstick. Here . . .' Mrs Rose clicked open her compact, and passed it to Felix. 'You've got plenty of time to touch up. We're awfully early.'

'I know.' Felix frowned at herself, and tried a photograph face in the powdery mirror. They should have waited outside for the others. It was sunny outside. Warmer too.

'You look beautiful. You really do. And I like your hair that way. Not quite how . . .' Mrs Rose's voice trailed off, and she gathered herself, and coughed, and then began to look about curiously. Felix knew what her mother was thinking. Of course this wasn't how she'd ever imagined her daughter getting married. In a navy blue silk two-piece, a modest hat, no veil, no guests to speak of, and a gloomy register office in Stepney with a parquet floor that could do with a polish. Well, it was what Felix wanted, so there was an end of it. No fuss.

They both caught sight of a swollen-eyed bride sitting

opposite, and looked away simultaneously. Her coat could no longer button up round her waist, but she was putting a brave face on things. The only way Felix could tell who she was about to marry was that one of the three young midshipmen hanging round her kept putting his arm around the girl and telling her to cheer up, and that he was bound to be promoted soon, what with the war coming, and all. And that he'd make her proud of him yet. There were other forces' uniforms in the room too, and various ranks.

'How many do you think are ahead of us?' Felix asked her mother. 'Did you notice?'

'Three or four, I'd say. So busy for a weekday morning. Do you think it's always like this? Oh, don't fret, dear. They'll be along soon.'

Felix rearranged her skirt. How she hated waiting.

Hushed and shrill, voices rose and fell around them. Groups of guests knotted protectively around their own bridal couples, and shyly acknowledged the others' from time to time.

George's brother arrived first, panting a little, and calling over his shoulder to his family to hurry up. Felix stood up and immediately felt wobbly with recognition. It was less a physical resemblance than the similarity between their voices. A particular inflection. Their laughs. Frank even ran his fingers through his hair in the same way George used to. When his wife Margaret burst in, moments later, a child on one hip, another dragging on her thigh and three more bringing up the rear, the family seemed to fill up all the rest of the space in the room, and everybody stared. An official came out of a door and shushed the whole waiting room, with a pointed glare in their direction, and said the noise was disturbing the ceremonies. But Frank had just George's knack for defusing awkwardness too. He got everyone smiling again, quietly, and Felix gave him and Margaret and each child a hug, down to the very littlest girl, who was only slightly snotty today.

'We're so glad you could all come.'

'I don't think George would have forgiven us if we hadn't,' said Frank, easily. 'He was terribly fond of you, you know.'

'Yes, yes, I do know. As we loved him.' And Felix glanced round, embracing her mother in her words, and Mrs Rose nodded approvingly. So Mother was right. George had only ever confessed his full intentions to Neville. And Neville wasn't here to spoil things. He was the one in battledress now. He'd joined up as soon as the army recruitment drive began, and was off at training camp already, unable to get away even for a family wedding. Or so he claimed.

'You're looking wonderful, isn't she, Margaret?' said Frank. 'Quite the blushing bride. Well, apart from the blushing, actually.'

'Thank you.' Felix hoped Nat would agree. It felt years since she'd been so dressed up, even if this wasn't her mother's idea of a wedding gown. For the twentieth time, she glanced over to the doorway leading from the hall, and finally she glimpsed Nat's face, looking for and then finding their party. Close behind him was his sister Rachel, her smile bigger than ever and looking just as well tailored. They began to make their way across the waiting room, and Felix saw immediately that Nat did agree with Frank, and also that everything would be all right.

She signalled with her eyes that perhaps they shouldn't kiss until the ceremony was over. All through the greetings and handshaking and introductions, she was aware of the light pressure of his hand on her back, and felt reassured. She hadn't seen him for a week: Rachel had insisted on keeping that custom, at least. It had seemed an age. Felix loved the way Nat bent to talk to each child, and how they responded so seriously to his questions. Nat's face was bright and glowing. He'd been in a rush.

'What kept you, darling?' she whispered, when she got the chance. 'Parents?'

'No, I had an interview in town at nine. Do you remember that design department job I put in for, in Whitehall? They called me in at the last minute.'

'And?'

'It was all going well, until they found out about the Party, and Spain. They said they'd write, but I think it's no go. Should have guessed. Surprised they hadn't done their homework already.' Nat spoke lightly, but Felix could feel the strain in his body.

'Oh, darling.'

Her mother nudged her. 'Come on, dear. That's you they're calling now.'

'*Mazel Tov!*' said Rachel, hugging Felix and Nat together.

'Well, that was certainly short and sweet!' said Frank. The tallest girl, Elsie, was tugging at his elbow.

'Is it over already?' she kept saying. 'Is that all?'

'I'm afraid so,' laughed Felix, happily arm in arm with Nat. Nothing to stop them. Her ring kept catching her eye, and she noticed Nat, noticing. 'Shall we say it all over again to make it longer?'

'He didn't half rattle it off!' said Nat. 'Thought I'd mess it all up at that speed. *I do solemnly declare that I know not . . .*'

'*Of any lawful impediment . . .*'

'Now, now!' interrupted Mrs Rose. 'I don't think you two are taking this seriously enough.'

'Oh, Mother, we are,' said Felix, staring at Nat, suddenly solemn. A horrible pit had opened up inside her. It was time to meet his parents. Rachel had persuaded them not to sit shiva, not to mourn the loss of Nat as if he were dead. There had been weeping and wailing, of course, but Rachel had quietly reminded them, over and over again, how much there was to be grateful for. And at last Mrs Kaplan had agreed – not to come to the wedding, but at least to see Felix afterwards.

Rachel took one look at Felix's white face, and said quickly, 'I'll go ahead. Make sure. Don't worry. They'll love you.'

'See you later then,' said Frank, tactfully ushering everyone else away, and sounding more like George than ever. 'And congratulations, Mr and Mrs Kaplan!'

Felix was vaguely aware of her mother's anxious face, mouthing the same words, and discreetly blowing her a kiss. Then the next wedding party came tumbling down the steps and hid them from sight.

'Oh, Nat,' she said, quietly, arranging his tie and feeling shockingly like a wife. 'Do you think they really will understand?'

'I don't know. I don't know. I hope so. I think my dad does. But if they don't, it's just too bad. It doesn't matter. We're already bound together. We already were, before today, and there's nothing anyone can do about it. You know that.'

Felix nodded. It was true, she thought. In good ways and bad.

Before they kissed, they both glanced up to check the skies. The habit was hard to break. With one hand, Felix kept her hat secure on her tilted head; the other tenderly cradled the back of Nat's head. She let his arms take the weight of her body. She knew he'd never let her fall. And if tonight she woke in a sweat from a nightmare, she wouldn't be alone. Nat would understand why she cried out in the dark, and what she saw and heard. Anger and grief nearly overwhelmed her every time she thought about Spain. Knowing that Nat felt the same helped her to bear it. They would learn together what to remember and what to forget, and, if they could, how they might begin to overcome their bitterness and their regrets. That war was over. Franco had won. But the fight wasn't finished.

'I couldn't love anyone the way I love you,' said Felix into Nat's neck. She felt her limbs weakening as his pulse quickened.

Nat steadied her on her feet, and then looked at her in the way he had that always made her reach up again for one more kiss.

'Come on then,' she said at last, inhaling him. 'It's not going to be as bad as all that, is it?'

They walked down East Arbour Street, past children playing on pavements between flat-fronted terraces. A small and ragged gang of boys was clambering over a shiny black Model Y Ford parked on the cobbles, waiting to take a wedding party away. They scattered at Felix and Nat's approach, and regrouped around the car as soon as they had passed.

Felix felt decadently, extravagantly happy. She was ready for anything, she decided. And then she frowned.

'This isn't the way to your parents', is it? Shouldn't we have turned back there?'

'Probably.'

'You know we should have.'

Nat wouldn't look straight at Felix. He just kept on walking, a secret smile on his face.

'Don't worry,' he said. 'It's just a little detour. Won't take long.'

Felix knew it was more than a little one, but she was glad to delay. She was happy just to be alone with Nat, and walking through London under clear skies. They skirted the back of the hospital, and kept walking along Fieldgate Street, and he kept on refusing to give a straight answer to her questions.

'Nearly there,' he said, as they turned left into Whitechapel Road.

Still Felix couldn't think where he was taking her. The light only dawned when she saw the squared arch of mint green tiles framing the shopfront. A smartly dressed commissionaire stepped out to greet them, complete with gold-braided epaulettes, kid gloves, two rows of gleaming buttons and a peaked cap marked 'Boris Studios'.

'Mr and Mrs Kaplan?'

'That's right,' said Nat, shaking his hand confidently before turning to Felix. 'I have a feeling my mother might find it easier to forgive us if she knows we've been to Boris Bennett for our wedding photograph.'

Felix stared through the polished plate glass at rows and rows of frames, all flowing satin and ribbons and tumbling bouquets and Hollywood smiles. She couldn't quite see how she and Nat fitted in with these couples, but she liked the idea. Hastily tidying her hair in her reflection, she adjusted the angle of her hat while the commissionaire stood by, polite and expressionless.

'How do I look now?' she said, taking Nat's arm again.

'How do you feel now?' he asked her, very seriously.

HISTORICAL AFTERWORD

'Through Spain, my generation came to know the taste of defeat for the first time: we discovered that you could be right and still be beaten, that force could overcome spirit, and that there were times when courage was not rewarded.'

Albert Camus, 1945

The volunteers who went to save democracy in Spain were sent home before the war was over. In September 1938, when the Battle of the Ebro was still raging, the Spanish Prime Minister agreed to withdraw the International Brigades, hoping Hitler and Mussolini would also withdraw their troops. This didn't happen.

Some Brigaders would go back to their countries, some into exile, some to concentration camps. Many were already prisoners of war, or missing. At a farewell parade in Barcelona, cheered by thousands, surviving volunteers were addressed by the Republic's most gifted speech maker, Dolores Ibárruri, *'La Pasionaria'*.

'Go proudly,' she told them. 'You are history. You are legend. You are the heroic example of the solidarity and the universality of democracy . . . We will not forget you; and, when the olive tree of peace puts forth its leaves, entwined with the laurels of the Spanish Republic's victory, come back!'

The Republican Army was forced into retreat in November 1938. But the Spanish Civil War only ended on 1st April 1939, when the USA joined Britain and France in recognising Franco's regime. By this time Czechoslovakia was in German hands. Britain's policy of appeasement had been abandoned.

Almost as many Republicans were executed by Franco's regime after the war as had already been killed in combat. As many again were interned in concentration camps in southern France, where precise death rates have yet to be established. Spain remained a dictatorship until the death of Franco in 1975.

THE SPANISH CIVIL WAR

A BRIEF CHRONOLOGY

1936

February: General election in Spain won by Popular Front

July: Military uprising in Morocco (Spanish North Africa) spreads to mainland Spain, but rebels quickly defeated in Madrid and Barcelona; Start of airlift of Army of Africa (under Franco's command) from North Africa to Seville; *Hitler and Mussolini send military aid to rebels*

August: Execution of Federico García Lorca; March on Madrid begins, followed by aerial bombardment of capital; *Britain and France announce arms embargo*

September: *Non-Intervention Committee meets in London for first time (27 countries eventually sign the agreement, including Germany, Italy, the Soviet Union, Britain, France, Portugal and Sweden); Soviet Union agrees to send arms to the Spanish Republic;* Franco is appointed supreme commander of rebel Nationalist Army

October: **International Brigade volunteers** start arriving in Spain

November: Republican government retreats to Valencia; **Battle for Madrid** begins; *Hitler sends Condor Legion to Spain; Germany and Italy recognise Franco*

1937

February: Republican forces stem rebel offensive at **Battle of Jarama**; Málaga falls to Nationalists with Italy's help, and refugees are bombed

April: Saturation bombing of Basque capital **Guernica**

May: Barcelona 'May Days': civil violence between Republican factions

July: Battle of Brunete, Republican offensive west of Madrid

October: Rebels capture all **Northern Spain**

1938

January – February: Battle of Teruel – city captured by Republicans, then re-taken by Nationalist forces

March: *Hitler invades Austria;* Bombing of **Barcelona** by Italian planes; France re-opens border with Spain

April: Republic physically divided as Franco reaches the Mediterranean; Nationalists attack **Valencia**

May: *Vatican recognises Franco as head of state*

July: *Plan to withdraw foreign combatants from Spain approved by Non-Intervention Committee, but then ignored by Germany and Italy;* **Republican Army launches the Ebro offensive**, hoping to save Valencia and reverse the direction of international diplomacy

August: Franco rejects all peace initiatives

September: *France and Britain agree to Hitler's annexation of Czech Sudetenland at Munich conference*

October: As **Battle of the Ebro** continues, non-Spanish volunteers for the Republic are withdrawn from active service; International Brigades' Farewell Parade in Barcelona

November: Republican Army forced into retreat back across the Ebro river; Barcelona and Valencia bombarded;

Kristallnacht: anti-Jewish pogroms in Germany, Austria and Sudetenland

1939

January: Franco captures **Barcelona;** Mass exodus of refugees towards France

February: First concentration camp for Republican refugees opens in France; Republican parliament meets in Spain for the last time; Nationalists take **Catalonia**; *Britain and France recognise Franco's regime*

March: Republicans surrender in Madrid; Refugees attempt to flee Spain in huge numbers; *Hitler enters Prague, Czechoslovakia*

April: Franco announces the end of the war; *USA recognises Franco*

ACKNOWLEDGEMENTS

I really hope you'll want to find out more about the International Brigades and the Spanish Civil War. Here are some very good places to start:

Antifascistas: British & Irish Volunteers in the Spanish Civil War in Words and Pictures, by Richard Baxell, Angela Jackson and Jim Jump (London: Lawrence & Wishart / IBMT, 2010)

The Spanish Civil War: A Very Short Introduction, by Helen Graham (Oxford: OUP, 2005)

www.international-brigades.org.uk

http://www.spartacus.schoolnet.co.uk/Spanish-Civil-War. htm

From the outset, I wanted to make *A World Between Us* as accurate as I possibly could and so I've drawn on the lives and work of a huge number of people. Prepare for a long list, starting with the volunteers, journalists and other supporters of Republican Spain, whose courage and commitment moved me to write this book in the first place. These include Ted Allan, Jay Allen, Arturo Barea, Winifred Bates, Leila Berg, Alvah Bessie, Hetty Bower, John Cornford, Virginia Cowles, Len Crome, David Crook, Patience Darton, Penny Feiwel, Aurora Fernandez, Martha Gellhorn, Walter Gregory, Nan Green, Jason Gurney, Charlotte Haldane, Joe Jacobs, Lou Kenton, Bernard Knox, John Langdon-Davies, Emmanuel Litvinoff, James Neugass, Hank Rubin, Reginald Saxton, John Sommerfield and Tom Wintringham. A few real people appear in the novel: Dr Bethune, Ilsa Kulcsar, Arturo Barea, 'Rita', and the journalists and sea captain in Bilbao. The racehorse and her owner were also real.

I've immersed myself in the work of some outstanding historians of the Spanish Civil War and its era, particularly Richard Baxell, Paul Preston, Angela Jackson, Helen Graham and Jim Jump, but also including Sally Alexander, Anthony Beevor, Tom Buchanan, Nicholas Coni, Jim Fyrth, Juliet Gardiner, James Hopkins, Nick Rankin, Hugh Thomas and Herbert Southworth. Huge thanks to Richard Baxell and Jeremy Scott for generous and invaluable help with maps and fact-checking, and also to Jessamy Harvey for making sure my Spanish made sense. I'm extremely grateful to the following libraries, museums, archives and organisations: British Library, Guernica Peace Museum, Hunterian Museum, Imperial War Museum, International Brigade Memorial Trust, London Library, Marx Memorial Library, Jewish Museum, Royal London Hospital Museum, St Bartholomew's Museum, and Wellcome Library.

Friends young and old have been incredibly generous with suggestions, information, books, comments on early drafts and general encouragement, and I'd like to thank Dominic Anderson, Simon Banfield, Paul Barnes, Charlotte Baxter, Christopher Cook, Laura Davies, Fátima Duerden, Lydia Durkin, Emily King, Iris

Mathieson, Frank Radcliffe-Adams, Polly Radcliffe, Michael Rosen, Rivka Shaw and Fabian Thomas. Natasha Lehrer, Richard Taylor, Tig Thomas and the Finsbury Group (Keren David, Fenella Fairbairn, Jennifer Gray, Becky Jones, Anna Longman and Amanda Swift) were all brilliantly constructive readers. Most heartfelt thanks too to my agent Catherine Clarke and everyone in the amazing Hot Key team, particularly Sarah Odedina, Georgia Murray, Jet Purdie, Jan Bielecki, Kate Manning, Sarah Benton, Megan Farr and Naomi Colthurst.

Finally, four generations of my family have been involved in this book in various ways, and I couldn't have written it without them: Jack, Maire, Lucy, Nick, Polly, Nic, Antonia, Luke, Phoebe, Adam, Rufus, Solomon and, above all, Martin. The loving and intelligent support of my daughter, my sister and my husband, and my three sons too, has been utterly unstinting. It leaves me lost for words.

LYDIA SYSON

Lydia Syson is a fifth-generation Londoner who lives in Camberwell. She was once a World Service radio producer, and left the BBC after the birth of the first of her four children. Then she wrote a PhD about explorers, poets and Timbuktu and a biography of the eighteenth-century 'electric' doctor, James Graham, telling the full story of his extraordinary Celestial Bed. *A World Between Us* is Lydia's first novel.

Find out more about Lydia at:

www.lydiasyson.com

twitter @LydiaSyson

A scene from the Syracuse Stage production of "K2."

Photo by *Susan Piper Kublick*

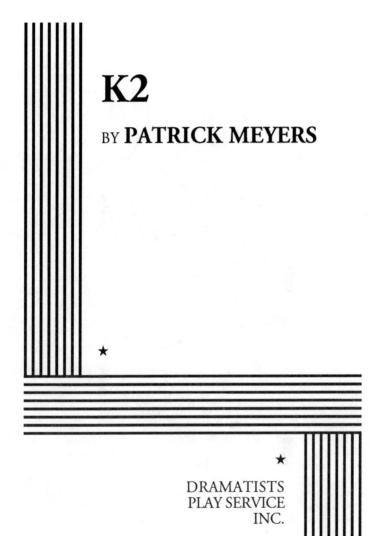

K2

BY **PATRICK MEYERS**

★

★

DRAMATISTS
PLAY SERVICE
INC.

K2
Copyright © 1980, 1982, 1983, Patrick Meyers

All Rights Reserved

K2 was presented on Broadway by Mary K. Frank and Cynthia Wood, by arrangement with Saint-Subber, at the Brooks Atkinson Theatre, in New York City, on March 30, 1983. It was directed by Terry Schreiber; the set was by Ming Cho Lee; costumes were by Noel Borden; the lighting was by Allen Lee Hughes; the audio composition was by Herman Chessid; the sound was by David Schnirman; and the assistant director was William S. Morris. The associate producers were Shawn Beary and Charles H. Duggan. The cast, in order of appearance, was as follows:

TAYLOR . . . . *Jeffrey De Munn*

HAROLD . . . . *Jay Patterson*

K2 was originally produced by Arena Stage, in Washington, D.C.

Place: A ledge, eight feet wide and four feet deep, located on a six hundred foot ice wall at 27,000 feet on K2, the world's second highest mountain.

Time: September 4, 1977.

AUTHOR'S NOTE

To Irene . . . a real friend.

When Rod Marriott, the dramaturg for Circle Repertory Co. in New York, called me in mid February of 82, and asked if I would like to stage the first production of K2 at Theater by The Sea in Portsmouth, New Hampshire, I was initially very interested. The play was already slated for two productions in the spring; at Arena Stage in Washington, D.C., and Syracuse Stage in Syracuse, New York. However, this one would proceed both of those and be the most "regional" of all the productions, far from the New York critics. It would be an opportunity to see what worked and didn't work, and have a chance to fix it—a process, I have learned, that is devoutly to be wished for.

But when I asked how many days of rehearsal we had, and the reply came back "nineteen", the first question I wanted to ask was, "Rod have you lost your mind?". K2 is a very demanding play.

Since the Broadway production opened in March of 83, much attention has been focused on the awsome efforts of designer Ming Cho Lee, who created a wall, well beyond my wildest dreams. In the Portsmouth and Syracuse productions, the designers had smaller spaces and smaller budgets, and were also able to create beautiful and imaginative sets. The wall in Portsmouth was only 16 feet, but the climbing there was just as exciting as it is on Ming's 55 foot, crystal masterpiece. In Syracuse the set was totally abstract — made entirely of steel and fiberglass — a frozen, existential, no man's land.

Creating a set for K2 is an exciting challenge for any designer, and it's one that can be responded to in various ways, and with various resourses. But what all four productions have had to face, with an equal degree of energy and commitment, is the climbing reality of the play. The actors must learn climbing technique. They must learn to use climbing gear and ropes. And Taylor must climb a 90 degree face. It is this physical commitment to a very athletic and frightening reality that makes K2 an extremely demanding work.

I'm glad now that I overcame my doubts about Rod's sanity and said yes, because that production gave me the experience and the courage I needed when I walked into Arena Stage's, Kreeger Theater and saw Ming's monsterous set. I'd already had to write "filler" dialogue in Portsmouth to cover dead spaces in the climbs, and now before my very eyes stretched a wall three times the height. It took awhile but my imagination finally responded to Ming's, and I went back to the script, rewriting so that Taylor could use more climbing aids, thus getting up and down much faster. Exit "filler" dialogue.

We did do it in nineteen days in Portsmouth. The first time we didn't have to stop the play because Taylor was in danger, was opening night. I remember it as a very involving evening in the theater.

Patrick Meyers

K2

At Curtain: The house lights dim and then we hear a loud gust of wind blow them out. The first notes of a Japanese flute are heard, a low, haunting sound. The curtain slowly rises to reveal the wall, lit in deep blues by the light of the moon. A small rumble is heard in the distance, and then a showering of snow falls onto the ledge. The flute winds higher and higher, mixing with the wind, as slowly, in a rainbow of colors, the dawn breaks on the icy, crystal face. Finally, bright yellow rays cut across the ledge, spreading slowly over the entire wall. There is a beat of complete stillness, and then slowly the mound of snow on the ledge begins to move and break up. A man's head, and then torso, rises from the mound. Taylor sits looking into the sun for a long moment, a sleepy smile growing on his face. He looks up and then begins to giggle softly. Suddenly he is digging into the mound around him feverishly.

TAYLOR. Harold wake up. Harold . . . morning . . . Harold. Made it . . . Harold . . . alive . . . alive Harold! (*He has uncovered a body which he yanks to a sitting position, wiping snow from the face and shaking it.*) HAROLD BE ALIVE!
HAROLD. Hu . . . Tay . . . lor . . .
TAYLOR. (*Hugging Harold to him.*) Yeah . . . yeah, Tay-

lor. Made it Harold . . . alive. (*Turning Harold's face to the sun.*) Feel buddy . . . Oh Jesus . . . it feels . . . Oh Jesus . . . feel buddy.

HAROLD. Yeah . . . yeah.

TAYLOR. Gonna make it now buddy. Gonna make it off this mother. (*Hugging Harold again.*) WE'RE ALIVE!

HAROLD. Uh . . . huh.

TAYLOR. (*Propping Harold up against the wall.*) History . . . history buddy! (*He begins digging in what's left of the mound, pulling out various pieces of equipment.*) History! . . . Hornbein . . . Unsoeld . . . Jerstad . . . and Bishop . . . 28,000 feet on Everest . . . no tent . . . no bags . . . one night. We didn't break that record buddy but we got second place. We have now definitely got second place — Poor old Buhl standing on that ledge all alone, all night on top of Nange Parbat, he is from this day forward relegated to a lowly third . . . You and me Harold, no tent, no bags, one night . . . You and me Harold . . . (*Taylor sticks a piece of beef jerky he has taken from a pocket into Harold's mouth.*) History Harold . . . at 27,000 feet.

HAROLD. (*Chewing dreamily.*) Uh . . . huh.

TAYLOR. (*Chewing on his piece of jerky for awhile.*) Now we gotta get off this fuckin' mountain. (*Taylor looks at Harold's leg.*) How's the leg?

HAROLD. Huh? (*Taylor takes off his down filled mittens to reveal black silk gloves. He rummages in a pack.*)

TAYLOR. Here! (*He takes a small green cylinder with a black hose and mask attached out of the pack and places the mask over Harold's mouth. He turns the nozzle.*) Breathe. Breathe deep buddy and come back to me . . . Earth to Harold, Earth to Harold. (*Taylor starts to giggle.*) Oh Christ. (*Harold begins to wake up from the oxygen and see the view. He lets the oxygen mask drop away as he stares in wonder. Taylor puts it back over his mouth.*) Breathe! If we don't wake up we're gonna be in a lot of trouble Here. Hold it. (*Taylor places Harold's hands on the cylinder and mask.*) Got

8

it? (*Harold nods.*) Good. Breathe. (*Taylor gropes in the pack until he finds another cylinder.*) Hypoxia won't cut it now. Maybe three hours before it starts snowin' again . . . enough . . . they'll be comin' up to six. They know we're in trouble . . . they hafto. (*Taylor puts the mask from the second cylinder over his mouth and turns the nozzle. They sit breathing the oxygen in deeply for awhile, then Taylor shuts off his nozzle and does the same for Harold.*) Not too much . . . we're gonna need it goin' down . . . Harold? (*Harold smiles dreamily.*) You gonna be alright?

HAROLD. Yeah . . . hunky-dory.

TAYLOR. Let's see the leg. (*He gently straightens Harold's left leg and puts it in his lap. Then Taylor slowly unzips his left overboot.*) You wanna take a look? (*Harold nods and Taylor unzips the leg of Harold's suit.*) Thank god for E.H.A.'s. Wearin' these fuckers for the summit was your idea Harold. (*Slapping Harold's face.*) You saved our miserable lives . . . you realize that? (*Harold smiles.*) We'd've froze for sure last night without these babies. You ready?

HAROLD. Yeah. (*Taylor delicately peels back the heavy woolen sock from Harold's leg and pulls the leg of the suit open. We can see that the leg is badly broken.*)

TAYLOR. . . . Holy shit . . . we gotta get off this fuckin' mountain.

HAROLD. Stupid. (*Taylor puts the sock back on, then the overboot, and zips the pant leg up again, talking rapidly while he works.*)

TAYLOR. Can't do anything for it now. Have to get you off fast as possible. They might be able to save it. The quicker we get to base, better chance you've got. So just hang in there . . . Harold . . . just hang in there. . . . all right?

HAROLD. I'm okay. It's just stupid. I should have known you were still on the rope.

TAYLOR. What the hell's it matter now? Right now we got to get off this mountain. Right?

HAROLD. Right.

TAYLOR. Okay. Equipment inventory, situation assessment.

HAROLD. (*Shaking his head.*) Water.

TAYLOR. Dehydration! Good. Very good. Water first. Yes. We are gonna help each other beat this mother. Good. (*Taylor unzips the top of his suit still further and reaches inside.*) Shouldn't be frozen, it's been layin' on my belly all night. (*Taylor pulls an insulation wrapped canteen out and takes off the cap. he drinks.*) Yeah, oh yeah. Drink. Not too much. (*Harold drinks.*) Not too much. (*Taylor takes the canteen away from Harold, screws the cap on and gives it back.*) Okay. Now, equipment inventory, situation assessment. (*Taylor grabs a pack and starts taking things out of it.*) Two ice axes . . . two oxygen bottles . . . climbing rope, 120 feet . . . Ice screws . . . Three . . . Ice hammer . . . thank god. Mine's gone. I threw it right off the fuckin' mountain when we went. (*Holding up a small tube.*) Sun screen . . . (*He takes Harold's mittens off and hands him the tube of sun screen.*) Save enough for me . . . Nylon tubing, thirty feet. These are thirty feet right?

HAROLD. Right.

TAYLOR. That should be enough if we need a sling. Two meat bars! You dirty fucker . . . holding out again. A little piggy to the end. We'll eat 'em before we go. One Pentax. You didn't use this on the summit did you?

HAROLD. No. Just back up, in case you screwed up your roll.

TAYLOR. (*Tossing the camera into space.*) Fat fucking chance.

HAROLD. We get back Cindy's going to kill you.

TAYLOR. We get back it's going to be because we carried us . . . and as little else as possible down this bastard. (*Taylor takes the other pack.*) Okay. What I got? Ice screws . . . two. Good. (*He rummages awhile, then all at once he is frantic, muttering to himself.*) Oh no . . . oh no . . . oh fuck, no . . . (*Totally frantic.*) oh holy fuck, no . . . no, no, no, no.

HAROLD. What is it?

TAYLOR. (*In utter disbelief.*) No rope . . . there's no rope in here. (*Howling.*) I forgot my back up rope! Oh . . . God Damn Mother fucking Son of a Bitch! (*He suddenly loses his breath and grabs the oxygen, turns the nozzle and puts the mask over his face. After a moment he puts it down.*) Mistake. Can't get upset about anything. We just have to work with what we've got. (*Pause.*) Harold, we've only got one rope.

HAROLD. Put some sun screen on.

TAYLOR. (*Taking the tube from Harold.*) Right. Sun screen. (*He puts some on his neck and face.*) Okay. We still got only one rope.

HAROLD. See what else is in the pack.

TAYLOR. I'll see what else is in the pack. Alright! Four carabiners. With the two on my rack and . . . (*He checks Harold's belt.*) You've got one . . . that's seven beaners. Enough. Enough if we have to take you down in a sling . . . And I really can't see any other way we're gonna get you off this wall. Unfortunately, we don't have half the rope we need to run through the little buggers but we've got plenty of beaners . . . Yes! Well if nothing else, we can play horseshoes with the little fuckers.

HAROLD. Maybe I could make it on the rope.

TAYLOR. Yeah, sure Harold. I'd rather not repeat yesterday's experience if you don't mind. You need a sling. You're a wreck. You NEED a sling.

HAROLD. How's your shoulder?

TAYLOR. (*Rubbing his shoulder absently.*) Great. Fine. Does wonders for the deltoids—havin' somebody stomp on 'em with crampons. Yeah. They're just wonderful.

HAROLD. Yeah . . . well . . . I broke my leg.

TAYLOR. Right. That makes 'em feel a lot better. (*Noticing holes in the fabric on his shoulder.*) Look at those holes . . . brand new, state of the fuckin' art, expedition parka, and you punch fuckin' holes all through it.

HAROLD. I thought you were off the rope.

TAYLOR. Forget it. (*A beat, and then Taylor starts laughing. Harold joins in. They stop.*)

HAROLD. What are we laughin' at?

TAYLOR. We've only got one rope.

HAROLD. Maybe we can still make a sling and use just one rope.

TAYLOR. Come on Harold! We're gonna be lucky to find one more ledge between here and the bottom of this wall that'll hold both me and you all trussed up in a sling, let alone three!

HAROLD. See what else is in the pack.

TAYLOR. I'll see what else is in the pack. One camera containing records of a triumph that others may never see . . . one rain poncho. You've got yours under you. They'll come in handy to make the sling that can't be used BECAUSE we've only got one fucking rope. It's no good. (*Taylor puts the pack down and stares into space for a moment.*) It's no good. I gotta go back and get the other rope. (*He takes the ice screws and carabiners, and puts them on his gear sling.*)

HAROLD. Taylor, you can't go up this wall. We're both half frozen! We're exhausted. Your shoulder's racked up. We can't go up this monster!

TAYLOR. Speak for yourself John . . . we're gonna go down the god damn wall aren't we?

HAROLD. That's different and you know it! It's a lot easier goin' down on a rappell than it is tryin' to . . .

TAYLOR. RIGHT! RIGHT! YOU TELL ME HOW EASY A RAPPELL IS HAROLD!!! Let me explain this to you all right? SITUATION ASSESSMENT! We've got one one hundred and twenty foot rope. The wall we are on is 600 feet if it is a fucking inch! We are maybe half way down it . . . if we are lucky. We couldn't have fallen more than twenty, twenty five feet to this ledge. We'd've bounced right off the motherfucker if it'd been any farther than that. That's three hundred feet to go—one more ledge if we are lucky! The rope will be doubled using a beaner as a pulley for the sling . . . one one hundred and twenty foot rope will become just sixty feet long. One ledge Harold, if that . . . We need two ropes to be in striking distance of that ledge. God help us if it's not there. Do you understand now Harold? Do you understand? (*We hear the wind. Taylor looks up, then down at the ledge they are on.*)

HAROLD. I thought you had a ledge. I thought you were off the rope. I couldn't see you in the snow. There wasn't any tension!

TAYLOR. I had a crack. I was takin' a little breather. You should've called down to me.

HAROLD. . . . I know.

TAYLOR. Wait a minute . . . Harold . . . what would you say the odds are of two climbers on a six hundred foot, ninety degree ice wall coming off their rope . . . and then surviving the night with a temperature somewhere between forty and fifty degrees below zero in nothing but Emergency High Altitude suits, overboots, and a couple of fucking ponchos . . . what would you say the odds are of that happening?

HAROLD. No odds. Too improbable.

TAYLOR. No odds . . . no odds. I'm goin' up there and get the rope. With the luck we've had so far, I may dance up the son of a bitch. On belay.

HAROLD. Belay on. (*Taylor taps the R. ledge with his ice axe.*) Rotten! Yep! Rotten ice . . . oh no you don't baby, you've won all the rounds you're gonna get from me. Cruise on the crack. (*Taylor moves over to the L. side of the ledge.*) She's up there, probably just beyond that overhang. I can't climb up and tie this rope off to it, cause with it doubled I'd still be about eighty feet short of this ledge and that's too big of a jump even for me . . . I'm just gonna have to pull the bastard free. It's our only chance. (*Taylor puts his ice axe and ice hammer in his tool belt, then he begins testing the face of the wall for hand holds.*)

HAROLD. Take care.

13

TAYLOR. I'll take care . . . you entertain me. Tell me stories you've never told before, big sprawling lies about your life, or interesting trivia . . . yeah, better yet, let's have some interesting trivia. (*Taylor discovers a jagged piece of ice to belay the rope on.*) Well will you look at this . . . a little hooker . . . all right! I wasn't kidding about talking Harold. I know I ususally demand total silence while making my deft moves, but right now I think I need some company . . . So talk!

HAROLD. Right. Once upon a time there was a cyclops with a glass eye named Rex . . . who loved to eat pussy. Not only did Rex love to eat pussy but he would take out his glass eye and insert it in all the young maidens he'd meet, where it rolled playfully about while he licked thus producing a double fun treat. Unfortunately for this myopic misfit, to wash his face was an unusual feat, and his eye socket got so funky, that his whole face began to reek. (*Harold starts laughing weakly, and Taylor, in spite of himself, joins in.*)

TAYLOR. Harold! For Christ's sake you're gonna kill me with your crazy shit. Jesus!

HAROLD. Sorry . . . just drifting back to younger days.

TAYLOR. Younger days . . . Christ. Tell me how you got into physics Harold. I could never understand how a depraved literati got into something as straight as physics.

HAROLD. That statement reveals a lot about your conceptual understanding of the universe.

TAYLOR. Enlighten me buddy. Enlighten me.

HAROLD. Right. (*Harold takes oxygen again.*) I got interested in physics in the seventh grade. It was there I first grasped the American concept of education. It relied solely on the theory that if enough facts, data, information, input, etcetera were pumped into the organism it would begin to correlate the material, interrelate it in such a way that a connective fabric would appear and enable the organism to engage in the civilizing pastime of problem solving.

14

TAYLOR. (*Working through a hard pitch.*) Yeah, right . . . problem solving.

HAROLD. Now at first that seemed . . . a quaint idea. I mean all around me were a bunch of confused little dunderheads, their pubescent brains being pureed by a "Kitchen Magician" of unrelated facts. I was also slipping into this apparent miasma of disassociated data when . . . one day, in the school library. I came across a physics textbook that explained Albert Einstein's Unified Field Theory . . . I found God.

TAYLOR. Harold you're crazy.

HAROLD. No. God. A believable God. A fluid, flexible, mutable, ever changing, always constant God. God, as a subatomic intelligence that pervades, is the very core of the physical universe. A God forever exploring all the possibilities of existence . . . A God with the balls to hoist the main sail and head for infinity!

TAYLOR. Harold, we're climbin' a mountain remember? See if you can't stay a little more in touch with our present reality.

HAROLD. Right . . . Anyway, the American educational system was modeled it seems, on the ultimate universal concept of reality, not yet understanding the connective fabric was God, not being able to fathom that Neutron, Proton, and holy Electron held the real trinity . . . going on blind faith. And it was the not understanding, the not knowing that was creating all the chaos of crossed purposes. Witness all the young dunderheads crashing recklessly off into life — a condom in one hand a qualude in the other . . . Stumbling off to insanity. I went to college . . . I dove deeper into physics . . . I discovered that Albert had failed in the face of Quantum Mechanics . . . I saw God die . . . almost before he was born.

TAYLOR. You're losing me Harold.

HAROLD. Quantum mechanics . . . A branch of physics

15

that deal with physical phenomena that do not adhere to the main law of physical science — CAUSE AND EFFECT — a cornerstone of physics, of all science, smashed to pieces by anarchist phenomena from the very universe that gave them birth. For years, all through college, I wandered, a bitter, confused atheist in an existential world of quantum reality, seeking an answer . . . some escape from the emptiness.

TAYLOR. Oh Christ! I don't believe this wall.

HAROLD. I became a hippie, then a bum . . . finally at the end of my transient rope . . . zonked on peyote . . . Mescolito . . . It came to me. There was no answer, it was NOT understandable!

TAYLOR. (*Disappearing.*) . . . That explains everything.

HAROLD. It was BLIND FAITH! Blind faith was the plain brown wrapper that carried the supreme intelligence, the cosmic glue . . . and the dunderheads, the sweet, sweet dunderheads took on new meaning. All their ignorant suffering was anything but "in vain" . . . for the MISERY, the PAIN, the LOSS were the fuel for faith — the blind, catalytic, life force beating through the cosmic frame . . . the ENERGY for metamorphosis . . . life looked pretty strange in that new light . . . I went back to school, got my PhD. I picked up Albert's trail, seeking the hidden variable that would explain away quantum insanity — doubting I'd ever find it, doubting blind faith would ever be explained.

TAYLOR. I GOT IT! I GOT IT HAROLD! Thank you Jesus, thank you. . . . all right . . . all right . . . okay you bastard. Harold pray I can pull this son of a bitch free. Come on you mother. . . . COME ON . . . GOD DAMN YOU, COME ON! COME ON YOU BASTARD!!

HAROLD. Take it easy Taylor! Take it easy!

TAYLOR. COME ON YOU BASTARD!!! COME ON!!! (*A few chunks of ice fall past Harold.*) Oh my god . . . oh my god . . . TENSION! (*Harold quickly tightens the rope.*) Just relax . . . it's okay . . . it doesn't matter.

HAROLD. Are you all right?

TAYLOR. Yes . . . I'm just fine . . . I'm just fine . . . and I'm coming down slowly . . . I'm coming slowly down . . . slowly down . . . slowly. A journey of a thousand miles begins with one step . . . one small step for mankind . . . a giant step for man . . . (*We can see Taylor again. He is moving carefully down. He has snapped the rope through a carabiner at his highest point and Harold is playing out rope, slowly lowering him as he climbs back down the wall. He stops at ice screw and unsnaps the rope from it.*) A horrible thing . . . a temper . . . horrible thing. Only thing it's good for is P.D.s and scum . . . Hell haith no fury like an assistant D.A. . . . Maybe it's my Italian blood . . . all that tomato sauce. Yeah it's gotta be the tomato sauce. You know how most families have orange juice for breakfast? We had tomato sauce . . . nice big glass of tomato sauce in the morning . . . you ever take a good look at a tomato? Nasty little fruit . . . yeah, it's gotta be the tomato sauce . . . funny the things you talk about when you're about to die . . . cocksucking rope! (*He reaches the ledge and drops the beaner and ice screw next to Harold who places them on the part of the ledge which will later disappear in the avalanche. He vomits.*) Oh god . . . she's a bitch . . . a nut bustin' bitch. (*Taylor sits, totally exhausted.*)

HAROLD. Taylor . . . I've got an idea.

TAYLOR. Oh Yeah . . . an idea?

HAROLD. We could take the rope we've got, secure it here and you could make a descent as close to its full length as you can and still find another ledge or a crack. Then you could signal and I'd release the rope and you could fix it and probably get within forty feet of the bottom of the wall. Then you get off and drive on down.

TAYLOR. . . . Yeah . . . yeah, that's a great idea. Yeah, right, uh huh, and then you just hop off the ledge and I catch you . . . is that right?

HAROLD. No. You go down to six where Rod, and Stew, and Earl are coming to help us and you bring them back and take my crippled ass off this wall. It's better than sitting here sniveling Taylor.

TAYLOR. Who's sniveling. I'm not sniveling! And your great fucking idea is totally fucking ridiculous. In the first place there are now a little over two hours of sun left. After that it's wall to wall snow, in case you forgot Harold. In the second place there is no way I could get down this wall and down to six and get back here and get you off this wall in two measly, fucking hours. I would be lucky to get to six in two hours . . . asshole. Sniveling—shit. And in the third place we don't even know Rod, Stew, and Earl are comin' to six. For all we know they're back at base camp jackin' off!

HAROLD. You got a better idea?

TAYLOR. Yeah, as a matter of fact I do! We wait a little longer—say another half an hour, and let the sun work on the ice—and then I go back up and try the rope again.

HAROLD. Gee Taylor that's a great idea . . . knowing as we do how effective the sun is at twenty seven thousand feet.

TAYLOR. FUCK YOU!

HAROLD. You really do have a rotten temper.

TAYLOR. Listen, can you really be so very dumb that you don't realize that if I leave you here that that's that. It's curtains for you old buddy. The end. Do you really think you could make it through another night up here? Are you out of your fucking gourd? Your veins will freeze. You know that don't you? Now if you want to play martyr you're gonna have to make it home to darling Cindy, and get hit by a car 'cause I ain't gonna play Harold, I ain't gonna play. And let me tell you one other thing . . . I haven't lost faith—you know, that crap you were goin' on about while I was on the wall—I still have faith in my ability to face this challenge and win . . . and winning means getting me and what I care about off this wall . . . I was just making a little joke when I referred to dying. It was a joke. I didn't realize you were so sensitive about the subject. I apologize.

18

HAROLD. I'm not so sensitive . . . I think about it quite often as a matter of fact. More than you do I think.

TAYLOR. I doubt that Harold. Death is my job, it's what I'm paid for. (*Pause.*) Every day I go into court and put at least a couple of lousy scum on ice. I salt their tails for two, five, ten, twenty years at a wack, Harold. You have any idea the kind of dent twenty years of prison puts in a man's life? Usually I don't get to kill 'em all at once but I take chunks out of the fuckin' scum, I take as big a chunk as I can get . . . and I think about it all the time.

HAROLD. I never realized you were so . . . possessed.

TAYLOR. Possessed? Yeah. Well . . . I try to keep it to myself. I know I wouldn't get much sympathy from our hip young friends. Earl'd have a coronary if he knew what I thought of his do-gooder horse shit . . . You don't know what it's like Harold. Day in, day out, the arrest jackets, you wouldn't believe the things some people will do to others . . . and I gotta see the slimey bastards all spruced up in the court room tryin' to slide out of it. It's worse than bein' a cop. (*Pause.*)

HAROLD. (*Absently.*) Yeah . . . I never really thought about it. I guess your job is pretty . . . unpleasant.

TAYLOR. Listen Harold, you don't know what's goin' on down there all around you every day, every night — while you sleep, make love with Cindy, eat Chinese food, play with atoms at Lawrence Radiation Center. All around you all the time, you don't know buddy. Sure you read about some of it in the papers, selected atrocities for your viewing pleasure, Stew, Earl, all a ya, sittin' around bitchin' about crime in the neighborhood and social injustice all in the same breath. Christ, if you guys had any idea of what's really goin' on out there under your fuckin' noses, you'd be so damn scared you'd shit and die . . . there's a war goin' on down there — and the barbarians are winning! They're kickin' our civilized asses all over the streets . . . you know that out of every ten faces I prosecute — one is white, two are brown, and the other seven are black? What does that tell you Harold?

HAROLD. What do you think it tells me?

TAYLOR. I'm asking.

HAROLD. It's not a real tough one to read Taylor . . . we're a racist society.

TAYLOR. "A racist society". . . . That's just the self-conciously hip answer I would expect from a white middle class liberal. I'm not talking about moral culpability you frigging clown, I'm talking about what is. I'm talking about what the fuck is going on. You think makin' the free lunch a little bigger is some kind of real swell humanitarian act don't you? That's the way to solve the problem right? Hmmm? (*Harold does not respond.*) Let me tell you what your god damn bigger and better free lunch has produced. It's produced a black male, average age thirteen to twenty-five, average weight one hundred and thirty to two hundred and twenty pounds, who has the reflexes of a rattler, the strength of a rhino, and the compassion of a pit bull. He can rip off you and your grandma before you can count to one and he'll take it all—your money, your clothes, your assholes—both of 'em—and he'll get her false teeth! That's what you get when you take away somebody's dignity and try to make it up to 'em by givin' 'em a free bag of groceries and a place to sleep . . . and I put 'em away every day. I make sure they get their three squares and a place to flop behind fifty foot walls with some gun towers up top. That's what you pay me to do Harold, and I do it extremely well. I do it to clean up after all you pollyanna jerks . . . I do it for you and Cindy, Harold. I do it to "protect and serve" what little of our society is left. (*A pause in which we hear the wind again.*)

HAROLD. You don't do it for me.

TAYLOR. Yes, I do, yes I do. You'd just rather not know about it. (*Harold takes some oxygen.*)

HAROLD. Taylor, you're a Quinn Martin Production you know that? I had no idea you were so consumed by such a tragical, romantic world view. "And I put 'em away . . .

20

every day." Hey, let me tell you something Taylor . . . (*Harold laughs maniacally.*)

TAYLOR. Why don't you just rest awhile Harold.

HAROLD. Let me tell you who you really do it for . . . (*Harold cracks up again.*) You do it for the gadgets Taylor. You do it for the gadgets—so all the little gadgets can live and prosper. It's all about the gizmo pal. We are only here, our only purpose for existence at this point, is to design, manufacture, package, transport, sell, service, dismantle, reassemble . . .

TAYLOR. Why don't you just take it easy. (*Harold starts making little machine noises and playing with imaginary gizmos.*)

HAROLD. "Well hey, looky here at this gizmo! What is this dang thing? Interestin' little doodad ain't it? Think I'll tinker with it here this afternoon . . . What's that? Ya say it's time to die? Well I'll be durned! Time sure flies when you're havin' 'Gizmo fun'."

TAYLOR. Where do you get this shit?

HAROLD. Where do I get it? From the Gizmo Kings—same place you do. And they got it from the Doodad Barons before them, Yayuh, Yayuh, all the way back unto the dirty gadget people living in preindustrial filth in eastern Europe. We are the culmination of a long line, the quintessence of Gizmo consciousness.

TAYLOR. You're the quintessence of horse shit.

HAROLD. Nooo, nooo Bub! We got a zillion different little gadgets to keep your mind off the fact that it's all getting tooo big tooo fast. Why there's even the "Auto Suck," which is also designed to take care of your anxiety over it getting too big too fast! You know, "The Auto Suck," the little gadget you plug into your car lighter and stick on your dick, so that while you're racing from one doodad to another, you can shoot your cookies on all the pretty girls you don't have time to stop and fuck. And believe me, gizmo broadcasting knows how obsessed you are with sex, because they've shot a lot of

21

hot neon pussy through your tubes, tryin' to get you to buy every doodad under the sun . . . so they have created the auto suck especially for you . . . but I digress . . .

TAYLOR. . . . No shit.

HAROLD. You think I'm some doomsday Sci Fi freak who has slipped over the edge, don't you, old buddy? Where as you are the real thing huh? A Real Disillusioned, blood and guts individualist, right? . . . . O.K. let me ask you one question Mr. Disallusioned D.A. . . . if you were given the choice of developing a bomb that would blow away all the things, you know, houses, cars, machines, etcetera, and leave the people . . . or of developing a bomb that blew away all of the people and left all the things, which would you choose? That's not so hard is it? Well is it?

TAYLOR. The Neutron bomb . . . right?

HAROLD. Very good Taylor . . . I work at the Lawrence Rad. Lab remember? We developed the Neutron bomb. Do you know what the Neutron bomb is, hmmm? The Neutron bomb is the Great Gadget, the protector and sustainer of all gadgets . . . the one designed to decimate all life without so much as scratching any of the precious little gizmos crammed on our earth . . . (*Seductively.*) Listen big boy, we can drop you in your tracks without so much as altering the flesh tones on your Sony Trinitron . . . THAT'S REAL . . . the culmination of Gizmo Madness. And you puttin' away a few gadget stealing niggers, who can't afford to buy their doodads from the Gizmo Kings—and then sticking them in prisons where the Doodad Barons can sell more gadgets to keep 'em down . . . shit, blood! That's all part of the Gizmo Plan, baby. It's all a part of the Gizmo Plan!

TAYLOR. Harold . . . you're totally nuts.

HAROLD. Yeah . . . and you . . . you are just an old fashioned romantic.

TAYLOR. Right. I spend my whole life in the sewer of our criminal justice system hoppin' from one turd to another and I'm a romantic. Christ!

22

HAROLD. You take our present situation . . .

TAYLOR. No, you take our present situation!

HAROLD. You climb up an ice wall to try to pull down a rope that was tied off to two locking D's attached to two tube screws firmly sunk in rock solid ice . . .

TAYLOR. You got a better idea?

HAROLD. And now big strong Taylor is just gonna yank it free with one hand while clinging for dear life to some half-assed driven ice screw with the other. You are the Clint Eastwood of mountain climbing buddy. That's a fact.

TAYLOR. So give me a better suggestion Harold! Give me a better suggestion.

HAROLD. I already have.

TAYLOR. Oh crap! And you've got the gall to call me a romantic. You fucking clown. You and your gizmo theory both belong in Disneyland. Any other bright ideas?

HAROLD. You're missing an increasingly obvious fact in your situational analysis. Real obvious.

TAYLOR. Oh pray tell. And what might that be, oh wise and wonderful one?

HAROLD. I can't tell you. You have to see it for yourself.

TAYLOR. Oh . . . okay . . . is it bigger than a bread box?

HAROLD. Yes.

TAYLOR. Harold, right now I don't feel like playing twenty questions anymore. I am going back on the wall now and try the rope because it's the only thing I can think of to get us off this mountain. Now if you have any helpful suggestions . . . just . . . FUCKING . . . SAY . . . SO! (*Taylor uncups rope from anchor screw and unties figure 8.*)

HAROLD. (*Searching through his pack.*) Take the nylon tubing with you and tie it to the rope. Then come back to the ledge and we can both pull on it from a secure position.

TAYLOR. . . . Very good idea. Thank you. (*Reaching across Harold's broken leg, Taylor takes the nylon tubing from him.*) This is not bigger than a bread box.

HAROLD. (*Looking at his leg.*) No. But you're very close.

23

TAYLOR. You're nuts buddy, stone nuts. (*Taylor clips the nylon tubing onto his gear harness and prepares to climb with ice axe and hammer. As Taylor begins to climb, Harold assists.*) Let's see . . . when we last left young Harold he had found the solace of the mustard seed, and everything looked peachy keen for the tike . . . . . . So . . . tell me what happened after you discovered blind faith.

HAROLD. I played their album day and night.

TAYLOR. . . . . . . Harold . . . do your bit huh? Let me hear the next installment of the "Atom Cracker Suite".

HAROLD. Right. I knew that it came from the heart—blind faith.

TAYLOR. Good. That's very good.

HAROLD. . . . from something the heart knew. What did the heart know I wondered? And as I wondered, it became obvious that my mind was not in this with me. My wiz bang wonderful mind didn't really want to know. I started hanging out in coffee houses after work—drinking mulled wine—I stumbled around the lab with warm sangria hangovers. Other researchers avoided my hideous breath . . . I was alone. Then one night, just as my head was about to come to rest on the simulated oak table at a Jack In The Box, little Cindy Yee appeared in my life . . .

TAYLOR. Oh crap Harold. Is this gonna be a love story?

HAROLD. Yep.

TAYLOR. Oooooh. . . . christ.

HAROLD. I was in love and I didn't care about figuring out a thing for the first time in my life. I wasn't trying to make it all fit, have it make sense . . . I wonder what she's doin' . . . this moment? (*Harold looks up at the sun.*) It's about one P.M. Pakistani time—twelve hours difference, she's probably feeding piggy boy right now. You think I'm a pig, you should see Eric chow down.

TAYLOR. I've seen it. It's a sight I'll never forget.

HAROLD. Fat little piggy is probably stuffing his fat little facey at this very moment.

TAYLOR. Well, we got the kid in it too. Harold, this love story is gettin' to be some sappy shit.

HAROLD. AAAH YES! Sappy shit . . . you have met my child . . . . . . It was close, when he was born. It was really close. They both almost died. Cindy's water broke before she went into labor and she got an infection, Eric got an infection, and he was comin' out all upside down and months of Lamaze training were shot to hell. They finally gave her a C-section to get him out. It was very close. That experience changed something for me, you know. It changed something. When they went for the C-section and I had to leave the operating room, I went into the little chapel they've got off to the side there, and I got down on my knees, you know, and I felt like a fool, like some prehistoric creature with his tail fried by the first fire, screamin' at the heavens to make it go away. I felt the futility in every word, Dear God, Dear God, Oh Please God . . . please God, please, please — and I knew it was hopeless, that it was all so much bigger than what I wanted, so very much bigger than my desires. But I wanted her, and I wanted my son, and I prayed even though it was futile . . . even though I knew it wouldn't change a thing . . . . . . I said "please God."

TAYLOR. I got the rope.

HAROLD. Good.

TAYLOR. I'm tyin' the nylon off to it.

HAROLD. Great . . . God answered me . . . He answered me with the only answer he's got, and I felt the fabric for the first time. I felt the cloth come up in me and my knees didn't end at the floor and my hands didn't stop at the rail. I went on and on, through the tile and the walls and up the steel, through the sheets and the blood, and I was in my wife and in my son and I would never leave them ever ever ever. Never again! Never again . . . if I covered their bodies with my white sheet face, if I wheeled them below on my stainless steel legs, if I held them alone in my cold stone embrace . . . I would never . . . (*Taylor rappells back to the*

25

ledge in three easy jumps.)

TAYLOR. (*Unhooking from the rope.*) So, uh, Cindy and Eric made it through and you're now living happily ever after with mortgages, baby cribs, and college funds right? . . . Hello Harold? . . . Harold? (*Taylor gets the oxygen and brings it to Harold.*) Here. Just breathe in slowly okay? You're gettin' a little tired now. You need some food. We both need some food. I'll get the meat bars. (*Taylor gets the meat bars.*)

HAROLD. Good idea. See, you have 'em occasionally.

TAYLOR. (*Unwrapping the bars.*) What?

HAROLD. Great moments.

TAYLOR. Thanks. (*Taylor hands Harold a meat bar.*) Here. You okay? (*Harold nods.*) Okay. Chow city. (*They eat, chewing slowly, staring into space. Taylor grimaces at the taste.*) Good huh?

HAROLD. Yeah.

TAYLOR. We'll brace ourselves against the wall as well as we can and pull together on a four count all right. (*Harold nods. They eat awhile longer.*) You know Harold, as love stories go . . . yours is a pretty nice one . . . I don't know, I . . . I could never love as much as you and Cindy . . . I'll tell you, I watch the two of you a lot of times and you make me sick with your exclusive shit. You know, like your very own special world that nobody else can comprehend and all that crap. I peer in and it looks like one of those pink, Valentine, hands cards with the diamond ring and the couple at sunset . . . My relationships with women are battles . . . wars. Cold and simple. I enjoy them as that. So do they — the women — a good willful struggle of ideas over a couple of drinks, culminating in a ruthless, using fuck. That's my idea of a good relationship.

HAROLD. (*Chewing and staring absently into space.*) Taylor, you're such a pig.

TAYLOR. Yeah, I know. It gets me laid a lot. I can drop into any singles bar in San Francisco, establish myself as the

26

resident pig with a few crude remarks, and in seconds I am surrounded by young lovelies ready to do battle . . . and ready ultimately to bend their pliant bodies around my phallic reasoning. It's a gas. I guess I'm kind of your thinking man's Norman Mailer.

HAROLD. Aren't you lonely?

TAYLOR. Of course I'm lonely. So fucking what? That's the kind of question somebody asks when they're living in a pink hands card. Christ, Harold. Who do you know that isn't lonely, besides you and the other sappy couples like you, who've given your hearts away to each other for safe keeping. You feel good now, hand in hand on the sunny beach. I see ya. You feel wonderful, just wooonderful dancin' the night away. But wait till she goes and takes your heart or you go and take hers . . . I don't believe your fabric crap Harold. Cindy and Eric made it. They made it! But someday somebody's gonna leave and I don't wanna hear about it. I'd go through any hell before I'd go through that. And I pick ladies who feel the same and we lash out at each other's bodies and minds . . . and that's how we relieve the frustration and the anger, that it costs so much. Love costs too much. It's way overpriced . . . but I'll tell you Harold, stirring its juices with rage makes for one incredible hump . . . a steamy willful, punching animal fuck. I got to admit, I'm addicted.

HAROLD. It's called rape.

TAYLOR. Yeah, but we agree on it over Margaritas. We both contract for—and get—our own brand of relief.

HAROLD. You bore me shitless with your fear. You always have. (*There is a beat.*)

TAYLOR. Harold . . . I know what you're tryin' to do. (*They finish their meat bars in silence. Taylor takes out the canteen and drinks, then hands it to Harold who also drinks and puts the canteen away.*) Ready?

HAROLD. Yeah.

TAYLOR. One, two, three, PULL—all right?

HAROLD. Yeah.

TAYLOR. Can you think of anything else?

HAROLD. . . . Debris . . .

TAYLOR. . . . Right. (*They both put their sunglasses on and pull their scarfs up over their faces and then put up their hoods.*) Okay . . . okay . . . (*Taylor grabs the nylon cord which has been dangling down the cliff off to one side of the ledge. Harold also grabs ahold. They brace themselves.*) . . . as Gary Gilmore last said . . . Let's do it! . . . One, two, three, PULL! One, two, three, PULL! (*They are straining now with everything they've got.*) One, two, three, PULL! (*Suddenly the nylon cord gives and the rope goes snaking past them through the air and disappears into the clouds. The nylon cord becomes taut again as it arrests the rope's fall. Harold and Taylor sit holding the cord tightly as some debris —chunks of ice—go flying past.*) Success! (*A rumbling of splitting ice and tearing snow can be heard faintly.*) . . . Oh no . . . oh no . . . Holy Fucking Christ no . . . oh my god . . . (*Suddenly the whole face of the wall is engulfed in falling white. It is a massive avalanche. Harold and Taylor disappear beneath a thundering waterfall of ice. When they reappear the rope they were holding is gone as is the piece of ledge on which their equipment was placed. The other rope still hangs down the wall as it has since Taylor's first ascent. Harold is unconscious, blood trickling down his forehead from underneath the pack. Taylor sees the rope and equipment are gone.*) . . . Oh Jesus . . . (*Taylor takes Harold's head gently in his hands.*) Harold? Buddy? Harold? Oh come on Harold wake up. Harold please? (*Taylor takes the pack carefully off of Harold's head and inspects the wound.*) That's not too bad . . . not too deep buddy. Come on Harold. (*Patting his cheek lightly.*) Come on, Come on Harold. Come on buddy, wake up. (*Harold regains consciousness.*) Yeah. There we are. Back on good old planet earth. Hi buddy. Surprise! We're still alive.

HAROLD. Unnnn . . .

TAYLOR. Maybe there's something . . . I'll rip off some

poncho, make a bandage for your cut. (*Taylor takes the poncho out of the pack.*) We still got one rope . . . Thank god . . . we still got one rope. (*Taylor tears a strip of the poncho off and ties it around Harold's head.*) Fucking mountain. God damn stinking fucking mountain. Stinking fuck hole of a mountain . . . Stinking fucking, fuck hole of a mountain . . . you got conked pretty good didn't you? Lousy stinking, fucking mountain wants to kick my ass.

HAROLD. Success. (*Harold laughs weakly.*)

TAYLOR. That's right, rub it in. Rub it in real good. We lost the rope, we lost the oxygen, we lost about every god damn thing except our lives . . . and now we're probably gonna lose those too . . .

HAROLD. You found it. (*Harold chuckles weakly once more.*)

TAYLOR. Huh?

HAROLD. It's bigger than a bread box. (*Harold passes out.*)

TAYLOR. Harold? (*He shakes Harold.*) Don't take off on me now God Damnit!

HAROLD. (*Regaining consciousness.*) I'm tired Taylor . . . I'm tired . . . I just wanna . . . (*Harold passes out again.*)

TAYLOR. WAKE UP! (*Harold does.*) You stay awake FUCKFACE! We're gonna get out of this god damnit! EQUIPMENT INVENTORY, SITUATION ASSESSMENT!

HAROLD. Right.

TAYLOR. Now we got a rope, a hundred and twenty feet, RIGHT?

HAROLD. Right. (*Taylor begins searching in the snow around him.*)

TAYLOR. . . . we got the hammer, I know we got the hammer. I know it's here . . . I put it down when I sat . . . . . ALL RIGHT! (*Taylor pulls the hammer out of the snow.*) Now . . . one pack, one poncho, a canteen, and uh . . . your ice axe Harold? Your ice axe is laying right beside you . . . isn't it?

HAROLD. Huh?

29

TAYLOR. (*With increasing intensity, finally approaching dementia.*) Your ice axe Harold! I'm asking you about your crummy fucking ice axe. It's next to you in the snow there isn't it? Just say yes. Say yes you stupid fucking jerk. Say it before I throw you off this ledge you fucking crippled clown! (*Harold just stares woozily at Taylor. Suddenly Taylor grabs him by the collar and begins shaking him violently.*) SAY IT! SAY IT! SAY IT! SAY IT! SAY IT! SAY IT!

HAROLD. . . . help . . . Taylor . . . help me . . . help . . . please . . . (*Taylor stops shaking Harold.*)

TAYLOR. . . . Oh God . . . oh my God . . . (*Taylor moves away from Harold.*) . . . oh no . . . no, no, no, oh god . . . I'm sorry Harold . . . I'm sorry.

HAROLD. . . . You can make it. You can still make it but you gotta go now . . . now. (*Harold searches in the snow around him.*) Here. It's here. (*Harold pulls the ice axe out of the snow.*) I got it Taylor. Look, you got a chance. You could get down before the snow. You could . . . if you're lucky.

TAYLOR. No . . . no, no, no . . .

HAROLD. You could. Do it like I said before . . . you could make it.

TAYLOR. It's no good. We're dead. We're dead.

HAROLD. Secure the rope here and . . .

TAYLOR. The screws! They're gone Harold . . . It's all gone.

HAROLD. What about the wall? (*Harold looks up at the rope.*) There must be some left on the wall.

TAYLOR. No.

HAROLD. Look.

TAYLOR. No.

HAROLD. Look!

TAYLOR. I don't wanna . . .

HAROLD. All right, stay here and die! But you can't snivel Taylor. You can't snivel.

TAYLOR. I'll fuckin' snivel if I want to . . . You fucking clown! . . . asshole.

30

HAROLD. You don't wanna die.

TAYLOR. (*Taylor raises Harold's ice axe menacingly.*) . . . Shut your smug fuckin' mouth. (*Taylor realizes what he is about to do and drops the axe.*) . . . This is insane . . . What am I doing up here? I don't believe it . . . . this just doesn't make sense, I mean this is my fucking hobby for Christ's sake. It's not my GOD DAMN LIFE! It's not . . . this is nuts. I want off this Son of a Bitch right now god damnit! I'm not kiddin' . . . HELP!

HAROLD. (*Laughing weakly.*) Come on Taylor, give me a break.

TAYLOR. HEEEEEELLLLLLPPPPPP!!! (*There is a beat.*) . . . Just like my Chevy. (*Taylor looks around behind him at the wall.*) Mmmmm, hmmmmm . . . mmmmmmmm, hmmmmm. Just like my Chev. You want me to lose it don't you? (*Picking up the ice axe again.*) You want me to beat you don't you? Well I'm not going to. Nooooo, I'm not going to. Oooh, I'D LIKE TO, YEAH! But I'm not going to . . . oh no, no, no.

HAROLD. Take it easy . . . Taylor. Take it easy.

TAYLOR. Eeeasy . . . right. Eeeeasy. Bud'll beat my BUTT huh? (*Taylor taps the ledge with the axe.*) Ya hunk a junk. Uh, huh. Yeah.

HAROLD. Taylor relax.

TAYLOR. I'm not gonna dent your hide. I'm not gonna beat your god damn fenders in. Ooooh noooo. I'd like to . . . OOH YEAH! Not this time, you ain't gonna get me this time you son of a bitch . . . (*Suddenly Taylor is swinging the axe wildly into the wall behind him.*) SON OF A BITCH, YOU DIRTY SON OF A BITCH! I'LL KILL YOU, I'LL KILL YOU, I'LL KILL, KILL, KILL, KILL, KILL, kill, kill, kill . . . kill . . . kill . . . (*Worn out, Taylor stops.*)

HAROLD. Taylor . . . you're going crazy.

TAYLOR. Right. (*Beat.*) Right. (*Beat.*) Right.

HAROLD. . . . Look . . . I don't care if you wanna delude yourself until you freeze to death but . . . I don't want to hafta listen to you whine about hobbies and help . . . I don't know you. I thought you were a climber for Christ's sake! Mountains are metaphors buddy in case you forgot—the purest, simplest metaphors on this whole crazy planet. The higher you go the deeper you get. It's that goddamn simple . . . and when you can't run away from where the hell you are . . . then guess what? You have to be there! Where are we Taylor? Where are we?! (*Taylor curls up as if to go to sleep.*)

TAYLOR. You're not gonna die Harold. You're not gonna die.

HAROLD. You're a romantic fruitcake. What happened to you? You're retarded. Your emotional growth is stunted. You're a feeling midget. YOU'RE NUTS! How old are you thirty-eight? And you still don't know that there are consequences? CONSEQUENCES! Every action produces an equal and opposite reaction. Cause and effect. Cause and effect!

TAYLOR. (*His voice is small like a child's.*) . . . You said cause and effect didn't work anymore. Remember . . . you said . . .

HAROLD. Taylor . . . come on.

TAYLOR. . . . That's what you said.

HAROLD. (*Softly.*) Look . . . I didn't finish the story. We found the Quarks . . . hey buddy, we found the Quarks . . . Einstein was right. There is a hidden variable . . . a subatomic, non-local, beyond space and time particle that has the information . . . that carries the truth, the truth to explain away quantum reality's random madness. A physicist by the name of Bell put us on the track in '74 with the photon experiments . . . Two light particles, once in contact, will continue to react as if still in contact, no Matter How Far Apart they are in space . . . "In a universe filled with dark cathedrals of the heart . . . I find the same sacrament on every altar, the same unleavened truth waiting for lips to part . . . I am God . . . Oh God help me . . . I am God."

There is method. There is method all around us. We found God's house buddy, and we called it—Quarks. (*Harold laughs softly to himself.*)

TAYLOR. . . . Quark . . . (*Beat.*) . . . quark, quark, quark, quark, quark . . .

HAROLD. See if there are any screws left on the wall.

TAYLOR. I can't go on that wall again . . . I can't.

HAROLD. (*Reasonably.*) Just look and see.

TAYLOR. (*Taylor rolls over shakily and looks up the wall.*) Yeah . . . I can see three . . . and the one I belayed with.

HAROLD. . . . Thank God . . . three . . . we can get three. That's all we need.

TAYLOR. . . . one rope . . . and three screws.

HAROLD. (*Quietly.*) . . . No odds Taylor . . . no odds

TAYLOR. . . . No odds . . . no odds . . . (*He goes to the edge of the ledge and looks down.*) I guess there'll just have to be three more ledges between here and the bottom right? . . . No odds.

HAROLD. Right . . . Get on the wall and I'll tell you what happened to Rex. How's that for a terrific deal? (*There is a brief pause and then Taylor goes over to the rope and looks up the wall.*)

TAYLOR. It better be entertaining.

HAROLD. You're gonna find it inspirational. (*They are both beginning to breathe in a labored way now. Taylor starts climbing with ice axe and hammer. Harold assists pulling him up by taking rope in as he goes.*)

TAYLOR. SO TALK!

HAROLD. Well . . . Rex had problem and of course he was the last to know . . .

TAYLOR. . . . the last to know . . .

HAROLD. One day he was sitting under a tree staring up out of his funky, vacant socket when something splattered all over his forehead . . .

TAYLOR. . . . splattered . . .

HAROLD. . . . And suddenly his nostrils were filled with the sweet smell of apple.

TAYLOR. . . . apple . . .

HAROLD. (*There is a pause. Harold is fading now.*) I don't think I ever got over being the 'bright boy'. I can see it up here. I can see it so clear . . . the Quarks and neutron bang, and all the little gizmos down there. I thought they needed me to explain 'em. Shit, I thought my job was to explain it all. And I had the answers. I had the answers to all the questions. I found the Quark. I am one of the discoverers of the Quark. I was the answer man . . . I was the answer man. I never grew up . . . it's so clear up here. It doesn't need me to explain it. I mean it all goes on. It goes on whether I understand it or not. It goes on. Understanding has no meaning . . . holding on, holding on . . . just holding on . . . . that has meaning.

TAYLOR. I got one Harold! I got one!

HAROLD. Great . . . (*The wind.*) Listen, I want you to give a message to Eric when he gets older . . . I want you to tell him that life's about holding on. Tell him . . . Will you do that for me Taylor?

TAYLOR. Oh my God!

HAROLD. Taylor?

TAYLOR. HAROLD! FAAAAALLLLLIIINNNNGGGG!!!! (*Taylor falls from above and then is dangling on the rope. Harold, now momentarily brought back to alertness by the situation is straining with everything he has to hold Taylor on the other end of the rope.*)

HAROLD. Taylor! Taylor! Are you all right? TAYLOR! (*Taylor has curled himself into a fetal ball at the end of the rope.*)

TAYLOR. (*In total withdrawal.*) Uuuunnn . . . Uuunnn . . . un.

HAROLD. TAYLOR ARE YOU OKAY?!!

TAYLOR. (*An enraged primordial.*) AAAH! AAAAH! AAAAAHHHH! (*Now whimpering like a puppy.*) nnnn . . .

nnnn . . . nnnn . . . nnnn . . . nnnn . . . nnnn. (*Only Taylor's whimpering and the wind are heard for a beat.*)

HAROLD. . . . All right . . . all right . . . just rest . . . just rest. Listen Taylor . . . Taylor can you hear me? Taylor I know you're scared but the worst is over now. Listen Taylor, listen. The fall is over and I've got you safely by the rope so just reach out, reach out to me buddy. Swing over this way and reach out to me. Come on Taylor! Come on, you can do it. Come on! (*Taylor makes a few groping gestures and begins to swing himself in a pendulum motion, back and forth, closer and closer to Harold.*) That's it! That's it! (*Harold takes the other end of the rope, doubling it to form a sort of loop, and throws it out to Taylor each time he swings in toward the ledge. After several failed attempts, Taylor finally grabs the rope and Harold pulls him in!*) ALL RIGHT! ALL RIGHT! (*They lie together, exhausted on the ledge. There is a beat.*) We should have stuck with Go-Karts . . . . (*Harold grabs the single screw on Taylor's gear sling.*) You got one . . . you got one. (*Taylor pushes Harold away and unties from the rope. They sit staring out for a moment.*) I'm not gonna make it Taylor. It's obvious if you stop to think about it . . . I'm gonna die today Taylor . . . All right?

TAYLOR. You're not gonna die Harold.

HAROLD. For God's sake, do I have to give you a biology lesson to get you to understand? When the organism is damaged to the point where it can no longer obtain and use the materials necessary to support cell life — it doesn't. It dies. (*He hands Taylor the canteen.*) Here . . . just take it easy for awhile . . . rest awhile . . . before you go down. (*Taylor drinks the last of the water and then drops the canteen over the ledge.*)

TAYLOR. I'm not goin' Harold. I'm not goin'.

HAROLD. . . . Okay. I just wish you'd make up your mind. One minute you're screamin' you don't wanna die, and bawling like a two year old, and the next minute . . .

TAYLOR. It's not gonna work Harold! I'm not gonna get

35

mad and leave you . . . okay? You are one superior mother-fucker, you know that? You know how you can't STAND my fear? Well buddy that's what I can't STAND about you. You . . . are one smug, condescending son of a bitch . . . . . . You don't have any idea of what you're asking me to do! You don't have the slightest idea of what you are ask-ing me to live with . . . every lousy minute of the rest of my life. Stop being so NOBLE and maybe you could see that. I don't have a Cindy, Harold, and I never wanted one. I only ever wanted one goddamn real friend . . . Harold you're my friend . . . my friend. I AM NOT gonna spend the endless seconds of the rest of my days with the fact that I left you to die on some stinking mountain while I scurried back to life! I'm not gonna wake up and brush my teeth with that. I'm not gonna drive to work with that. I'm not. You understand now you stupid ponce . . . hmmm . . . can you understand that?

HAROLD. . . . . . Yes.

TAYLOR. Great. (*There is a long pause in which they are both still and we hear the wind, again.*)

HAROLD. Look Taylor . . . I don't want to be desperate now. I want to let it go with a little grace. It's too precious, it's too phenomenal a gift to claw at and beg to stay . . . I want to thank life for not being a rock . . . I want to see Cin-dy . . . I want to touch her . . . comfort her, help her. I want to hold her and tell her I love her and I'm thinking of her . . . that I'm caring till the last second . . . And I want her to know that I know . . . I messed up . . . I took it for granted . . . livin' on the outside of our happiness. I want to apologize for bein' a smug son of a bitch . . . I want Eric to know his daddy was his daddy . . . I want him to know I . . . grieve . . . that I won't be there to share his growing up. I want to hug him one more time . . . hello and good-bye . . . that's what I want . . . and I can have it all . . . I can have it . . . if you go back . . . if you live with what you'll have to live with . . . I can have it all Taylor . . . if you go back . . . if you just go back. I want it . . . I want it bad . . . I want it bad. (*Everything is completely still for a timeless moment.*)

TAYLOR. . . . . . . All right . . . all right . . . let's do it fast. Come on man, you gotta help me. (*Harold draws on the last strength he possesses.*)

HAROLD. . . . I'll help . . . . I can help . . . . . . equipment inventory, you got one screw.

TAYLOR. One screw. (*They laugh. Taylor pulls down the climb rope which remained attached above. Harold assists by unclipping from the rope and handing his coil to Taylor. After clipping into the anchor screw, Taylor throws the rope over the ledge.*)

HAROLD. Okay . . . situation assessment . . . take your time . . . try to find a crack within twenty feet of the end of the rope. Drive the screw and give the rope a couple healthy snaps . . . I'll let it go . . . by the end of your second rappell you'll be about forty feet from the base of the wall. Here, run this through your gizmo. (*Harold hands Taylor the rope and he runs it through his figure eight descender.*) Crampons tight? You've got the axe . . . it'll be enough . . . you'l. make it . . . try not to get lost Taylor. I don't want you droppin' into China.

TAYLOR. I'll be all right.

HAROLD. Ready? (*Taylor nods. They sit staring at each other for a moment.*) Thank you. (*Taylor nods.*) Take care of yourself Taylor.

TAYLOR. . . . you too.

HAROLD. Go.

TAYLOR. Right . . . . I love you . . . . . .

HAROLD. I love you too . . . Go. (*Taylor slips over the ledge in one easy motion and is gone. Harold sits for a long moment looking down the cliff after him. Harold is breathing more and more spasmodically, his chest rising and falling rapidly. He leans back and closes his eyes and eventually his breathing slows, calms.*) Oh Baby. Sweet Baby . . . hey. Hey. I was gonna write you a letter.

Yeah . . . you know me Al. Better late than never . . . right? I heard something real sad but I knew you'd wanna hear it . . . There's this little guy called the Japanese glacier fox . . . this little guy is really pretty . . . really special . . . long fine silky hair . . . the purest white . . . you can spot him for miles when he's below timber line . . . You look so nice. You look so warm. I got you now. (*Harold feels the rope.*) Tension. Great. Go Taylor . . . go, go, go . . . SO apparently Darling . . . some of these little nippers are born albinos, but it's in the summer so that's all right cause the snows are melted and they spend a lot of time in their burrows when they're young and in the fall and winter they kind of quasi-hibernate . . . but when the spring comes, the young albino foxes go out with the other foxes to romp and run and play . . . the glare of the sun off the spring glacier snow . . . burns their albino retinas to a crisp within a couple of days . . . and they are blind . . . sad baby. I know . . . I know. It's all right . . . (*Harold strokes the rope.*) . . . and for awhile they live in the burrow and the other foxes feed them . . . bring back food for them . . . that's nice . . . that's real nice . . . but a day comes when they feel their way out of the burrow, into the light . . . and start down, letting the earth pull them, just going down, to where they have to go. (*Harold feels the rope again.*) Go home Taylor, go home . . . and if nothing takes advantage of them, stops them and kills them, they make it to the base of those purple Japanese mountains—out—onto a brown sandy Japanese beach. I love you. I love you . . . And they sit there and curl their plume white tails around their feet and wait, staring blindly at the rolling Japanese sea . . . and they never move a muscle—not a muscle—once they face the sea . . . they sit . . . and let the waves rise around them . . . till they're gone, till they're gone. . . . the Japanese fishermen see one sometimes—once in a great while . . . at dawn . . . sitting . . . waiting . . . on the beach. (*The rope snaps sharply twice.*) Taylor found a crack. Taylor's got a crack baby . . . I love you. (*Harold unties the rope and holds it closely to him.*) Taylor's goin' home . . . Taylor's gonna see your pretty smile. Taylor's gonna be warm again. (*Harold's breathing starts to become violent again. He closes his eyes. It calms.*) Hold on . . . hold on . . . I have to hold on. Help me hold on honey. I want to stay with you now. I want to be calm like the little fox . . . and stay with you . . . I love you forever . . . forever. (*The rope snaps sharply in Harold's hands.*) . . . You know what I know? I know why the little fox sits so still . . . My One . . . It's because he knows he'll be back . . . and he'll have eyes next time. (*Harold throws the rope into space and it disappears.*) . . . He knows he'll have eyes next time. (*We hear Harold softly, very softly, as the lights dim out in blues.*) . . . hold on . . . hold on . . . hold on . . . hold on . . .

FINIS

COSTUME PLOT

BLUE

TAYLOR:
T shirt
Athletic cup
Cotton shorts
Cooling shorts with nylon pockets and suspenders
Cotton vest
Cooling vest with pockets
Black cotton turtleneck shirt (no sleeves) with crotch strap
Shin guards
Knee pads
Silk socks
Wool socks
Blue quilted pants (zip up inseams) with button suspenders
Blue quilted parka (distressed holes right shoulder)
Blue hood for parka
Black suede gloves (velcro across wrist)
Blue mittens with leather palms and fur backs
Neck bandana (black)
Green poncho
Hat
Super gaitors
White Kolfach climbing boots
Crampons with leather straps (chrome)

RUST

HAROLD:
T shirt
Cotton shorts
Cooling shorts with nylon pockets and suspenders
Cotton vest
Cooling vest with nylon pockets
Black cotton turtleneck shirt (no sleeves) with crotch strap
Shin guards
Knee pads
Silk socks
Wool socks
Rust quilted pants (zip up inseams) with left leg rigged for broken leg with button suspenders
Broken leg piece
Rust quilted parka
Rust hood for parka with detachable fur trim
Black suede gloves (velcro across wrist)
Rust mittens with leather palms and fur backs
Neck bandana (black)
Red poncho with rigged tear strip
Knitted brown hat with pocket for blood pack
Super gaitors (one left rigged for easy access)
Kolflach climbing boots
Crampons with leather straps (chrome)

PROPERTY PLOT

PROP PRE-SET

Poncho (green) [placed UL of trap door-folded neatly]

Harold's day pack (large — orange Chouinard)
(on bottom of pack)
Ice screws (3-top R side of pack)
Ice hammer (center)
(In loose color coded pockets on bottom of pack)
Sunscreen tube (CR)
Meat bars (2 wrapped together in foil)
Nylon webbing (permanently wrapped center under ice
    hammer)
(on top of pockets)
Climbing rope (live end up wrapped tightly)
Ice axe (54 cm)
Camera case
(outside pocket)
Oxygen bottle w/
    Tubing and mask (R side)

Harold's pack should be zipped up L side /unzipped R side/un-
zipped oxygen bottle

Taylor's day pack (small-blue Chouinard)
(inside)
Poncho (red) w/
    Rip-away (marked for easy sight)

Camera case
Oxygen bottle w/
  tubing and mask
Carribiners (4-3 in 1)
(lying on top of pack)
Ice axe (46 cm blade facing L)

Ice screw (permanently fixed UC wall)
Carribiner w/
  Nylon webbing (5 ft. long)

Preset on heaven's gate 7
Blue rack w/
  Carribiner
Red nylon tubing attached to 50 feet of climbing rope
Rubber ice axe
Carribiner w/
  Rubber ice screw
Water bottle w/
  Gatorade
Check oxygen bottles to be sure parts are secure and clean
  every night
Check tubing set on stage for vomit bottle make sure there
  is gatorade in bottle and tubing is clean.
Cover props and crack at break-a-way with snow. Place snow
  in footholds above ledge.

Harold
Blue gear sling w/
  Carribiner (1)
Sit harness w/
  Locking D w/
    Figure 8
(back of harness)
  Carribiner
Chest harness w/
  Runner (tied w/water knot)
Gator (left leg unzipped top two snaps undone)

Blood pack in pocket on jacket
Sunglasses (ski goggles)

Taylor
Blue gear sling w/
   Carribiners (2) w/
     Ice screws (2)
Sit harness w/ (carribiner-left side w/figure 8)
   Locking D (2-one with traverse cable)
Wrist device (black) w/ [running down left sleeve]
   Cable (for traverse ball)
Utility belt w/
   Carribiners (2) [one sewn to each side above holsters]
Sunglasses (goggles-ski)
Beef jerky (wrapped in foil-in inside right jacket pocket)
Water bottle w/ (inside jacket left) [⅓ filled]
   Gatorade
Traverse ball snapped up in jacket for easier access

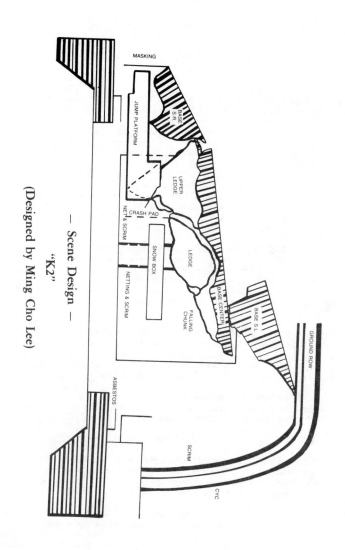

— Scene Design —

"K2"

(Designed by Ming Cho Lee)

DRAMATISTS PLAY SERVICE, INC.
e South, New York, NY 10016 212-683-8960 Fax 212-21
masters@dramatists.com   www.dramatists.com

NEW PLAYS

★ **SHEL'S SHORTS by Shel Silverstein.** Lauded poet, songwriter and author of children's books, the incomparable Shel Silverstein's short plays are deeply infused with the same wicked sense of humor that made him famous. "...[a] childlike honesty and twisted sense of humor." –*Boston Herald.* "...terse dialogue and an absurdity laced with a tang of dread give [*Shel's Shorts*] more than a trace of Samuel Beckett's comic existentialism." –*Boston Phoenix.* [flexible casting] ISBN: 0-8222-1897-6

★ **AN ADULT EVENING OF SHEL SILVERSTEIN by Shel Silverstein.** Welcome to the darkly comic world of Shel Silverstein, a world where nothing is as it seems and where the most innocent conversation can turn menacing in an instant. These ten imaginative plays vary widely in content, but the style is unmistakable. "...[*An Adult Evening*] shows off Silverstein's virtuosic gift for wordplay...[and] sends the audience out...with a clear appreciation of human nature as perverse and laughable." –*NY Times.* [flexible casting] ISBN: 0-8222-1873-9

★ **WHERE'S MY MONEY? by John Patrick Shanley.** A caustic and sardonic vivisection of the institution of marriage, laced with the author's inimitable razor-sharp wit. "...Shanley's gift for acid-laced one-liners and emotionally tumescent exchanges is certainly potent..." –*Variety.* "...lively, smart, occasionally scary and rich in reverse wisdom." –*NY Times.* [3M, 3W] ISBN: 0-8222-1865-8

★ **A FEW STOUT INDIVIDUALS by John Guare.** A wonderfully screwy comedy-drama that figures Ulysses S. Grant in the throes of writing his memoirs, surrounded by a cast of fantastical characters, including the Emperor and Empress of Japan, the opera star Adelina Patti and Mark Twain. "Guare's smarts, passion and creativity skyrocket to awesome heights..." –*Star Ledger.* "...precisely the kind of good new play that you might call an everyday miracle...every minute of it is fresh and newly alive..." –*Village Voice.* [10M, 3W] ISBN: 0-8222-1907-7

★ **BREATH, BOOM by Kia Corthron.** A look at fourteen years in the life of Prix, a Bronx native, from her ruthless girl-gang leadership at sixteen through her coming to maturity at thirty. "...vivid world, believable and eye-opening, a place worthy of a dramatic visit, where no one would want to live but many have to." –*NY Times.* "...rich with humor, terse vernacular strength and gritty detail..." –*Variety.* [1M, 9W] ISBN: 0-8222-1849-6

★ **THE LATE HENRY MOSS by Sam Shepard.** Two antagonistic brothers, Ray and Earl, are brought together after their father, Henry Moss, is found dead in his seedy New Mexico home in this classic Shepard tale. "...His singular gift has been for building mysteries out of the ordinary ingredients of American family life..." –*NY Times.* "...rich moments ...Shepard finds gold." –*LA Times.* [7M, 1W] ISBN: 0-8222-1858-5

★ **THE CARPETBAGGER'S CHILDREN by Horton Foote.** One family's history spanning from the Civil War to WWII is recounted by three sisters in evocative, intertwining monologues. "...bittersweet music—[a] rhapsody of ambivalence...in its modest, garrulous way...theatrically daring." –*The New Yorker.* [3W] ISBN: 0-8222-1843-7

★ **THE NINA VARIATIONS by Steven Dietz.** In this funny, fierce and heartbreaking homage to *The Seagull*, Dietz puts Chekhov's star-crossed lovers in a room and doesn't let them out. "A perfect little jewel of a play..." –*Shepherdstown Chronicle.* "...a delightful revelation of a writer at play; and also an odd, haunting, moving theater piece of lingering beauty." –*Eastside Journal (Seattle).* [1M, 1W (flexible casting)] ISBN: 0-8222-1891-7